A LOVE OUT OF TIME

A LOVE OUT OF TIME

Rick Adkins

iUniverse, Inc.

New York Lincoln Shanghai

A LOVE OUT OF TIME

iUniverse books may be ordered through booksellers or by contacting:

iUniverse
2021 Pine Lake Road, Suite 100
Lincoln, NE 68512
www.iuniverse.com
1-800-Authors (1-800-288-4677)

ISBN-13: 978-0-595-36682-8 (pbk)
ISBN-13: 978-0-595-81104-5 (ebk)
ISBN-10: 0-595-36682-1 (pbk)
ISBN-10: 0-595-81104-3 (ebk)

Printed in the United States of America

For Bronda

Acknowledgements

With appreciation and gratitude to Debra Adleman of the Susquehanna County Historical Society in Montrose, Pennsylvania for providing information on Montrose and Susquehanna County in the 1890's; to Keris Smith of the Susquehanna County Department of Economic Development; to the Montrose United Methodist Church; and to Katie Dann at Group Lotus Plc.

PROLOGUE

▼

The construction site was large, the heavy equipment moving in symmetry as the workers moved around them in the heat of the summer sun. The backdrop of Philadelphia shimmered on the horizon. At one end of the site, the small construction trailer with the logo 'Highland Limited Construction' sat isolated from the activity.

Inside the air conditioned comfort of the trailer, the foreman, Ray Kemper, sat at his desk and studied the cylindrical container again, shaking his head. "You say you're sure about where you found this?"

"Yeah, *under* the foundation of that old building in the southeast corner," replied one of his bulldozer operators, Rodriguez, who was standing in front of the desk. Rodriguez had notified the foreman, who had sent Rodriguez to the foreman's office. "Billy had given me the all clear, and I started clearing the foundation from the pit. Found this thing about four feet down, below where the subfloor was. Just about dead center of where the old building had stood. I wouldn't have seen it but the shiny reflection caught my eye."

"Yeah, that's what Billy told me when he gave this to me earlier." Kemper shook his head again. "This just doesn't figure," he said with a sigh. "That building was erected around 1895 or '96. I looked at the subfloor myself yesterday and didn't see any sign of cracks or breaks. That subfloor was as solid as the day it was poured before we broke it up. Did you find anything else around this thing?"

"No, just that cylinder. The ground hadn't been disturbed, I can tell you that."

"OK, thanks," said Kemper, and Rodriguez nodded and left. This is too strange, Kemper thought to himself; this looks like modern stainless steel, very lightweight, and, as far as I know, stainless steel like this didn't exist in the 1890's. But, he told himself, I'm no expert on that. The information etched into the surface of the cylinder was just as baffling. Initially, the thin film of dirt had hidden the etchings. It was only after he had brought the cylinder to the trailer and cleaned it up that he had seen the strange inscription, which he prudently had told no one about. He had placed a call to the project's architect, who was coming in from Richmond anyway and was due to arrive within the hour. But, he had given no details about the find. He had just told the architect that something had come up, and that they needed to discuss it.

He picked up the cylinder again and studied it closely. The cylinder was about two feet long and eight inches in diameter, rounded at both ends and with no visible seam anywhere. It was surprisingly lightweight. He had tapped on the cylinder with a pen but could not tell if there was anything inside. The outer surface was somewhat dull in places, with just a few spots where the polished surface shone through, and he agreed that it had been pure luck that Rodriguez had found it at all. It could just as easily have been dumped and hauled away, but Rodriguez had called Kemper and asked him to stop at the excavation on his morning rounds.

A knock on the door interrupted his thoughts, and he looked up to see Paul Melton step inside. Melton, in his late thirties, was the chief architect on the project, and Kemper had worked with him before. Although fairly young for a project of this size, Melton had proven himself to be competent and had the full trust and support of his architectural firm. Kemper's crew had first worked with Melton about five years previously and Kemper had found him to be as intelligent and knowledgeable as any of the seasoned, older architects he was used to working with. Once construction had started, though, about two months ago, Melton had only stopped by once. The two shook hands and Melton settled into the chair across from the desk.

"Not any problems, I hope?" Melton said, and Kemper shook his head.

"No, everything is right on schedule. We should have the new foundations ready by the end of the month. I called you because of something we found when we were excavating for the parking garage. You asked us to let you know if anything unusual turned up during construction. I figured you meant in relation to the project, but I thought this might qualify." Kemper lifted the cylinder and handed it to Melton. "Any idea what this thing is?"

Melton took the cylinder, looked it over and shook his head. "No, not at all." He looked at Kemper with raised eyebrows. Kemper said, "One of my operators found this buried underneath the foundation of that old building that we tore out on the southeast corner."

"So? Maybe one of the crew that built that building dropped it there, way back when. They find anything else along with it?"

"No, just this. But look at the inscription."

Melton pulled out his reading glasses and held the cylinder under the desk lamp. Neatly etched into the surface was: "H. Parkwood, TSP, Phila, Penn."

"What do you think?" Kemper asked, and Melton shook his head. "Strange. Maybe your crew is playing a joke on you."

"No, I know these guys. They're not the joking type. And they said they found it a couple of feet *under* the foundation. Seems to me that someone must have deliberately put it there for a reason. Besides, that old building was erected back in the mid 1890's. Whatever it is, it's been laying there for well over a century."

Melton shrugged. "I don't think it's anything important." He shook the cylinder but could hear nothing inside. He looked more closely at the cylinder. "But how do you open the thing? I don't see any seams or cracks. Looks like it's just a hunk of scrap metal."

"What about the inscription?" Kemper asked.

Melton shrugged again. "If it *was* buried in the 1890's, I'd seriously doubt if this TSP still exists, since they must have had something to do with it. I don't recall that name coming up when I studied the old plans for the buildings that were in this area, but that doesn't mean anything. Records weren't too meticulous back then."

Melton put the cylinder down on the desk and looked at Kemper, a slight smile on his face. "But, I just had an idea. A friend of mine was an associate history professor at one of the universities down in Pittsburgh. On the side, he's into history and artifacts and is especially interested in the late nineteenth century—his specialty, so to speak. He does preliminary field survey work for the state Archaeological Society at certain sites around Pennsylvania. He came into some money and decided to get out of teaching, although he still maintains ties with the school. Still lives nearby there, too. We met because on one of my early projects the construction crew found a 19th century settlement, and the whole project came to a halt so that my friend could bring his people in and excavate the find, under orders from one of those historical groups in Washington that have a lot of pull with the local government.

"At first, I was really upset because I could see the cost overruns climbing up out of sight while the crew was idle, but he had the site cleared in less than two weeks. In the end, the property owners were credited with the donation of the finds to a local museum, which gave them lots of good PR so it all worked out. I told my friend that if we ever found anything else like that at one of our sites, we'd let him know. That's another reason I asked you to let me know if anything unusual came up. I didn't want us accused of destroying an old Indian burial ground or something like that." He looked at the cylinder again. "But I'm betting that this is nothing but scrap. If it's all right with you, I'll see that he gets it. Maybe he can make something of it."

Kemper nodded. "Sure," he said, "I don't have any use for it," and placed the cylinder into a small carryall, which he handed to Melton. "Sorry to have called you all the way out here for nothing."

"No problem. I've been meaning to take a look at the project anyway, I just haven't found the time. Care to show me how things are going?" Kemper nodded and led the way outside, where Melton put the carryall into his car trunk. Kemper handed him a hard hat and the two walked toward the construction activity.

CHAPTER 1

▼

It was nearly three weeks later when Melton was traveling through Pittsburgh. He passed through the outskirts of the city, guiding his car through the light evening traffic as he headed for the older residential area near the university. Melton had telephoned Matt Collins the day after he had gotten the cylinder from the construction site, only to find that Collins was off on yet another site inspection in the northwestern part of the state. He had left a message on Collins' voice mail and upon his return Collins had telephoned him a few nights ago, inviting him over.

A light shower had started when Melton pulled up to the huge old frame house, half hidden by the oaks and elms so prevalent in this part of the city. He retrieved the carryall from the trunk and made his way up the steps to the porch. He had hardly finished ringing the doorbell when the door was opened by Matt.

"Good to see you again, Paul," Matt said, extending his hand and smiling. "It's only been, what, two years?"

"Yeah, just about," Melton replied, following Matt into the foyer. The two had formed an easygoing friendship, and could pick up the conversation where they had left it off if it was two weeks or two years since they had last seen each other. "Any luck up north?"

"No, it was a false alarm," Matt said. "Someone thought they'd found some really old remains. Dug up a couple of skeletons and word of it made its way to me. I went up but it turns out they'd just disturbed an old nineteenth century graveyard. The local government took over and relocated the remains, but I decided to spend some time going through the old records in the basement of their County Courthouse. You know, I figured since I was there..."

"So you still take the history thing seriously?"

"Where it looks promising or where it piques my interest, I do. That area was settled several hundred years ago. Lots of information, if you can find it, and the occasional artifact that turns up makes a good addition to my collection."

"Oh, yes, *the collection*," Melton said. "You said you'd give me the tour when I came by."

"No problem," Matt said, heading for the kitchen. "Care for something to eat?"

"No, but I'll take a beer if you have one." Matt pulled a couple of bottles from the refrigerator and offered one to Melton. "I've got things pretty well catalogued now that I've got some spare time," Matt said, and motioned toward the basement door. "Come on down and check it out." Melton picked up the carryall and followed Matt down the stairs.

"I try to keep the humidity to a minimum," Matt said as they descended the stairs. The basement was well lit and somewhat cool. "Some of these items are very fragile, but they don't qualify as museum material. So, I keep them for my personal collection."

The basement was at least forty feet square, with shelves around all four walls and several freestanding workbenches in the center, each holding a different collection of items. In addition, there were several pieces of electronic equipment scattered here and there. The shelves were about three-quarters full, each piece with a small placard adjacent to it with information on the artifact. Matt stopped at one of the nearby workbenches and picked up an old revolver. "Civil War," he explained, although the piece looked as new as the day it was issued. "I found this stashed away upstate in an old condemned clapboard house, along with a full uniform, medals, ammunition, the lot. Found out it belonged to a major in the 5th Pennsylvania Regiment by the name of Grosvenor who served at Gettysburg. The uniform is in pretty good shape, considering its age, but all of the metal artifacts were in very good condition. Didn't take much at all to get them looking like new again." He put the revolver down and picked up a couple of the medals. "Campaign ribbons," he explained, handing them to Melton, who put the carryall onto the table to examine the ribbons. "Grosvenor made it through the war unharmed, and made a fortune which, according to my research, his descendants squandered. Even lost the family farm, now abandoned, which is where I found all of this."

Melton had carefully replaced the medals on the table and turned to the shelves. "What else have you got down here? This looks like a pretty interesting collection."

"It is," Matt replied, "but a lot of the museums want one of a kind items. Actually, these nineteenth and early twentieth century pieces are fairly common, if you look around enough. Whenever I make a find, I offer it to a few of the local museums to see if they're interested. What they don't take, I usually keep. There's a little bit of our history in all of these things."

"Speaking of a little bit of history," Melton said, picking up the carryall and reaching inside, "this is what brought me out here tonight." He handed the cylinder to Matt, who looked at it with a puzzled expression. Melton smiled and said, "You asked me to let you know if anything unusual ever turned up at one of our construction sites. I think this qualifies."

"What is it?" Matt said, looking the cylinder over.

"I was hoping you could tell me," Melton replied. "Our crew was excavating the site of our new office complex and found this. The strange part is that it was found centered *underneath* an old foundation. The old building was erected near the end of the nineteenth century, and my crew said that the foundation was as solid as the day it was poured. So, whatever this thing is, was placed there *before* the foundation was poured. I thought maybe you'd come across something like this before."

Matt frowned. "No, this is new to me. I've found a fair number of old strong-boxes, and bottles with artifacts inside them, but nothing like this." He read the inscription and looked up at Melton. "TSP. Ever heard of this outfit?"

"No, and there was no mention of it in the old plans for the buildings we razed, but that doesn't mean anything. My foreman thought it looked out of place and gave me a call, and I called you. I think it's just scrap metal."

"I don't think so," Matt replied. "Look at the obvious finishing that has been done to the metal, and no evidence of seams. I can't think of anything belonging to that period that it could be." He hefted the cylinder and said, "Very light-weight. Definitely odd. What do you want me to do with it?"

"Whatever you want. It's yours. I thought you might find some information on the company, or whatever it was, from the inscription. It's got to be local judging from where we found it. I figured you might turn up something when you go digging around in the university archives, or wherever it is you go digging around."

"Thanks, I will," Matt said. "And I'll let you know if I find out anything." Matt paused, thinking to himself, then said, "Parkwood, Parkwood…wait a minute. I had a Professor Parkwood back when I was studying at the university— he taught physics. Most of it was way beyond me; I barely passed the class. Maybe this belonged to one of his ancestors." He placed the cylinder onto the workbench and said, "By the way, check out these old plans I found a couple of months ago." He walked toward a cabinet on one wall and removed a cardboard tube, one end of which he removed and pulled yellowed rolls of paper from inside. "I think these are part of the original plans for the old Flatiron Building in New York City." Melton's eyes lit up. Matt knew that Melton's interest in historical architecture almost matched his own for artifacts and collectibles. Matt found an empty workbench and spread out the plans, and before long Melton had verified that the plans were indeed what they appeared to be. The two men spent the next hour looking them over.

Looking at his watch, Melton said, "I've got to get going. Early meeting tomorrow." He looked anxiously at the plans as Matt rolled them up and replaced them in the cardboard tube. "What are you going to do with those?"

"Well, I've got no use for them." Smiling, he handed the tube to Melton. "Keep them. They're yours. Show them to your buddies at the office."

Melton was pleased. "Well, thanks, Matt," he said with feeling. "I've got just the spot for these on one wall, after I get them preserved and framed. Thanks."

Matt followed Melton up the stairs, and the two waved as Melton made a dash for his car through the rain, which had become steady. Matt watched as the taillights from the car disappeared around the corner.

CHAPTER 2

▼

It was past 1:00 am as Matt sat hunched over the workbench, a strong desk lamp illuminating the work area. The cylinder sat on a thick cloth, and Matt was making detailed measurements of its dimensions. He had long ago given up on keeping himself to any particular schedule, instead sleeping when he needed to and working on whatever his current project was. Any research he needed to do at the nearby university was no problem; he practically had the run of the place regardless of the hour.

He had been working with the cylinder for over two hours. He had been surprised to find that the cylinder appeared to be made of stainless steel. His first task had been to thoroughly clean the surface, then photograph it from several angles with the digital camera and transfer the images to the PC sitting nearby on a small desk. Once he had the measurements, he would transfer those to the PC as well and have the PC extrapolate all of the information, which would give him a three dimensional model to add to his files. Finishing the measurements, he took the cylinder over to an x-ray console and placed the cylinder inside. He had decided to take a few slides from different angles and study them at his leisure.

He was beginning to feel a little tired as he operated the x-ray console, and was about to call it a night when he decided to give the x-rays a quick look. Flipping on the viewer, he brought up the first x-ray and was brought wide-awake by what he saw.

Despite the fact that no seams were visible on the cylinder, he saw what appeared to be a threaded section around the middle of the cylinder. Adjusting the magnification, it was clear that the cylinder was actually made of two perfectly matching sections.

Impossible, he said to himself, I don't recall ever seeing anything with tolerances this close manufactured in the nineteenth century, and certainly not made out of lightweight stainless steel. But he was also startled to see that there were what appeared to be papers of some sort rolled up inside the cylinder.

Removing the cylinder from the console, he carried it over to the workbench and fastened one end vertically into a vise after wrapping it with cloth so that the vise clamps did not damage the cylinder. He was careful not to over-tighten the vise, which could also damage the cylinder. He then attempted to unthread the cylinder halves by hand.

Despite his best efforts, the threads would not budge. He grabbed a rubber-strapped adjustable tool from the rack at one side and fastened it around the top end of the cylinder, to give more leverage, and gave it another try. Still, the cylinder resisted his efforts.

Well, so much for that, he thought, and was thinking of the best way to cut open one end of the cylinder when he decided to try something different. Removing the tool from the cylinder, he flipped it over and applied pressure in the opposite direction. At first, nothing happened, and he was about to give up when he gave it one more push. Suddenly a thin line appeared around the center of the cylinder, and he felt the top section begin to turn.

A couple more turns with the tool and he was able to remove the tool and turn the top section by hand. It was obvious that the reverse threads had been machined to exacting tolerances, since each full turn of the top only widened the threads by a millimeter. He continued turning until a good three inches of threads were showing, and suddenly the top of the cylinder came loose. Gingerly he lifted the top section, looked inside it but, seeing nothing of interest, set it onto the bench.

There were several thick pages rolled up inside the cylinder, the top halves sticking up out of the lower section. He pulled on a pair of disposable latex gloves and slowly pulled the rolled papers out of the cylinder. He was aware that paper could, and often did, disintegrate quite easily from age, but this appeared to be fairly thick cotton bond and in good condition. He unrolled the papers and placed them onto the workbench, using a couple of thick rulers to hold down the edges.

At first, Matt had thought that there might be something of real value inside the cylinder. Otherwise, why would someone have gone to all this trouble to make sure that the contents remained sealed, even from a casual attempt to open it? But, as he studied the papers, his hopes fell. The top page was simply a letter of some sort, written in longhand. Matt scanned the writing. There was no salutation; the writing simply began, "There have been unexplained outages with the equipment. I have lost the ability to communicate and I have been unable to get the project operational again. I am hoping that you can perhaps accomplish something from your end, if this is found in time. I am off to Scranton to do my research but hope that you will have an answer for me upon my return. Enclosed is the latest information that I logged before the failure." It was signed simply, "Ben." The remaining pages were all covered in mathematical equations and what appeared to be computer code, but Matt disregarded this last as impossible. Simply a coincidence, he was sure, but he was no expert on code or the mathematics that he saw on the pages. There was no explanation as to why the pages had been so meticulously preserved. The writing on the pages was clear and concise, the ink well preserved. But, as a precaution, he took the pages to the PC scanner and scanned the images into it. He had learned a long time ago that old papers, and the ink that was on them, could often fade into oblivion in a few short weeks.

Satisfied that he had gotten all of the pages scanned, he rolled the papers again and replaced them in the cylinder, screwing on the top section until the two halves met. He reached for the phone and was about to call Melton when he glanced at his watch. It was after 3:00 am, and with a smile he replaced the receiver. He didn't think Melton would appreciate a call at this time of morning, and besides, it could wait. He wanted to get over to the university library later in the morning to see if he could turn up any information on this TSP. He shut down the PC and the other machines that were running, and walked up the stairs to the main floor, turning off the workroom lights as he left.

CHAPTER 3

▼

It was four days later and the search was not going well. Matt had initially gone online and ran exhaustive searches for Philadelphia history from the late 1800's, to no avail. The university had, over the years, acquired quite a few historical documents of various types that had to do with Philadelphia as well as Pittsburgh. These were housed in the dingy sub-basements of the university library, and he had spent hours poring over the old documents and newspapers, including what meager telephone records there were from that era, again to no avail. He could not find a single entry for TSP.

Closing the latest loose-bound volume and placing it back on the shelf, Matt heaved a sigh and shook his head. His eyes were red-rimmed and slightly blood-shot from reading the mostly hand-written records of a bygone era. He could feel that the search here was going to lead him nowhere, a feeling that he had gotten two days earlier. But, his training had kept him going on the off chance that something would turn up. Early in his career, he had given up too easily and someone else had come in, picked up where he had left off, and taken the credit on a project that should rightfully have been his.

Fortunately he had learned from that mistake and, in time, had developed a sixth sense about this kind of research. But that sixth sense just didn't seem to be working this time. Matt picked up his backpack and slung it over one shoulder. He trudged up the stairs to the first floor of the library and was slightly surprised to see the library with a fair amount of students bustling back and forth. He looked at his watch and saw that it was just after 2:00 pm. Heading for the main desk, he caught sight of Melissa Trumbull pointing a student in the direction of the reference section. As she turned she glanced in Matt's direction and a look of concern crossed her face.

"You look like crap, Matt," she said as she moved over to where Matt was standing. Melissa was familiar with his methods but didn't necessarily approve of them. "When was the last time you slept?"

"I don't know...yesterday sometime," he said tiredly. "I'm coming up with a big fat zero here." He rubbed his eyes and looked up. "Listen, I've decided to continue this research later. I think I might have better luck if I check in at the Historical and Museum Commission in Harrisburg. Besides, I've got another assignment from the State Historical Society that they want me to check out later this week, out near Philadelphia."

"How long will you be gone this time?" she asked. Melissa was a good friend, one that he had known for years, and she also acted as his unofficial secretary when he was working in the field. Besides, she still held hope that Matt might someday show more than a friendly interest in her.

"Not too long this time, I think," he replied. "If nothing turns up the first couple of days I'll head on back."

"Dinner next Monday?" she asked hopefully, and Matt nodded. "Sure, if I'm back," he said, then, "this *is* still Tuesday, isn't it?" Melissa smiled and nodded, and Matt said, "OK, I'll give you a call sometime Saturday. I'm going to get some sleep and get packed, and leave first thing in the morning. I'm going to drive down this time. If nothing turns up I'll head back Saturday evening. That should give me enough time to check this out."

"Good luck," she called as she watched Matt walk toward the exit, and with a wave of his hand he was out the door.

After a brief walk across the commons, he opened the front door to his house with the key and bent to pick up a small pile of mail that had built up below the mail slot. Sorting through the mail, he saw that there was nothing urgent and threw the stack onto the kitchen counter. He grabbed a beer from the refrigerator and headed upstairs to the shower. Half an hour later, he stretched across the bed and was asleep within minutes.

The following morning Matt felt like a new man. He was up around eight, and it didn't take him long to pack his field gear: his laptop computer, a few notebooks, his cell phone, and a dozen other small but necessary items. Picking up the knapsack, he headed for the garage where he kept an extra set of clothing ready, packed and placed into a carryall. He returned to the basement and retrieved the cylinder, placing it in the back with his equipment. He entered the garage, pausing for a moment to activate the house alarm system, and placed the items in the back of the SUV.

Matt thought about the drive ahead. His current field vehicle was a two-year-old four wheel drive SUV, since his fieldwork usually took him off-road into some rough country and the SUV was the best choice for that type of driving. He also owned, but rarely got to drive, a much sportier Lotus Esprit. Consequently, the odometer on the dark red car showed barely 10,000 miles, and the car was in virtually the same condition as when he'd bought it new almost four years ago. It sat gleaming under the garage lights. Not this time, he thought to himself, as he slid into the SUV's seat. He checked the gauges as he switched on the ignition, then hit the button for the garage door. As the door slowly rose on its track, he eased the SUV out and slowly idled toward the street. The garage door slowly closed behind him and the security system for the house activated automatically as he pulled away. He headed for the interstate and east toward Harrisburg. A steady rain started and continued as he drove.

He made a mental note to take the Lotus for a cruise when he got back. The car was one of the few extravagances that he allowed himself, although he could have purchased any of a dozen other sport models in that price range. He had immediately zeroed in on the two-seater as he was killing time one day at a local dealership, and when it was delivered the following week he had taken a sabbatical and found himself cruising down I-95 to the Florida Keys. The trip had given him time to clear his head after Carolyn's death.

He had been dating Carolyn off and on for a few years, both of them wishing that the relationship could become more serious; but their work often took them in different directions for weeks at a time, and they both knew that a marriage would be hard pressed to survive such long periods of being apart. They had discussed it at length and had decided to maintain the status quo for now, maintaining their own separate living arrangements but spending what time they could together as they grew closer. He had planned on another two years of field work and then asking to be permanently assigned to the in-house staff at the university, while Carolyn's prospects at the insurance company where she worked appeared to be headed toward a vice-presidency here in town. Once they had gotten their respective career goals locked in, they had planned to settle down together.

It had been a bare three months after their discussion when Carolyn's commercial jet had gone down during a storm while flying over the Rockies on a return trip from San Francisco. Matt had learned of the crash while watching the evening news and he had immediately caught a flight to Colorado. Upon his arrival he had been whisked into a private room at the airport and had been given the news—there had been no survivors.

For weeks after that, he was numb to everything around him. His colleagues at the university had been there for him but, as so often happens, after a few months they slowly drifted away and returned to their own lives, leaving him alone. Not that he had noticed—he had thrown himself into his work, and in the ensuing months he got the reputation of being the university's best field man. But, to him, there was only work and sleep—nothing else seemed to interest him. Also after a few months, some of the more eligible females had made attempts to get him interested, but he just didn't have the heart for a relationship and they finally gave up. He had volunteered for the lengthy field assignments and the other field personnel gladly let him take their assignments, content to stay at home with their families.

He leisurely cruised across I-76, giving thought to his research plan as he drove. He was in a much better frame of mind after a good night's sleep, and rather than put off the research on TSP, he hoped to be able to devote a few hours to it while he was in Harrisburg. It would save him another trip, and he just might find something. He knew, through telephone contacts, the administrator of the Historical and Museum Commission, who was also a senior member of the state's Archaeological Society. Matt had supervised several projects for the Society, and felt sure that his reputation would allow him access to the archives. He should be able to locate any information on TSP in a fairly short time, if there was any information to be found.

The rain was steady for the length of the trip but, despite the wet conditions, he pulled into the outskirts of Harrisburg around three o'clock. After filling the SUV with gas, Matt pulled into a diner and ordered a late lunch. While he was waiting for the food, Matt placed a call to the Commission offices and asked for its interim Director, Dr. Simonson. He found that Simonson had left for the day but would be back in the office at eight the following morning. Matt left his name and cell number with the receptionist, and a message for Simonson that he would stop in around nine o'clock.

The following morning, Matt drove to the Archives building down on North Street. Although he had never visited the facility, it was an invaluable resource and had extensive information available online which he had used many times before. The Archives was also a repository for manuscripts and records of families and businesses with historical significance for Pennsylvania, and it was also connected with the National Archives and Records Administration in Washington. There were virtually millions of pages of documents, manuscripts, and reels of microfilm with untold thousands of images of things like deeds, wills, mortgages, estate papers, and the like. The Archives also held over a million special collection items such as photos, maps, audio recordings, and motion picture films—practically anything a researcher would need. If the Archives didn't have the information available, then it probably did not exist.

Matt saw the tall, monolithic building in the distance as he threaded through the downtown streets. Although he had never met Dr. Simonson, he was sure that his reputation, and their mutual acquaintances, would gain him quick access.

And he was not wrong. As soon as he gave the receptionist his name, she rose and ushered him into the elevator, taking him up to the fifth floor offices. There, she turned him over to Connie Samuels, Dr. Simonson's secretary.

"Mr. Collins, it's so good to meet you. Dr. Simonson is looking forward to your visit. He's meeting with one of our benefactors who dropped in unexpectedly, but he should be back in just a few minutes. Can I get you anything?"

"No, thank you, I'm fine." Matt was shown into Dr. Simonson's office, where he sat down in one of the comfortable leather chairs in front of the desk.

Just as he had gotten settled, Matt heard Miss Samuels saying, "Yes, sir, he just arrived. He's waiting in your office."

Matt heard the door open behind him, got up and turned toward the door. He was surprised to see a man not much older than himself, dressed in a business suit, walking toward him with an outstretched hand and a big smile.

"Matt Collins? I'm Henry Simonson, but please call me Hank. It's a real pleasure to have you here."

"Why, thank you, Hank," Matt replied. Simonson went behind the desk and sat down, motioning for Matt to sit as well.

"I must say I envy you, Mr. Collins. Ever since I became the interim Director of the Archives, I'm tied to this office most of the time. I miss getting a chance to do field work like I used to. Your reputation, of course, precedes you."

Matt laughed. "Thanks…and call me Matt. As you can probably tell, I'm doing some field work this trip," Matt said as he indicated his jeans, casual shirt, and work boots.

"Yes, I understand that's why you came. Anything, anything you need, just say the word."

"I really appreciate that," Matt said. "I'm headed over to Philadelphia tomorrow for an assignment from the Historical Society, but I'm also looking into another matter that was brought to my attention by a friend. Since the Archives are on the way, I thought I'd take advantage of the opportunity and stop in."

Dr. Simonson leaned forward. "Anything specific? As you know, we have extensive holdings here, and I know where most of the items are catalogued—in fact, I helped set up the current filing system."

"I'm looking for information on a company that operated around Philadelphia in the 1890's. It was called TSP. I checked in my university archives but came up blank."

"TSP? Doesn't ring a bell. Of course I couldn't possibly know everything in the Archives. But," he said, rising from the chair, "I'll be glad to narrow down your search area. Come with me and we'll head over to that section."

Matt followed Dr. Simonson through the outer office and onto the elevator. They went down two floors and exited. Matt was astonished. The research area was brightly lit and roomy, a far cry from what he usually dealt with in ill-lit basements.

"Let's see," Dr. Simonson was saying. "The Philadelphia archives from around 1885 to 1900 are in this section." He pointed out different areas to Matt. "Here are the paper archives. Over here we have the microfilm readers. We haven't completed transferring all of the documents yet," he added by way of explanation. "And over here we have photographs and the like. Where would you like to start?"

"I think the newspapers first. And the telephone records."

"Right here," Dr. Simonson said. He looked at his watch. "I leave around four o'clock today. If you haven't finished by then, I'll stop in on my way down. Otherwise, please check in with me if you finish before then."

"I will, and thank you," Matt said, shaking the man's hand. Simonson turned and left.

Once Matt had gotten his bearings, he began quickly and methodically going through the old documents. He had done this type of research hundreds of times before, and knew where to look and what to look for.

After two hours, he realized that there was nothing to be found among the old newspapers. He then switched to the telephone records, all of which were hand-written, and looked for clues. Again, nothing. Matt thought it was odd that a business would have no record of its existence anywhere, not even a single entry.

Matt then moved to one of the terminals on a nearby desk, typed in TSP, and waited for the search engine to complete its task. After a few minutes, the readout "No files found" appeared on the screen. He tried again but the results were the same.

With a sigh, Matt picked up his belongings and headed for the elevator. He looked at his watch and saw that it was nearly three o'clock. Dr. Simonson should still be in the office, Matt surmised.

He was, and Matt briefly explained that he had come up empty. Dr. Simonson shook his head. "Sorry, but it just may not be there in the first place. Well, we can't solve all of these research questions." He motioned Matt to the elevator. "I'll ride down with you. I just need you to sign the visitor log in the lobby. Almost forgot about it myself. We need to keep track of who comes in and has access to the Archives. It's one of the newer Government regulations, if we want to keep getting that grant money."

"Of course," Matt said, and followed Dr. Simonson to the reception area in the lobby. Matt took the pen and was about to sign the log when a gust of air from the front door blew the facing page over the current day's page. Matt was about to turn it back when he froze. There, dated two weeks prior, was an entry that was signed "H. Parkwood."

"Dr. Simonson, can you tell me anything about this entry?"

Dr. Simonson leaned over and looked at the notations at the end of the column that had been made by the receptionist. "Looks like this person was researching the same period as you, a couple of weeks ago. These code numbers at the end here allow us to track who was here, for how long, and what type of information they researched."

"Is there any way to get any more info on who this person was?"

"I'm afraid not, Matt. If the person shows a valid ID, by law we have to allow them access. It looks like this Parkwood made quite a few copies of old newspapers, judging from the copy fees we charged. Oh, and he came here from Philadelphia—or at least that's what his identification indicated."

Matt looked at the preceding pages but found no other entries with that name. "Looks like he only came in the one time."

"Is this significant?"

"No," Matt replied, and laughed. "Probably a coincidence. *Has* to be a coincidence. The name 'H. Parkwood' has something to do with what I'm researching—but I'm looking for something from the mid 1890's, not from a couple of weeks ago."

"Well, sorry we weren't able to help," Dr. Simonson said, extending his hand. "And, please, stop in the next time you're down this way."

"I will," Matt said, shaking the hand. "Thank you for your hospitality." Matt turned and headed through the doors to the parking lot.

CHAPTER 4

▼

As Matt drove toward his hotel, he puzzled over the entry in the visitor's log. Nothing made any sense other than a coincidence. For all he knew, there could be hundreds of individuals named 'H. Parkwood' in the United States, and several just in this area.

Matt stopped at a restaurant and ate a leisurely dinner, then returned to his room. On a hunch, he pulled the telephone book from the bedside drawer but saw that it was for Harrisburg. Frowning, he opened the phonebook and found the area codes for Philadelphia. He replaced the book, pulled out his cell phone, and called information for Philadelphia.

"Yes, I'd like a listing for Parkwood, first initial H." The operator checked and came back on the line. "Sorry, sir, but there's no listing for that name in the greater metropolitan area of Philadelphia."

On a hunch, Matt asked, "Could you check for a business listing? It's called TSP; I'm not sure what that stands for, if anything."

The operator came back. "Nothing in the white or yellow pages, but I do show an unlisted number for a TSP in Philadelphia. There's no address shown, but there's not a block on the number either. Could that be it?"

"Maybe. What's the listing?" The operator gave Matt the number and he thanked her and hung up.

He sat there for a few minutes and thought. Maybe whatever TSP had been in the 1890's, was now a business of some sort. He dialed the number and heard it ring six times before an emotionless computerized voice answered, saying simply, "Please leave a message."

Oh, well, Matt thought, can't hurt to try. "My name is Matt Collins. I'm try-ing to locate information on a person by the name of H. Parkwood with TSP. I've come into possession of a rather odd artifact that you might know something about. If you're at this number, please call me tonight or tomorrow morning. I'm in Harrisburg at the moment." He left his cell number and hung up.

The following morning he packed the SUV and checked out of the hotel, get-ting back on the interstate and heading for Philadelphia. The rain from the previ-ous day had stopped and the sun peeked through the clouds from time to time. Matt was glad to see the sunshine. A good six months of the year here was mainly spent under steel gray skies, and the sunshine was a welcome sight.

He was about thirty miles out of Harrisburg and had stopped briefly at a rest area when he noticed that his cell phone had received a text message. That was odd, he thought as he punched in the password and saw the message on the screen.

The message was short, simply an address on Front Street near the Delaware River in Philadelphia, followed by the name "Parkwood".

Well, well, Matt thought. Looks like I've hit paydirt. Obviously Parkwood *was* at the number he had called. He wheeled the SUV back onto the interstate, east toward Philadelphia.

Matt had visited Philadelphia many times in the past, and was more or less familiar with the area of the address in the message. Traffic slowed perceptively as he neared the metropolis, and he realized that he had arrived just at rush hour. Ninety minutes later, he pulled into the parking lot of the hotel where he usually stayed in Philadelphia and booked a room for the night. His bags were brought to the room and he tipped the bellman, locked the door, and headed for the shower.

Matt preferred this old hotel to the national chains because of the cozy atmo-sphere and the personalized service. It was more like a bed and breakfast, although every amenity was available. After getting out of the shower and dress-ing, he called room service and ordered a light dinner. While he waited for the food to arrive, he pulled his laptop out of its case and booted it up. He pulled up a map of Philadelphia from the files and zoomed in on his location.

As he had thought, the address given by Parkwood was within walking dis-tance, although he had decided to drive to it anyway. Matt thought about recon-noitering the address but decided to wait until morning to go there, since it was already evening and he still had to eat. He made a call to Melissa's voice mail, asking her to contact the Archaeological Society to let them know that he might be delayed for the assignment.

He answered a light knock at the door and found Room Service there to deliver his meal. He signed the slip, wheeled the cart inside, and closed the door.

The rest of the evening was uneventful. Matt turned in before ten, hoping to get an early start in the morning.

CHAPTER 5

▼

Matt was up by six and, following his morning workout, he showered, shaved, and dressed. He grabbed the knapsack containing the cylinder, along with the laptop and a few essential items, then went down to the breakfast room and had a light meal and some coffee. He then walked through the lobby to the reception desk and asked the girl at the counter to hold his room for another night.

Matt looked at his watch: almost eight thirty. He walked out to the SUV and, driving slowly, made his way to the address a few blocks away.

There wasn't much activity in this part of town. Matt had no trouble finding the address, a large six-story building devoid of markings. Only the top floor windows were functional; the other floors had their windows painted over. He parked at the front, picked up the knapsack with the cylinder, and went up to the solid double doors. There was nothing on the doors except a small placard that said, 'TSP'. He tried the doors but found that they were locked. He then saw a buzzer at one side and pressed it.

The small intercom box next to the button came to life. "What can I do for you, sir?" He looked up and saw a small video camera trained on the entrance area.

"My name is Matt Collins. I'm looking for someone named Parkwood. I was given this address."

There was a brief silence, then the voice returned. "Please wait a couple of minutes and I'll buzz you in." The speaker went dead.

Matt waited a few minutes, then heard the door buzz as the lock was deactivated. He pushed on the door and entered the foyer, the door closing behind him and locking again with a decisive click.

A long corridor stretched out in front of him, and in the distance he saw an elderly man walking toward him, a cane in one hand. The light was dim and it was hard to make out the man's features. He discerned a white lab coat, a pair of glasses, white hair combed back, and a noticeable limp. As he approached, the man held out his free hand.

"Matt Collins. It's been a long time."

Matt was confused. "Do I know you?" he said, squinting in the dim light to try and discern the man's features.

"I should hope you would remember me. Professor Henry Parkwood. I taught your first year Physics class at the University."

"Of course," Matt said, extending his own hand. "It's been, what, twelve, fifteen years? But what are you doing here? What's this all about?"

"In good time, Mr. Collins, in good time. Please follow me. I guarantee you're going to be surprised."

Matt followed the old man as he shuffled along the dark hallway. Without preamble, the old man began talking. "This is my research facility. Just a few years ago, I was finally able to develop the means with which to test my theories," Parkwood said. "I obtained a government grant and set up this facility seven years ago. To keep it operational, I've called in forty years' worth of favors so that I could continue my research. So far, I've been successful in keeping it operational. However, this research facility is operating on borrowed time. I'll explain about that later."

Parkwood stopped and turned to Matt. "I wasted many years, obviously thinking that my research would require colossal amounts of equipment and, of course, money, both of which I went through." He shook his head. "How wrong I was, at least in terms of our present experiments. The actual apparatus required is surprisingly simple. The only requirements, I later found, were a relatively large and stable power source, and a place to work without interruption or interference. This complex," he said, waving his arm around, "took two years to build. A couple of stories below us is our own generator room...unlimited power. A small nuclear reactor." He smiled at Matt's look of concern. "Don't be alarmed. It's as safe as can be, and not much bigger than a large industrial freezer. It is of course monitored constantly, but it provides us with more than enough perpetual power with virtually no maintenance. Surprising what the government provides funding for, as long as you have the right credentials. Although they have no idea about our current project." He moved forward again. Matt still had no idea what Parkwood was talking about. He *seemed* sane enough, but he was getting on in years. You could never tell.

Matt said, "Your theories? Professor, you're assuming that I know what you're talking about. I don't. And, if you remember I had a hard enough time just getting through your class. I'm afraid you and I never got a chance to discuss your theories."

"I apologize, Mr. Collins," Parkwood said, nodding. "You're right, I'm getting ahead of myself. Of course you wouldn't know what I'm talking about. But you will soon enough." They reached one of the doorways near the end of the hallway, and Parkwood punched in a combination code on the keypad next to the door. The door opened with a slight click and Parkwood pushed it open.

As they stepped inside, Matt could see a few workstations with computer terminals arranged in a semicircle facing the far end of the room. They were standing on an elevated platform, and one floor below Matt saw a few individuals that appeared to be technicians bustling around a large upright oval shape near the center of the room. The oval appeared to be made of highly polished aluminum or steel. The lights of the room reflected off of its surface. Otherwise, a few consoles lined the lower walls. In all, it appeared to be a rather Spartan research facility for some unknown purpose. None of the consoles below appeared to be actively operating.

Matt looked at Parkwood and said, "You don't seem to have too many people in this research facility."

Parkwood grimaced. "I will explain that shortly as well, Mr. Collins. In the meantime, pull up a chair." Parkwood did the same. He turned to Matt and said, "Mr. Collins, what do you consider man's greatest dream?"

Matt looked at him, frowning slightly. "I don't understand what you mean."

"Well, Mr. Collins, man has always aspired to do the impossible. Less than two centuries ago, powered flight was considered an impossibility. Less than a hundred years ago, common use of the computer was undreamed of. Eradication of disease, a longer life span, traveling the world in hours…all of these boons to mankind have been sprung upon us rather quickly during the last few generations, you'll agree. Even now the first manned flights to Mars are about to occur. Another hundred years might find us exploring our own galaxy." He paused. "Most scientific theories are what I would term 'forward-thinking'. So, what do you think is man's greatest aspiration?"

"I don't know," Matt said. "Immortality, I suppose, although even that would get boring after a few hundred years, I guess. A cure for all diseases, maybe. I've never really thought about it. My work keeps me busy enough. I've never had much time to theorize."

"Ah, yes, your work. I took the liberty of bringing myself up to date on you between last night and your visit this morning." Matt watched as Professor Parkwood picked up a sheath of papers from the table and read from them. "Matt Collins, age thirty-two, former assistant history professor at the University in Pittsburgh. Bachelor's in Arts and Sciences, Master's in History with a Minor in Archaeology. Member of the State Archaeological Society. Primary field of interest, late nineteenth century. Then some personal information: home address, vehicle registrations, engaged at one time…"

"That's enough," Matt said with a frown, interrupting him. Professor Parkwood nodded and said, "Yes, well…interesting, the information that's available nowadays." He placed the papers back on the table. "In the years since you attended the university, you've built up quite an impressive record, especially in regard to historical study of the nineteenth century. A practical man. I'm glad to see that at least part of my teaching was taken to heart by some of you students. As I said, most scientific theories are "forward-thinking." My own field of endeavor has turned out to be quite the opposite."

"Strictly speaking, so has mine," Matt replied. "My work allows me to understand, at least in a small way, the way man lived in one period of the past."

"But you have to rely on a chance discovery, and a few odd pieces of a puzzle, to be able to do that, am I right?"

"Well, yes, of course," Matt confessed. "I can't really know everything. No one can. It's only been during the twentieth century that we began keeping complete permanent records…photos, videos, recordings and the like. Further back than that, it's mostly just guesswork."

Parkwood gave Matt a serious look. "What if I told you that you could see exactly what life was like in, let's say, 1865?"

"I'd say you were mistaken," Matt said. "There are no comprehensive records of that era. With few exceptions, our understanding of life back then comes from personal letters, some from novels of the time, some from artifacts and still photos, but nothing very detailed." Matt was curious. "Why, have you found a cache of documentation or something that provides a detailed record of some event? I'll be glad to take a look at it for you. But, I have to tell you that there have been the odd finds now and then, where someone wrote down details of something…but never more than a few days or weeks worth, and nothing of any great consequence." Matt felt that he had discovered the old man's secret, and was about to explain to him that his discovery wasn't all that important. But, there was still the puzzle of the cylinder, and Matt wanted to get to the bottom of that mystery. So he remained silent.

"Of course you'd say that," Parkwood said. "Or worse, you'd think I was crazy." Matt sensed that Parkwood was going to say more, but the old man had apparently changed his mind. "Well, enough for now. Let's go back to my office and take a look at what brought you here."

Ten minutes later they were seated on either side of the large desk. Matt reached into the backpack, removed the cylinder and placed it on the desk. Parkwood looked at the cylinder, then at Matt. With a slight grin, Parkwood swiveled his desk chair around and opened one of the doors to the bookcase behind him. Inside, Matt saw another eight cylinders identical to the one on the desk, sitting upright in their wooden slots. Matt's eyes widened. "You've found more of them?" Matt asked. Smiling now, Parkwood closed the bookcase door and turned once again to the desk.

"This cylinder," Parkwood continued, tapping the cylinder on the desk with his finger, "came from this research facility. It has reverse threads that are machined so precisely by laser that when the two halves are joined and tightened the seam cannot be seen." Parkwood reached out and, taking the cylinder in both hands, gave the top and bottom a sudden sharp twist in opposite directions. The seam popped into view, and Parkwood slowly unscrewed the two halves. "And, if you haven't removed them, there should be papers inside. On those papers are most likely mathematical equations." Parkwood removed the top half and set it aside. The cylinder was empty. He looked up at Matt with a questioning look on his face.

"The papers are here," Matt said, again reaching into the backpack. "I did remove them, but I couldn't make heads or tails of what they meant." He handed the papers to Parkwood. "My only clue was the inscription on the cylinder, and I thought some research at the Archives in Harrisburg would shed some light on TSP, a company or business I assumed was from the latter part of the nineteenth century. Then I was fortunate enough to follow up a couple of clues and find you."

Parkwood smiled as he examined the papers and the short personal note. "As I explained, this facility did not exist until seven years ago. TSP did not exist as an entity until two years ago. The initials TSP, by the way, stand for Time Synchronization Project, which is what we've come to call it. These papers hopefully contain information that will assist us with a problem that has come up. Mathematically, it's against the odds that this cylinder was even found, although it was placed in an area where it had the best chance of being found. We had planned on just such a contingency but we had no way of knowing that any of the cylinders had been used—until you showed up with one. There are probably a couple of other cylinders, each identical, buried within a ten or twenty mile radius of this complex. The person who buried the cylinders would have chosen the most likely places for one or more of them to be found, based on information about current construction or excavation projects. Yours is the first, and none too soon." He examined the papers. "Was there anything else in the cylinder?"

"No, only the papers. Should there have been something else?"

"Possibly, but not likely. I had hoped that there might be something more personal but this cylinder was planted before any really serious problems arose, apparently."

Matt thought that the old man was rambling. Nothing that he said was making much sense. "You couldn't have known about those papers," Matt said. "This cylinder was buried in concrete over a hundred years old. It's been verified that the concrete was undisturbed. How could someone have gotten this cylinder underneath all that concrete without disturbing it?"

Parkwood looked up. "Because the cylinder was put into the ground just before the concrete was poured. This was one of our contingency plans in case a problem arose. The person who put it there couldn't have been sure that anyone would even find the cylinder." Parkwood looked up at the ceiling. "A ten thousand-to-one chance, and it worked. Coincidence? Or luck? Perhaps that's why the other cylinders are still out there." He looked back at Matt. "Mr. Collins, this facility is quite specialized, designed for one purpose but now used for something entirely different."

Matt was sure the old man was demented. "What, the past? I hate to tell you this, but this is not the way the study of history works. You can't sit at a console with a bunch of equipment and uncover the past. You have to get out there and look for it."

"Or have it come to you," Parkwood said.

Matt was now sure that the old man, if not totally gone, was certainly unbalanced. Matt got up. "Professor Parkwood, I'm serious about my work. I don't have time to play games." He headed for the door.

"I am serious about my work, too, Mr. Collins. If you leave now you will be turning your back on what could be your greatest find—and perhaps your greatest adventure."

Matt was reaching for the doorknob when he hesitated. There was still the question of the cylinder. His mind refused to believe the obvious explanation. Still…he turned to look at Parkwood.

Parkwood said, "The past, Mr. Collins. It's as close as a short walk down that hallway." Parkwood paused. "Humor me. I of course expected this kind of reaction. Let me prove it to you."

Matt shook his head in resignation. "Whatever," he said. "Show me your smoke and mirrors show. I might as well get something out of this trip."

CHAPTER 6

▼

They were back in the room near the end of the hall. Parkwood had motioned Matt to sit at one of the consoles, and had pulled a chair up to the console as well.

"What I am about to tell you is going to sound fantastic, and unbelievable," Parkwood said. "I only ask that you hear me out.

"As you know, my field has always been physics. When this facility was first created, I was attempting to perfect a way to transport solid matter through space and reconstitute it at the other end—a dream of many scientists over the past few decades, but with fairly recent technological advances my colleagues and I finally thought that we might be able to actually do it. This facility had six of these chambers, for want of a better word, all identical, with six of them arranged around the outer edge of this complex and six in an identical complex a few blocks away. They were all at one time operational to some degree.

"Last year, we activated one of the chambers that you see there." Parkwood pointed to the far end of the room.

"Of course, when we activated the first chamber we expected it to connect with its corresponding 'destination portal' in the other complex, and have the matter reappear there. However, the destination portal sat dormant. Nothing we did could get it to 'resonate' with the master portal. And yet, when we placed objects into the master portal they disappeared. We at first thought they were somehow being vaporized. Then, one of my colleagues constructed a high frequency transmitter, switched it on, and sent it into the portal.

"It disappeared, all right, but we *continued to receive the signal from it* through the portal. Well, we had a real problem on our hands. Where was it? The destination portal, where it should have ended up, was completely inoperative and empty. We then surmised that the transmitter had somehow been transported to a location independent of the destination portal.

"We shut down our equipment, and began trying to pick up the signal upstairs in our communications center. We thought the transmitter might have ended up somewhere in the vicinity of the complex. But, that was not the case. Since it was using a unique transmitting frequency, we even enlisted the aid of our contacts in the government, explaining that we had lost a simple tracking device and could they please help us locate it. None of those agencies was able to locate the signal anywhere on earth.

"After a few days, we re-energized the portal and, after some adjustments to the equipment, again picked up the signal. Obviously we knew that the transmitter was working, but where was it? It was then that another of my colleagues, at our senior staff meeting, threw out the idea that perhaps we weren't focusing in the right direction. She said we should think outside the box, so to speak, and suggested that perhaps it wasn't *where*, but *when*, the transmitter was sending its signal from. Most of us dismissed this possibility outright, but a couple of our team suddenly looked as if they had seen a revelation.

"As you know, my field is physics, and I am aware of quantum theory, but a couple of my colleagues were some of the acknowledged experts in that field. They literally ran for the computers and began checking the variables for the experiment. The rest of us stood and watched them as they checked this, verified that, and finally nodded to each other and said, 'It's possible.' They turned to us and said, 'We think she may be right.'"

Parkwood leaned back in the chair. "Well, you can imagine our reaction. Could it be? It was too fantastic, and yet these were the experts. Their opinion, with which I was finally forced to agree, was that with this equipment we had inadvertently created a temporal doorway—a passageway to another time. But, to where?

"We spent the night constructing another probe, this one with video, sampling equipment, and whatever else we thought might be needed, to find out where, or when, the transmitter had gone. We had no idea if the probe's equipment would be able to send back the data. We thought that it could, since the initial transmitter had worked, but that was a simple tone signal. And, of course, we had no way of knowing where the other end *was*. We still didn't know if there was air, and solid ground. The first probe could have been floating in space for all we knew, or buried deep underground. In any event, we launched the probe, and immediately began receiving telemetry and video. We were finally able to ascertain that there was air, what appeared to be solid ground, and that it was a cold climate. It was a week before we saw a man riding in the distance on a horse. That told us nothing, since we could have been looking at a real time picture, for all we knew at that point."

Parkwood shifted in his seat. "But nothing from the probe could tell us what year it had been sent to, if indeed it had crossed the time barrier.

"Finally, after much argument, we decided that one of us would need to go through the portal and gather the information that we needed. I knew that this would be the ultimate test, and would either be a success or kill the volunteer, who by the way was Barrett, one of my closest colleagues here at the facility. We outfitted him as best we could in protective gear, loaded him up with essential equipment, and one evening he stepped through the portal and vanished.

"We heard nothing for a couple of days, and feared the worst. Then, out of the blue we picked up Barrett's signal. We were able to maintain contact for a couple of days, off and on for a few minutes at a time, just long enough to learn that Barrett had landed near a small town in a remote part of Pennsylvania in early February of 1894. Thank God for that. One miscalculation and he could just as easily ended up floating in space, or in the middle of the ocean.

"But, our success spawned a new problem. In our rush to explore this incalculable opportunity, we had failed to think of the most obvious contingency: how to get our man back. The equipment allowed us to communicate with him but the communication became intermittent. And, we had been unable to reverse the process. This temporal doorway that we had opened only went in one direction—from here to there. Although we were able to receive electronic signals through the portal, actual matter was another thing. There was also no way, no place for anyone or anything to be able to return *through*. Barrett would be trapped there for the rest of his life if we weren't able to come up with a solution.

"Three quarters of our team set about to find out why the destination chamber hadn't worked on the initial experiment, while the rest of us monitored Barrett's progress. It took a few weeks, during which Barrett leased the farm with the substantial sum of money that we sent through to him." Parkwood smiled. "That money was printed right here. It was the only way to fund him quickly enough. As far as we can tell, we didn't upset the economy of that time period." Parkwood became serious again. "The team here finally found one possible solution, which it turns out was the only chance that we'd ever have to get Barrett back here. It was really very simple. We dismantled the destination chamber portal and sent it through, piece by piece, to Barrett. It would be up to him to reconstruct it at his end, and see if we could get it to work.

"Well, I can tell you that this in itself became a problem. The equipment didn't just go through and appear at Barrett's location. We'd send six pieces of equipment through at the same time, one right after the other, but they'd randomly appear at Barrett's end, sometimes hours apart and in different locations. The only luck we had was that all of the equipment materialized within a half-mile radius of Barrett's position at the farm. Because of that, he'd have to go on daily foraging runs around the farm and look for the components. We quickly began tagging the components with radio markers and he was able to zero right in on them. Fortunately the farm was in a rural area. After a few months of labor, Barrett got everything put together.

"We hoped that we would be creating a permanent link to 1894." Parkwood paused. "Well, permanent as long as there was a stable power source at the other end, and if we could get the equipment to work. Constructing a reactor in 1894 was obviously out of the question. There wasn't even enough conventional electrical power, and no way to obtain it anyway. We were finally able to construct a reliable source."

Fascinated with the story so far, but not really believing any of it, Matt played along. "A generator?" Matt asked, and Parkwood shook his head.

"No...too much fuel required. It was actually quite simple. Solar power. For all of the theory involved, this equipment operates on direct current, not alternating current. We'd have an unlimited supply of fuel for the solar cells, or would by spring in Barrett's time. At any rate, we kept at it, and so did Barrett; he refurbished the farm, replaced the roof of the barn with camouflaged solar cells, and got the whole thing set up. Another two months of work paid off when the equipment at his end finally became active. The simple solution, we learned, was that the temporal doorway to then, the one in this room, was unable to resonate with a destination portal that was located in the present, since by its very nature it was a doorway to another time.

"In non-technical terms, we had been trying to align the operating frequencies to match here on the master site and on Barrett's end. Simply stated, it turns out that these portals, for want of a better word, must be exactly one hundred eighty degrees off frequency from each other, so that each portal is a mirror image of the other. Well, it sounds simple but trying to balance the power, communications, and everything else required was extremely difficult, since adjusting one piece of the equation sent another piece out of sync. Even voice and data communications with Barrett at those low power levels would throw the whole apparatus slightly out of sync. Besides that, we had to re-synchronize everything every single day. Very frustrating. We finally programmed the computers to do this and, when we'd scan for and receive a signal from Barrett, we were fully operational within an hour. The computers locked on to the signal, compensated for the variables and kept everything stable for as long as possible. We were finally able to achieve stable transfers between the portals, but each transfer depleted the power cells at the other end and it took days or sometimes weeks for the power to build back up again."

"You see, although we had designed the equipment for matter transfer, once activated it became equipment for a temporal doorway, although we didn't know it at the time. Once Barrett activated the portal at his end, the whole thing began operating. His equipment is located in the cellar of the main farmhouse. The equipment unfortunately requires an inordinate amount of power to operate when transferring matter—less so when we simply communicate. Even so, we were usually able to maintain a good hour or two of contact daily with Barrett. We learned from our mistakes, but we were fantastically lucky that first time in that we got the whole system to work inside of eight months."

"And your man Barrett?" Matt asked. "Is he…"

"Oh, he was even able to set up another portal in another city. He came back within the year, with more data than we've been able to sort through. Unfortunately, he passed away recently, and unexpectedly, from a stroke.

"We at one time had both portals fully operational. Two were complete, Barrett's first one and the newer one that he set up later. We were able to duplicate the temporal doorways for the remaining four portals, but for some reason they never operated properly. Very unstable. We were finally forced to shut them down. The reason was that the temporal fields generated by the four one-way portals collapsed after they'd been operating for just a few months, and all four of them collapsed within a month of each other. Fortunately we didn't have anyone visiting those time periods or they would have been trapped when the doorways collapsed. For some reason that we don't know, these links to the past are not permanent. We've had the two remaining completed portals operational for about eighteen months, and so far they've been very stable. But, we've recently noticed serious fluctuations in the readings for the equipment. We believe that the remaining two portals will also cease to operate in the near future. Since the problems surfaced, we've only used the barest minimum of power to maintain communications. No transfers of people or materials". Parkwood paused for a moment and shook his head sadly. "Before the problems became apparent, and wanting to complete our research, we finally decided that we needed an individual willing to risk another journey through the remaining completed portal, just like Barrett had done."

"And?" Matt asked, intrigued by this implausible story but curious as to where it was going.

"My son, Ben, had worked with me closely from the beginning. He was concerned that we would lose the only opportunity we might ever have for such a fantastic experiment. So, on his own, he activated this portal and went through." Parkwood brightened. "Since only Barrett had done it before, Ben proved that, if the portals are stable and operational, there is no problem moving between now and…then."

"But Professor! Just for the sake of argument, since I'm still not convinced of all this, what about the risks to history?" Matt replied. "What if one of your people had changed something? Think of the consequences!"

Parkwood was expecting this. "Ah, yes, the Grandmother paradox, or whatever you want to call it, which goes something like: What if you went back in time and killed your grandmother before she had any children? Then you could never be born to go back in time and kill your grandmother. We argued the same point early into the first experiment, practically ad infinitum. But, these people you see around you are scientists, and committed to the same ideals as myself. We have come to find that travel in time is actually not much different than traveling to another city, for instance—*if* you take care not to make any changes. Then, you end up being part of what happened at that time and place in history. Besides, one theory even suggests that you *can't* change history. That even if you tried, you wouldn't be able to. Because it's already happened, from our perspective, and is inviolate. However, that's a theory that we absolutely do not want to test."

Matt shook his head. "Assuming this is all true, you still can't know that for sure."

"Well, we've never *tried* to change history. We were not there for that. Once we realized what we had here, we went there simply to observe." Parkwood leaned forward to the computer screen. "The two remaining operational portals are now connected to these dates and times," he said, pointing to the screen. "Although it is March here, Portal Two, the one in this room, is connected to a small town in northeastern Pennsylvania called Montrose, in August 1896. Portal One is connected to Philadelphia, also in 1896. Oddly enough, it's about three days ahead of this portal. Time at the other end, of course, progresses at the same rate as our time. So, next year our time, it will be 1897 at the other end. We had no control over where the initial transport took us." He pointed to the first entry. "Our earliest contact time for one of the portals was 1823, but that was one of the portals that collapsed. We have not made contact further back than that, nor have we tried. We've already amassed so much data that we'll never be able to sift through it all in our lifetimes." Parkwood pointed to another entry. "The strange thing, though, about these two remaining portals is that they are virtually parallel in time and within a few hundred miles from each other. Almost identical, which is most unusual. We were never able to explain that, since the time difference between all of the other portals was a couple of decades apart at the least, and geographically quite far apart."

"And the Philadelphia portal?" Matt asked.

"It's dormant at the moment; we decided that having just one portal operational in the same time period was sufficient. Besides, the Philadelphia portal will collapse and cease to exist within a few months, just like the others."

CHAPTER 7

▼

"Look, Professor, even if I believed all of this, and I don't yet, surely all of this is classified. Why are you even telling me about all of this?" Matt said.

"Because you are in a very unique position to help us...to help me," Parkwood replied. "As I said, our time has almost run out. Once the portals collapse, we are not constructing any new ones. Once they collapse, this facility will be shut down and dismantled. This is as it should be. You are right, the potential dangers of such a project are beyond belief if it fell into the wrong hands. No one, save a handful of my most trusted colleagues here, knows the full extent of the operation. I doubt that any of them alone could reproduce what we have here, nor could I again. Some discoveries are better left unheralded; this has turned out to be one of those."

Parkwood paused. "But, we have a problem. My son is currently conducting research, in 1896. The problem is that we haven't heard from him for the last three weeks. Then, a few days ago the equipment on that end simply stopped working. We checked but it's not a collapse of the time field like the others. It's as if all of the equipment at that end has simply been turned off. I fear that something may have happened to my son. We've scoured as many of the old newspapers from that era that we could find, those that still exist, and there's no mention of anything involving him." Matt realized that this explained Parkwood's presence at the Archives.

Parkwood got up and paced around the room. "He could be lying dead, for all I know, but again there's no mention of him in that era's news reports. It's as if he simply vanished."

"So send someone to find him," Matt said, and Parkwood nodded.

"Yes, exactly what we need to do. But, we have the bare minimum of personnel still here to be able to operate the equipment. None of us can be spared, or we would have done what you suggest already. No, none of *us* can go", Parkwood paused, looking at Matt, "...but you could."

Matt couldn't believe what he'd just heard. "You want *me* to get into that thing? Professor Parkwood, even assuming that I believed you, and that this is an actual portal to another time, I'm not trained for this kind of work. You yourself said how incredibly dangerous it could be if something were changed. I could change something and not even know it—and come back to a world that I don't even know, a world where I might not ever have existed."

Parkwood shook his head dismissively, then said flatly, "That shouldn't happen."

"*Shouldn't* happen?" Matt said, incredulous. "That's as sure as you are?"

"The very fact that we're here, right now, indicates that nothing occurred," Parkwood said. "Of course, there are theories about parallel existences and that sort of thing, but we've never had proof of that. We *do* have proof of this," he said, with a sweep of his hand, "proof that this works. It is my belief that there is one past, one present, and one future. I'm simply offering you the opportunity to visit some place unique." Parkwood paused, then continued. "And I'm asking you: help me, help my son. Help me to complete this great experiment so that it can come to a successful conclusion. I cannot leave my son back there. I can't go for him. I need someone like you, Mr. Collins—in fact, oddly enough it turns out that it's you in particular that I need. You're very familiar with that time period, how they lived, how they acted. You could blend in far more easily than any of us."

Matt's head whirled. The opportunity was fantastic, and yet so much could go wrong. Parkwood saw his hesitation and reached for the telephone. He punched in an extension and said in a low voice, "Please ask Sandra to come to my office." He hung up the phone and continued speaking to Matt.

"It should take you no more than a few weeks. Think of it as a vacation. Surely you could use some time away. And think of the information, the knowledge that you would obtain! Not to just study a culture, but to live and breathe it, to exist with it." Parkwood picked up a folder from the desk. "We can have you ready to go inside of seventy-two hours. A few inoculations, period clothing, some material for you to review about the region and the people you'd be dealing with. And information on how to get the portal at that end operational again. After that, once you're there, you can make your own decisions as to how you want to proceed." Parkwood placed the file back on the desk and sat down.

"Think it over, Mr. Collins, but don't take too long. I will need you to let me know by tonight if you do decide to do this." Parkwood looked up at Matt. "I'm not trying to pressure you, but if you don't help me, you may well be dooming my son to die over a hundred years before he was born. Please, Mr. Collins." There was a knock at the door, and a young woman in her late twenties entered and sat down in the chair next to Matt.

"Sandra, this is Matt Collins, one of my old students and something of an expert on the nineteenth century. It's all right, I've explained our experiments to him. You can speak freely." Parkwood turned back to Matt. "Mr. Collins, this is Sandra Parkwood, Ben's wife."

Matt turned to the woman and was about to say something when he saw the anxious look on her face. It was clear from her drawn face that she had been suffering from some kind of strain recently. She abruptly said, "Will you help us, Mr. Collins? Will you help me to get Ben back?"

Matt was nonplussed. "I…I don't know," he said, shifting uncomfortably in the chair, not looking at her. Matt looked up at Professor Parkwood. "You've got to admit, this is a lot to spring on someone so quickly."

"Why do you think I told you everything?" Professor Parkwood said. "When I heard you were here, with the cylinder, and then found out that you're one of the acknowledged authorities on that very time period, well, I didn't know what to think. Everything seemed to fall together. The right person, at the right place and time, someone who could specifically help us…

"Well, what *could* I think? Fate, karma, whatever you want to call it—I only knew that I had to try to convince you to do this, and quickly. Think of the opportunity, Mr. Collins! And it works out to everyone's advantage."

"I just don't know…" Matt said. He stood up. "Professor, I've always known you to be a man of integrity. But, this is just too fantastic. I'll need some time to sort it all out."

"Come with us," Professor Parkwood said, moving toward the door. "We'll give you the full tour, let you see the equipment, how everything works. And let you look at some of the items Barrett brought back. Those should convince you that this is real."

Matt followed Professor Parkwood and Sandra down the hall once again, only this time they led him down to the lower floor of the facility. As Matt followed them, he felt his eyes drawn toward the large shape at the far end of the room. The portal, although dormant, seemed to be an entity in its own right. He slowed, studying the huge shape, and then slowly walked toward it.

Professor Parkwood followed behind him but said nothing. As Matt neared the portal, his hand involuntarily reached up and touched the surface. It was cold, the polished stainless steel reflecting his image. He looked up. The portal was massive, bigger than it had looked from above, the opening a good fifteen feet tall and at least ten feet wide. The thing looked like a large silver oval dough-nut, deceptively simple in its design. "So this is it?" Matt said.

Parkwood nodded. "This is it," he said. "Not as complex as you had expected, is it?"

"I would have expected something more...complicated," Matt admitted. He turned away and walked with Parkwood back toward Sandra. She had moved ahead and opened a door that led into a large storeroom, standing aside so that Matt and Professor Parkwood could enter.

"Barrett sent back several items while he was there, and we keep those in here for research." Matt saw several areas: one held clothing, another held a stack of newspapers, still another held an assortment of tinware, a few guns, leather goods, and the like. Matt moved over to the newspapers and began looking through them.

"These could easily be reproductions, Professor," Matt said as he examined the newspapers. "The paper feels new, but that doesn't prove anything. The same goes for the clothing. But this..." He picked up one of the guns lying on the table, and immediately recognized a rare Smith and Wesson revolver that was in perfect condition. He examined the piece closely, then laid it back gently on the table. "That looks real enough," he said. "I know for a fact that only a few of those still exist, and none in as good a condition as this one. That one would be worth thousands to a collector."

"It's real enough, Mr. Collins, and as you can see it is in perfect condition. It should be; it is less than two years old—that is, from when it was manufactured in the 1890's." Professor Parkwood looked at Matt. "From your point of view, I can see how you'd be skeptical. Yes, all of these items could be clever forgeries. But, what purpose would I have in doing that? I tell you, these things are authen-tic. What can I do to convince you that this is all real?"

Matt was silent as he turned away. The whole concept of this facility was unbelievable, and yet he knew that nothing was impossible. If Professor Park-wood and his colleagues had perfected a way to travel to 1896, and if he *was* allowed to go...

But grave doubts kept coming to the fore. What if, as Professor Parkwood had mentioned, the portal collapsed while he was gone? He'd never be able to get back.

And then he thought: back to what? His life here was empty. His work brought him some measure of satisfaction, but since Carolyn's death he had become an empty shell. In a worst case scenario, would it be so bad if he never came back? He had no ties to keep him here. He'd just have to keep a low profile and live out his life.

Still, this—the here and now—was *his* time, and although he didn't know exactly what it was, his beliefs told him that he had been put on this earth for a purpose. Then again, maybe this *was* the purpose.

As he turned it over in his mind, he realized that what Professor Parkwood had said was true—this was perhaps one of the most unique opportunities ever offered to someone. Looking at it from that angle, Matt suddenly realized that he could not let a chance like this escape.

Professor Parkwood watched Matt closely as Matt thought it over. He pointed to a video monitor on a nearby computer desk and said, "Mr. Collins, look at this." Professor Parkwood activated the monitor and clicked the mouse. A recorded video began playing, and Matt could see a panoramic view of a 19th century town from a high vantage point.

"This, Mr. Collins, is from a small camera that Ben installed on the tower of the County Courthouse in Montrose in 1896. This feed was recorded just a few weeks ago, and transmitted to us by Ben before the equipment on that end failed." Matt marveled at the video, a view of long-dead townspeople going about their business—the images sharp and in full color, nothing like the old grainy, black and white films he had seen over the years from the late 19th and early 20th century. To have a chance at being a part of that, to live in that culture and interact with its inhabitants, was too great an opportunity to miss.

He turned back to Professor Parkwood and said, "If I agree to do this, what will I need to do?"

"We'll take care of everything," Professor Parkwood said with a smile, knowing that Matt had decided to help him. "Just go along with Sandra and she'll get you started." Matt nodded and followed Sandra out.

CHAPTER 8

▼

It was two days later and Matt hadn't left the confines of the facility. Professor Parkwood had sent someone to collect his things from the hotel and pay the bill, and his SUV had been brought down into the underground garage of the complex. Matt had also sent a message to Melissa, explaining that he would be out of contact for a few weeks, and that his research for the Archaeological Society needed to be postponed.

The facility had a small but well-equipped medical section, and Matt had endured a complete physical with the accompanying battery of tests. In addition, he had been inoculated against typhoid, diphtheria, smallpox, and other diseases and maladies that simply no longer existed in the 21st century. To go back and encounter a disease for which he had no protection could and probably would make short work of him. He was also measured for period clothing, which was procured from the samples that Barrett had brought back.

Matt spent much of his spare time poring over the old newspapers of the period, especially those relevant to Montrose. The staff had scanned and downloaded digital versions of many of the papers into one of the laptops that he would be taking with him. Fortunately, he was a fast reader and able to retain a lot of the information. The newspapers of that era were generally small weeklies, and usually consisted of a half-dozen pages at most. The papers gave a truncated account of life in Susquehanna County at that time, complete with weddings, births, obituaries, and quite a few social commentaries detailing gatherings among the wealthier residents. He learned the names of some of the principal citizens, and got a feel for the commerce of the city.

The official story would be that Matt was Henry Parkwood's nephew, come to town to look for his missing cousin, Ben Parkwood.

Professor Parkwood gave Matt the necessary background information: Barrett had purchased the Montrose farmhouse under the name of Henry Parkwood, and had explained to the locals that it was an investment property for Mr. Parkwood, a rich but somewhat eccentric type from Philadelphia. Barrett had presented himself as being Parkwood's business manager, which explained the renovations he was making at the farm. Barrett had explained that Mr. Parkwood and members of his family might be staying at the farm from time to time, and that Parkwood had wanted it renovated to his specifications prior to his arrival. Since Barrett could not accomplish setting up all of the equipment by himself, he had hired tradesmen from the area and had explained to them that Mr. Parkwood was trying out some new building materials at the farm. This explained the different material consistency of the panels for the barn roof, which were in actuality the solar panels.

Barrett had also hired miners from nearby Forest City to dig and reinforce a passageway between the cellar of the farmhouse and the barn. Once those tasks had been accomplished, Barrett was able to run the power cables himself and to assemble the portal in the cellar of the house, without assistance.

Matt had read through as many of the newspapers as he was able to chronologically, and was reading a weekly from the late fall of 1896 when Professor Parkwood knocked at his door. Parkwood entered and sat down across from Matt. "I see you're catching up on the local history of Montrose," Professor Parkwood said, indicating the computer. "The newspapers we scanned—the ones we were able to locate, that is—are through February 1897, well beyond the end of your stay. You'll be arriving in August 1896. Once there, you should have some spare time to review them further if you feel the need." Professor Parkwood shifted in the chair. "So, Mr. Collins, in less than twenty-four hours you'll be making a most unique journey. How do you feel about that?"

"Anxious, excited, and a little apprehensive," Matt replied.

"I envy you," Professor Parkwood said. "I only wish I could go. But you are the best choice for this mission. You should have more than enough time to carry out any research you might want to conduct while you search for Ben." He reached into a pocket and pulled out a list. "We've equipped you with several items that should assist you. Among them, a digital camera-recorder combination small enough to fit into your hand. Two laptop computers, either of which you should be able to use to reactivate the portal at that end if necessary. We obviously can't send any lethal weapons with you, but we've included a taser device should you need it. Won't kill anyone or anything, but it should render them helpless for a short while. No use taking any chances. We've tried to cover all possibilities." He handed the list to Matt.

"How long will I have, Professor?" Matt asked.

"It is imperative that you locate Ben and get both of you back here as quickly as possible. I've figured on you being able to accomplish this within three weeks. Our calculations indicate that this portal may, and I stress the word *may*, remain operational for approximately four more months. But, the closer you get to the end of the four months, the likelihood of your safe return diminishes greatly." He paused, then said, "This is all guesswork on our part. The portal may collapse next week, for all we know, or it could last another year. But, based on our best projections and the data from the other portals, you should have sufficient time."

"Provided I can find Ben," Matt said.

Professor Parkwood nodded. "Use whatever means at your disposal. You'll have access to approximately seventy-five thousand dollars, which in that time period should allow you to do whatever is necessary.

"I don't need to remind you to do nothing in that time period that might have an adverse effect on history. Try to blend in and maintain a low profile. Just do what you need to do and come back."

"I will," Matt nodded. "Is there anything else I need to know?"

"We've done all we can at this end. Now it's up to you." Professor Parkwood rose and looked at Matt. "If for some reason you can't find Ben, get yourself back here safely. Get a good night's sleep, Mr. Collins." He turned toward the door.

"Professor, the only way I'm coming back without Ben is if he's just not there, or if..." Matt paused. "What I mean is...I'll find him, sir. Count on it."

Professor Parkwood nodded wordlessly and left, closing the door behind him.

CHAPTER 9

▼

It was time. Matt had donned the period clothing for his trip through the portal. Since the equipment at the other end wasn't fully operational, it was likely that he would materialize somewhere around the farm. Exactly where, no one knew. If he were seen, he'd have to look like everyone else in that time period.

He had been provided two suitcases containing his clothing, a small case containing currency of the period, and two carryalls that contained the laptops and other electronics. All of this had been loaded onto a small, wheeled cart, which looked as if it had been built in that time period. If necessary, he could carry all of these items by hand but it would slow him down considerably.

"The farm is at these coordinates," Professor Parkwood said, indicating a marking on the map. He handed the map and a bundle of papers to Matt. "With the equipment inoperable at that end, there's no signal for you to home in on. The maps will help, but not much if it's dark, or raining when you arrive. Remember that there are virtually no road signs, no addresses, nothing to help you find your way after you get there. This is, however, a topographical map, so some of the local landmarks might help."

"I just hope you don't land me in the middle of a lake," Matt said jokingly, but when Professor Parkwood didn't smile Matt realized that was a possibility that did exist.

"We're ready, Professor," came a voice from one of the consoles, and Professor Parkwood replied, "Thank you, Dr. Stinnett." He turned to Matt. "Well, then, this is it. The rest is up to you. Good luck." They shook hands. Sandra had appeared at Professor Parkwood's side, and she quickly hugged Matt and said, "Thank you again."

Matt was feeling strangely optimistic, considering what he was about to do. He smiled at them both, then gave a thumbs up to the technical crew. The low hum from the equipment suddenly intensified as the portal was energized. "Wait for the energy field to equalize," Stinnett said. Matt could feel the static charge building up in the air. After a few moments, Stinnett again spoke up, looking at Matt. "Any time you're ready," he said.

Matt looked at the nimbus of what appeared to be static electricity dancing around the outer frame of the portal. He took a deep breath and slowly pushed the cart ahead of him. He came to the portal opening and paused, then slowly began walking again. It looked as though he was pushing the cart through a fog-filled doorway into a dark abyss ahead.

CHAPTER 10

▼

The sensation as Matt went through the portal was distinctly uncomfortable, but nothing nearly as bad as he thought it would be. It felt as if he was electrified, the hair all over his body standing on end. There was no pain, no nausea, but he kept his eyes closed as he walked the few steps into the portal. Once inside, he walked another five feet or so as if walking down a short corridor.

Then, just as abruptly as it had started, the sensation was over. Matt cautiously opened his eyes to find himself standing in a brightly lit room not much different from his own basement at home. He turned around and saw the portal apparatus behind him, and that it was empty—he could see through the opening to the far wall. Then he realized with a slight shock that he was no longer in the facility in Philadelphia, but was hopefully in the cellar of the farmhouse in 1896. He remembered that Professor Parkwood had told him that the transfer was in one direction only—from the present back to 1896—until Matt was able to reset the equipment at this end and allow the computers to realign the signals from the portals. When and if that happened, transfers should be possible in both directions. This was obviously the other portal.

Although it was very quiet in the room, Matt could hear an irregular, distant booming noise from time to time. It sounded like cannon fire, or explosions, and Matt wondered what the cause of that could be.

But first things first. Stinnett had said that he'd try to duplicate the transfer settings from the previous 'trips' as closely as possible, but this was fantastic luck. Stinnett unknowingly had sent him directly through the other portal, just as if it had been operating. A bulls-eye. But, unless he could get this one operating, he'd never be able to return to his own time.

Matt pushed the cart to the far end of the room, near three consoles arranged in a semicircle, and found the laptop computer just as Professor Parkwood had described. Matt saw that the screen was blank, and realized after several minutes of trying to get it to work that this particular computer was dead. He pulled one of the spare laptops from his supplies, disconnected the dead laptop, switched all of the cables from the console, and booted up the program as Professor Parkwood had shown him. To his great relief, the computer began to go through what was obviously its initiation sequence. Professor Parkwood had said that this would take some time, probably hours, so Matt pushed the cart to one side and appended a text message to the boot-up sequence so that Professor Parkwood would know that he'd made it safely. Once the portals were synchronized the message would be sent through. He then decided to explore the room.

The stairs leading up to the farmhouse were to his right, and to the left was another small room. Matt looked inside the room and found that it was a small bathroom, complete with a self-contained toilet, a sink and a large shower stall. Another adjacent room turned out to be a small sleeping area, with two single beds. At least he wouldn't be roughing it too much.

This cellar was about sixty feet square with a high ceiling. He looked up and saw florescent lighting recessed into the openings. The walls were smooth, and Matt saw that they were made of fiberglass panels, as was the ceiling. The floor was rough stone, with the exception of the work area around the consoles, which had been smoothed and finished. The console workspace was arranged in a semi-circle, and an ordinary office chair on casters sat behind it. Matt sat down and briefly examined the equipment.

Besides the laptop, there were a couple of small control panels. One indicated the amount of power available from the storage batteries; it read almost three-quarters. With the equipment off-line, the batteries hadn't been fed the current from the cells. It would be some time before they fully recharged. The other console held a clock and some nondescript monitoring equipment. He checked the console clock against his own pocket watch and noted that it was nearly ten p.m. here; he had left the complex in Philadelphia at about four p.m. in the afternoon. Smiling to himself, he reset the pocket watch to local time. Near the stairs to the upper portion of the house, Matt saw a couple of utilitarian carts holding a few small kitchen utensils: a microwave, coffee machine, a small hot-plate, and there was even a small refrigerator. Since the entire facility operated on electricity, there would be plenty of power for these items. He was surprised at the simplicity of the equipment; nothing at all like what he'd expected.

Matt rose from the chair and listened. In the stillness, he heard the strange booming sound again. Taking a small flashlight from the console, he quietly made his way up the stairs.

At the top, he switched off the lights in the cellar below and allowed his eyes to become accustomed to the darkness. Then, reaching up, he punched in the combination code he'd been given on the small illuminated keypad next to the door. The door popped open silently and Matt eased the door open until he could make out dim shapes in the darkness. Suddenly, a bright flash lit up everything for a second.

Matt breathed a sigh of relief. It was simply a thunderstorm, the lightning flashing intermittently and the thunder shaking the air around him. He flipped on the cellar lights again and, shining the flashlight into the kitchen, found the control for the main floor lights and activated it. At first, the lights came on very dimly, then brightened somewhat. Matt smiled. The lights were made to resemble gaslights, and the enclosed bulbs even flickered to simulate flame. To a casual observer, behind their opaque glass chimneys they would look real enough.

He checked the doors and windows and found them all secured. He then reconnoitered the main floor and the upstairs. The furnishings were Spartan, and he realized that Ben must have spent nearly all of his time down below. These things were just for show, but Matt didn't relish the thought of spending all of his time in the cellar of the house. He decided to use the master bedroom upstairs and divide his time between the upper and lower floors.

He retraced his steps to the cellar and checked the laptop. It was still going though the initiation sequence, so Matt grabbed his suitcases and carried them up to the second floor and into the master bedroom, a large room with double doors leading out onto a balcony. He spent a while unpacking his things, and realized that he felt tired; no doubt the stress and excitement of the last couple of days. He undressed, stretched out across the large bed and was asleep within minutes.

CHAPTER 11

▼

The thunderstorm had ended a few hours before dawn, but Matt had slept throughout the din and awoke feeling refreshed. He lay there for a few minutes, looking out the open window and thinking that all that had happened the night before was just a dream—when he was again aware of the silence. No, not silence, but...*peacefulness* was the only word he could think of to describe it. The birds were singing, and he could hear the clop of horses' hooves from a distance. But there was no background noise—no automobile traffic, no horns blaring, no airplanes overhead, no bustle of activity, although looking through the window he could see several people moving about in the distance. He moved to his kit and removed his shaving gear and, in the brightening light from the window, thought about attempting to shave. After a minute he picked up the kit and his clothing and headed for the cellar stairs.

Down below, the cellar was still brightly lit and held most of, to him, the modern amenities that he was used to. The scientific equipment took up most of the space along the walls, but he again noticed the small kitchen area in addition to the bathroom and bedroom areas tucked away to one side. The cellar was pretty well self-contained, the only external equipment being the solar cells on the roof above the barn and the storage batteries hidden away in the house upstairs. He had seen the barn from the upstairs window and saw that the roof had been painted to look like any of the other roofs in the town. Professor Parkwood had told him that, even without direct sunlight to keep them charged, the power cells' reserve capacity from a full charge should be able to provide power for all of the auxiliary equipment for up to a week. This time of year there was plenty of sunshine during the day to keep the cells fully charged constantly provided the equipment was on line.

He went into the bathroom and shaved in the bright light from the florescent tubes above, and then took a quick shower. Toweling off, he finished dressing in the suit he had worn the previous evening. He checked his appearance in the wall mirror to one side and, satisfied, returned to the work area. Matt pulled the documents from his carryall and inspected them again. The documents looked sufficiently used and worn, although he knew that they were less than a week old. His clothing, too, looked slightly worn but in good condition. He placed the documents inside his jacket and, checking his appearance one last time, he walked up the cellar steps to the kitchen above and locked the cellar door behind him. Matt knew that the magnetic locks would stop any intruders. He slid aside the false brick to one side of the door to check the combination keypad and, seeing that the indicator glowed red, replaced the brick. Heading for the foyer, he opened the front door and stepped outside.

It was a beautiful summer morning, and he paused for a minute to take it all in. The air smelled and tasted clean and fresh, like nothing he had ever quite experienced before. The sun sparkled in the sky, and he could see clearly to the horizon in every direction. No smog or pollution here, he remembered, and he suddenly realized that it had been years since he had felt so alive. Strange how he had been here for barely twelve hours and already he felt differently. He leaned against the porch railing and felt a smile involuntarily form on his face. It was as if all the cares and worries of his life had slipped away. It had been a long time, a very long time, since he'd felt anything like this.

Matt saw that the farm was located on the outskirts of the town, close enough to be convenient but far enough removed to afford at least some privacy. He walked around the house on the wide porch and saw that the porch, railing and overhang above circled the entire house, with the only breaks in the railing being at the steps at front and rear. He came back around to the front steps, and as he walked down and into the street he felt a spring in his step that had been gone for too long.

But now to business. Finding Ben Parkwood was Matt's primary task. Time enough to conduct his own research as the hunt for Ben progressed. Remembering the layout of the town from the map he had studied again the previous night, he headed toward the corner of Maple Street and Public Avenue some distance away. As he neared the town everyone he met smiled and nodded a hello, and he in turn did the same, again almost involuntarily it seemed. He reached Maple Street and turned east, toward the Courthouse, Library, and the First National

Bank he remembered seeing on the old map and in the old photographs. The Courthouse would be his first stop.

In 1896, Montrose, Pennsylvania was a small but growing town with a population of nearly 1,000. The town had been incorporated in 1824, but had grown primarily in the years after the Civil War. It was the oldest settlement in Susquehanna County and now, at the end of the nineteenth century, claimed the distinction of being the county seat. In the town proper, business consisted of numerous lawyers to handle the court-related activities, as well as several merchants and, of course, the newspapers. The repair shops for the Delaware, Lackawanna & Western railroad were also located nearby. Outside the town, there were many family farms as well as specialty trades such as harness making, blacksmithing, and such. The town's economy was thriving.

As he walked along Maple Street, Matt was again aware of the relative quietness. He was surprised at how accustomed he'd become to the background noise of the 21st century, the subconscious but unending din that he, like everyone else, had learned to block out and disregard. Although there was noise—horses, creaking wagons, people bustling about—the overall silence was still somewhat unnerving. Still, Matt decided that this was definitely something that he could get used to.

He reached the Courthouse, a beautiful old building with tall columns reaching to the skies, and as the clock on the building chimed 9:00 am he went up the steps to the entrance. Inside, he noted how relatively dark it was, but the people inside didn't seem to be having any problem going about their business. He headed for the main desk and was greeted by an older lady with horn-rimmed glasses.

"Good day, sir, and can I be of assistance?" The smile on the old lady's face was genuine, and he in turn smiled back.

"Yes, I certainly hope so. I just arrived in town last night. My name is Matt Collins. I've been given a partial share of my uncle's house here in town, and I needed to find out what I need to do concerning the deed and any other things I need to take care of."

"It's nice to meet you, Mr. Collins. My name is Martha Higby. Well, let's see—first you should visit the Assessor's office. That's up the stairs and to the left. Ask for Amanda, she runs the office. She'll be able to help you." She paused and said, "Who is your uncle?"

"Henry Parkwood. He owns the small farm just outside of town, past Wyalusing Street."

"Oh, yes, I know the one, although I didn't know your uncle. He lived some- where else, I understand."

"Yes, in Philadelphia. I'm from Pittsburgh myself. I was hoping to spend some time here and relax."

"Wasn't there another young man living there a while back?"

"Yes, that was my…cousin. Uncle Henry's son, Ben Parkwood. You wouldn't happen to know anything about him, would you?"

"Sorry, no. He kept odd hours, didn't get into town much, and I never got to know him very well. I understand he rented a horse and rode out of town two, three weeks ago, and no one's seen him since."

"Neither has my uncle," Matt replied. "One reason I came here was to find out what he's been up to."

"You don't suppose anything has happened to him, do you?" Mrs. Higby said with a look of concern.

"I doubt it," Matt said with a laugh. "He's a land speculator. Probably looking at farmland around the region. He's been known to disappear for days at a time. It's just that we haven't gotten a letter or anything for some time, and I was com- ing through here anyway so I told Uncle Henry that I'd check on him."

Mrs. Higby looked relieved. "Well, you might check at the Post Office. See if any letters are there."

"I will. Thank you, Mrs. Higby. Like I said, I was planning on staying a while. I need a rest."

"You'll find our town a nice place to do it. We pride ourselves on our friendli- ness. My son runs the bank, and takes care of being Mayor in his spare time too. Once you've gotten settled in, I'm sure you'd like to meet some of the other townspeople." She paused for a few seconds, then said, "By the way, the next few weeks are going to be hectic around here, what with the harvest and all. But after the harvest we're having a picnic and dance in the Town Square, all afternoon and evening, to dedicate the new Village Hall improvements. I'm sure you must have seen it after you arrived on the train. That would be a grand opportunity for you to meet everyone. That should be around the end of October."

"Thank you," Matt said, although she couldn't know that his arrival here wasn't as simple as getting off a train, he thought to himself. And, if all went well he'd be gone in a few weeks anyway. Nevertheless, he smiled at Mrs. Higby and said, "I'll try to be there. Upstairs, you said?"

"And to the left. Nice to meet you, Mr. Collins."

"Nice to meet you, Mrs. Higby, and thank you."

Matt went up the stairs slowly, inspecting the architecture and furnishings of the building as he went. Electric lights were scattered about, the bulbs putting out a weak light. He had noticed the old-fashioned telephone on Mrs. Higby's desk, and surmised that only the most influential businesses and wealthy families would have those. He also surmised that Mrs. Higby herself was one of the town's information centers. Although "town gossip" would be a more appropriate term, Matt knew that small towns like this depended on having two or three people that pretty much knew everything about anything that was going on.

He reached the top of the stairs and turned left toward a door marked "Assessor's Office, J. P. Milhouse." He entered the door and moved to a long counter at the front of a large open office where three girls were busy working with oversize plat books. A young girl of about twenty-five, obviously the senior employee of the three, looked up and said, "Can I help you, sir?"

Matt looked into her face and stopped dead in his tracks, awestruck. He found himself staring at one of the most extraordinarily pretty girls he had ever seen. He knew that most of the women of this era were somewhat plain and average looking, but this girl was beautiful even by the standards of his own time. There was an awkward silence as he stood there, mute, looking into that face, not understanding his own reaction. He abruptly came to his senses and felt an involuntary smile on his own face. He pulled the papers from his inside jacket pocket, but his eyes never left her face.

"Yes, I'm supposed to see Amanda."

"I'm Amanda," she said. "What can I do for you?"

"Oh. Well, Amanda, my name is Matt Collins. My uncle gave me an interest in his farm just outside of town. I understand that I need to take care of some deed paperwork." Matt handed the papers to her.

There was no returning smile on her face, but Matt could tell that she had noticed his reaction to her. He was surprised at himself and felt slightly embarrassed, but was relieved to see that she took the papers and concentrated on inspecting them in a businesslike manner. As the girl shuffled through the papers, Matt took the opportunity to study her closely. He saw that she was very attractive, the long lustrous black hair piled high upon her head in the fashion of the time. Her waist was unusually small, the result no doubt of the corsets he had seen in numerous books, and this served to enhance her hourglass figure. Her nails were short, with no polish, and she wore no rings. He noticed virtually no makeup at all, and the long lashes over her blue eyes gave them a pleasant, soft quality. The dress was a muted green, with white lace at collar and wrist and large puffy sleeves above the elbow. He couldn't see the rest of the dress behind the counter but knew that it went to the floor. There was no sign of a pendant or necklace around her neck, but the collar was high. She continued to check the documents, seemingly taking no further notice of him.

After a few minutes, a slight giggle from several feet away made Matt turn to his left where he saw two of the other clerks, both young girls, watching him as he was observing Amanda. He smiled at them, winked, and turned his attention back to the girl. She had turned and was giving them both an admonishing stare. He heard the two girls whispering to each other and giggling some more as they moved away.

"Yes, I think we can take care of all of this for you today," she said to Matt, glancing up at the clock on the far wall. "Come back this afternoon after three and I should have everything ready for your signature."

"Thank you, Amanda...?"

"I'm sorry, my name is Amanda Caruthers."

"Amanda Caruthers?" Matt felt a slight shock when he heard the name, and she must have noticed his reaction.

"Yes," she replied. "Have we met?"

"No. At least I don't think so. Of course not, I only got into town last night."

Matt's thoughts raced. Not expecting anything like this to happen, he was stunned to realize that this girl had been mentioned in one of the old newspapers that he had been reading just a couple of days ago. The brief article came flooding back into his memory: "A memorial service was held this week for Amanda Caruthers, who was the victim of a tragic fire recently." The article had not given any other information, and he couldn't remember the exact date of the newspaper—only that it was sometime during the coming weeks.

This was eerie, to say the least. It gave him a distinctly unpleasant feeling to come face to face with someone who he knew was going to die, and relatively soon. Of course, there were others in this town whose future for the next few months was similarly known to him. For instance, he recalled offhandedly that Mrs. Higby's son would win the next mayor's election, still a few months away; he knew that an unusually long summer would abruptly change into an early winter this year; and a dozen other inconsequential matters that would affect this town and the people in it.

But this was different. Knowing the finality of this girl's fate made him uncomfortable, especially so since he was speaking to her face to face. Still, Parkwood had made it as clear as possible: do nothing to affect any of the normal events in this era. To do otherwise might create serious problems for his own time.

Her voice snapped him out of his reverie. "Sir, are you all right?"

"Sorry, I was…after three, you said? Yes, of course, Mrs. Caruthers," Matt said.

"It's Miss Caruthers, Mr…Collins, was it?"

"Call me Matt," he said with a grin, and then remembered that people of this era weren't so familiar. There was an uneasy silence, and no change in her expression as she answered him.

"After three, Mr. Collins," she said.

"Uh, thank you," Matt said, standing there awkwardly for a few moments. This girl had stirred something inside of him. He wanted to speak with her some more, but couldn't think of anything else to say. Amanda was watching him with a puzzled look, and said, "Is there anything else?"

"No, no, thank you," Matt said, picking up his hat. He said, "After three, then," and turned and headed for the stairs.

As soon as Matt had descended the stairs, another burst of giggles came from the clerks. Amanda looked over at them and said sternly, "What on earth is so amusing?"

"You didn't notice, Mandy? I think the gentleman saw something he liked."

"Nonsense. Besides, I've never even met him before." Still, she had sensed something different about him, especially his reaction to her. But, she was sure it was nothing. "Let's get back to work, girls," Amanda said, and returned to her desk.

Matt reached the bottom of the stairs and was about to go out when he paused, a frown on his face. He was confused at the reaction he was having after meeting this girl, but then figured it was because of the knowledge he had about her. Still, he decided to speak with Mrs. Higby again. Looking around, he saw that the room was deserted. He headed through the door to the porch and was about to go down the steps when he saw Mrs. Higby sweeping one end of the wide porch. He turned and walked over to her.

"I just wanted to thank you for your help, Mrs. Higby. Being new in town, I wasn't sure how people would react to me."

"Oh, you'll find our town to be a friendly place, Mr. Collins. Why, I can remember when there weren't more than a couple of dozen families around here. Now, we've grown to be quite a town. Why, the membership at my church is the largest in the area." She paused. "Do you attend church, Mr. Collins?"

"When I can," Matt said, although he couldn't remember the last time he'd been to a church, not since Carolyn's funeral.

"Well, you'll have to give ours a try. It's the Methodist church right down the street," Mrs. Higby said, indicating a large ornate building a few hundred yards away.

"Yes, I will," Matt said. "Well, thank you again." He was about to leave when he turned to Mrs. Higby and said, "I hope you don't think this too forward of me, but what can you tell me about Miss Caruthers?"

"Amanda? A sweet girl. Hers is a local family, has been for years. She grew up here. Her father and mother own the General Store up the street. A nicer family you'll never meet. Let's see, there are the two oldest boys, Jack Jr. and Edward, they're both married and work for the railroad—they live in Harrisburg now. Then Amanda, Sallie, and Rebecca, they all still live at home with the parents."

"I made the mistake of addressing her as Mrs. Caruthers, and she made a point of telling me that her name was Miss Caruthers. I didn't want to say anything, but she's much too pretty…I mean, I would think she was married."

Mrs. Higby paused for a moment, then lowered her voice in a confidential manner. "Nothing I'm about to tell you is anything you wouldn't find out about sooner or later. Amanda was engaged some time ago, to young William Reed. William was a handsome lad, but he was always a gadabout, and so all the girls tried to catch him. All but Amanda. So of course he set about courting her. They were an item for quite a few months, and Amanda thought she had changed him into a more stable person. After all, a girl has to have a dependable man. Needless to say, they became engaged. But, she confided in me on more than one occasion. Deep down, she didn't believe he'd ever settle down. Then, last year, he suddenly up and runs off with Amanda's best friend. Not a word to anyone. Last we heard they were married and living somewhere in Indiana." Mrs. Higby shook her head. "Amanda was crushed, and wasn't seen for, oh, days and days. Of course the poor dear was embarrassed, especially when she found out later that those two had been carrying on behind her back. When she did go out and about again, there was something different about her. Several of the young men in town have tried to catch her fancy, but she's having none of that. Such a shame, though," Mrs. Higby said again. "She is such a sweet girl. And pretty, too."

"Yes, I noticed," Matt said with feeling, and was immediately sorry he had said it out loud. Mrs. Higby looked at him quizzically, then with a slight grin said, "Well, you have a good day, Mr. Collins. If you get a chance, stop in at the hotel restaurant for lunch. Most of the town's businessmen lunch there, perhaps you can meet some of them." She returned to her sweeping.

Matt touched the brim of his hat and made his way down the steps and along Maple Street toward the bank, thinking as he walked. So, it wasn't bad enough that this girl was going to die; she had already suffered a great loss, just like Matt. If nothing else, she was a kindred spirit of sorts.

As Matt moved along, he saw that most of the shops were already open, the various shopkeepers sweeping the porches of their establishments. Matt nodded to the passersby and looked with interest at the many displays in the windows. He stopped to look in the window of the confectioner's store and was awed at the rows and rows of jars along two of the walls, each filled with candies. Another wall was filled from floor to ceiling with bottles and boxes of medicines and such. From behind the counter, the proprietor, a Mr. Morris according to the information painted on the front window, smiled and nodded at Matt, and Matt nodded in return.

He continued along the street until he was at the entrance of the General Store. Large hand-painted letters on the windows proclaimed, "General Store", and below that, "J. M. Caruthers, Prop." There were several shoppers inside, and Matt entered and began looking around.

Although it was a large cavernous building, every available space seemed to be taken. He was surprised to see what appeared to be a little bit of everything on display, from blankets to harnesses to tin pots and pans, clothing, and even some furniture. Behind the long wooden counters on each side, tall shelves reached to the ceiling. At one end of the counter, he saw a man and woman trying to help several shoppers at once and doing a good job of it. He surmised that this must be Mr. and Mrs. Caruthers, and his guess was proved right when he heard one of the women say, "Mrs. Caruthers, has the material for my dresses arrived yet?"

"Why, yes, I believe it has," Mrs. Caruthers, a good-looking woman in her mid forties, said, and disappeared into a room behind the counter. She emerged a few minutes later carrying three bolts of cloth, which she laid out on the wide counter for the woman to inspect. Mrs. Caruthers looked up at Matt, smiled and nodded a greeting. Matt nodded in return.

He lingered for a while, marveling at the combination of items in the store, when he heard a voice behind him. "Is there something I can do for you, sir? I'm Jack Caruthers, the owner."

Matt turned and looked up at the man standing before him. Jack Caruthers was a few inches taller than Matt, and sported a small handlebar moustache. His hair was jet black and slicked back, with a part down the middle. His long-sleeved shirt was striped, and there were garters on the upper sleeves. The suspenders completed the outfit. Matt took all this in as he reached for the outstretched hand. "Yes, I hope so," Matt said as he shook the hand. "My name is Matt Collins. I just arrived in town last night. I was looking for the Post Office."

"Well, you've found it," Mr. Caruthers said with a smile, and motioned Matt to follow him. "Besides running this store and being on the town council, I'm also the local postmaster. We've got a small office here in the back."

Mr. Caruthers went behind the counter and turned to Matt. "Now, what can I do for you?"

"Well, my uncle Henry Parkwood sent his son, Ben, down here to Montrose a few months ago. Ben's a land speculator, and goes off for days at a time, but it's been quite a while since my uncle has heard from him. My uncle asked me to come down and look him up, make sure everything's all right. I thought Ben might have left a letter or something concerning his whereabouts."

"Let's see," Mr. Caruthers said, turning to the mail slots. "Nothing under Parkwood, and nothing under Collins. Let me check the miscellaneous mail." Mr. Caruthers pulled out a stack of envelopes and began rummaging through them.

"No, sorry, nothing here. Are you going to be in town long?"

"For a while," Matt said. "I've moved in to my uncle's house temporarily, the farmhouse outside of town past Wyalusing Street."

"I know the house. Quite a large place, but remote. Your wife and children come with you?"

"I'm not married," Matt replied. "Just me by myself."

"You'll probably need some help with a place that big. There's lots of boys in town that could help you out."

Matt smiled and shook his head. "Thanks, but not just yet. I just got into town last night. I'll need a couple of days to get my bearings. In fact, I imagine I'll be in and out of town quite a bit. If you do get anything from my cousin, would you please let me know?"

"I will," Mr. Caruthers replied. "Well, if there's nothing else, I've got to get back out front. My wife will be swamped."

Matt followed Mr. Caruthers to the counter, and Mr. Caruthers said, "Mother, this is Mr. Collins, just arrived in town."

"Pleased to meet you, Mr. Collins," Mrs. Caruthers said, smiling. "Staying long?"

"At least a few weeks, maybe longer."

Mrs. Caruthers said, "Welcome to Montrose, Mr. Collins," as she turned to help another customer. Matt glanced around at the people in the store. It was odd to see everyone dressed in classic 1890's clothing, but then he remembered he was dressed in like fashion.

Matt left the store and headed back toward the police station. He inquired about Ben Parkwood but gained no information. He then visited the bank, giving the manager, Mr. Higby, the paperwork that allowed him access to the funds that Barrett had deposited here. He also deposited the bulk of the money that Professor Parkwood had sent along with him, keeping a few hundred for himself. He saw Higby's eyebrows raise at the amount of the deposit, which far exceeded the sizeable balance that was already in the account. As the receipt was made out, he learned from Mr. Higby that there had been no account activity for nearly a month.

"But," Higby said, "Mr. Parkwood did make a rather large withdrawal the last time he was in."

"That's understandable," Matt said. "He deals in real estate and said that he was looking for some properties in the area. Maybe he just wanted to be prepared in case he came across a good deal."

Higby nodded. "Of course, he may have some competition. Our biggest land-owner in the area is old Josiah Green. For the last couple of years he's been buying up most of the properties around here. Doesn't like to lose, either. He owns probably five percent of Susquehanna County, one way or another. May not sound like much, but that's a lot of land."

"Yes, I guess it would be. Well, thank you for your help. And, if you don't mind, I'll check in every few days to see if there's any activity on the account from Ben."

"Fine, fine, I'll let you know," Higby said as Matt shook hands with him and left.

Outside, Matt pulled out the pocketwatch and looked at it. Nearly noon, and he was getting hungry, not having had any breakfast. He consulted the map and headed toward the hotel.

The restaurant at the hotel was nearly empty. Most of the townspeople who ate here would be coming in within the next hour or so. Matt caught the attention of the woman behind the counter, pointed at a window booth and raised his eyebrows in a questioning look. The woman smiled and nodded, at the same time picking up two plates and carrying them across the room to two gentlemen in business dress already seated at a table.

Matt seated himself so that he could see the entrance, and looked around at the layout. The restaurant was in a large L shape, allowing entrance from the street on one side and from the hotel on the other. Behind the counter, huge mirrors ran the length of the wall around both sides, and from his vantage point Matt could see the reflection of the passersby in the street outside. A chalkboard on an easel near the entrance proclaimed that day's lunch menu. After a few minutes the woman came toward him.

"My, looks like we're getting some early business today," she said. "My name is Mrs. Wharton. My husband and I run the hotel. You're new here, aren't you?"

"Matt Collins. I just got into town yesterday. I'll be staying a while."

"Well, it's good to have you here. Now, what can I get for you? Something to drink?"

The beverage choices this time of day were simple: beer, tea, and water. The bar was open but the harder liquor would be served later in the day and into the evening. Looking at the other table, Matt saw that the two men were having beer. Obviously this was the standard drink, so Matt opted for the same. He was surprised when Mrs. Wharton returned with what must have been a full liter of beer in a large mug. Matt sipped at the beer and nodded to himself. Not bad. He ordered the meat loaf, and Mrs. Wharton said, "A good choice. Made it myself just a while ago."

Matt sipped at the beer sparingly and watched for a while as a few more gentlemen and a sprinkling of ladies entered and were seated. Before long the food came, and Matt was surprised at the generous portions. He ate slowly and watched as the restaurant filled up. He listened in at the bits of conversation he heard from the other tables: talk of the railroad, various legal matters, and quite a bit of personal information about residents in and around the area.

Matt leisurely finished the meal and, despite the amount of food he had consumed, still found himself hungry. Mrs. Wharton came to remove the plates and said, "Anything else I can get for you?"

Matt looked up and smiled. "You know, I'm in the mood for some dessert. Do you have any pie?"

"Any pie?" Mrs. Wharton said. "Only the best pie in the county. What's your preference?"

"I think apple," Matt said, and Mrs. Wharton nodded and said, "Be right back."

From a couple of booths behind him, Matt picked up on a conversation. "Well, you know, Mandy, you need to make plans for the dance." Matt turned to glance at the reflection in the large mirror behind the counter and saw that Amanda Caruthers was seated with two other young ladies. He hadn't seen them come in.

One of the young ladies was talking animatedly. "It'll be here before we know it, and," the girl lowered her voice conspiratorially, "I heard there might be some young men in town from Philadelphia." The other girl nodded in agreement.

Matt heard Amanda sigh. "Sarah, will you two *please* stop trying to play matchmaker for me? I'll be going to the dance, or at least the picnic, if the new dress Mother ordered for me gets here in time. But I don't want to be bothered with a lot of strange men. I'll be attending with my family."

"Oh, Mandy," Sarah sighed. "That doesn't sound like it'll be much fun." She turned to the other girl. "What about you, Lucy?"

"I wouldn't mind meeting a tall, handsome gentleman from Philadelphia, except that Michael might not like it."

Lucy and Sarah giggled, but Amanda remained neutral. "You shouldn't make him jealous," Amanda said.

Lucy replied, "Maybe that's just what he needs. I've been seeing him for almost two years now, but he never seems to want to get serious. After all, I'm almost twenty-three."

There was an awkward silence at the table. Lucy must have realized that what she had said could be taken the wrong way by Amanda; although the situation with Amanda's fiancé was common knowledge, it was never spoken of, especially around her.

The silence was broken by Mrs. Wharton bringing their lunch. As she set the plates in front of them, Sarah turned to Amanda, changing the subject. "Tell us about your dress, Mandy."

"Oh, it will be gorgeous," Amanda said with feeling. "Light blue with a frill…"

Matt's eavesdropping was interrupted by the arrival of Mrs. Wharton with the pie. "Just let me know when you're done," she said, and Matt nodded. He ate hurriedly and, when he finished, rose from the table and unobtrusively went around the corner to the counter, out of sight of the three girls.

"What do I owe you, Mrs. Wharton?" he asked, and counted out the amount along with a generous tip. Matt looked into the mirror, put on the hat and adjusted it, and went outside.

Matt spent the next couple of hours walking about the town, getting his bearings and marveling at the architecture of the buildings. It was a strange combination; the ornate, beautiful buildings, such as the churches and the government buildings, were mixed in with squat, square nondescript buildings that were purely functional. He surreptitiously pulled the digital camera from his jacket pocket and took a few photos as he walked.

Much later, Matt pulled the pocket watch from his vest and saw that it was nearly three thirty. He headed back to County Courthouse and went inside. Mrs.

Higby was no longer there, and he walked past the deserted reception desk and up the stairs.

Entering the Assessor's Office, he saw that Amanda was reviewing paperwork with an older couple. There was no sign of the other girls. He sat down on one of the benches and watched her as she worked.

The eerie feeling returned. It was odd to know that this girl was destined to die within a few months and that he knew with certainty that it was going to happen. Human nature being what it is, he idly wondered to himself what he could do to protect her from that fate. Any reasonable person would do the same, he thought, and then caught himself. He realized that he was in a unique position, to know for a fact that someone he had met was going to die, and soon. It was true that he didn't know exactly where or when, but he knew nonetheless that it would happen.

On the other hand, Matt felt himself almost mesmerized by her beauty. No woman before or since Carolyn had produced an effect on him like this, and if he were honest with himself he would admit that even Carolyn had not created a feeling inside him like this. His relationship with Carolyn had grown over many months' time; but this girl, right from the beginning, had bowled him over for some unknown reason.

Because of this, Matt was confused by his reaction to her. But as he sat there with his thoughts, Professor Parkwood's warnings kept intruding.

As for Amanda, she had seen Matt come in and take a seat as he waited. She briefly glanced in his direction from time to time. His reaction to her earlier in the day had puzzled her, and she had thought about him more than once in the ensuing hours. She wondered if they had met before, but try as she might she was unable to remember ever meeting him. Still, he was rather handsome, and the fact that he was a stranger newly arrived in town intrigued her.

She was finishing up with the couple. "I'll see that these are sent to your lawyer," she said, "and he can review them and make any necessary changes. He should be in touch with you in a week or so."

"Thanks, Miss Caruthers," the man said, and he escorted the woman out the door.

Matt got up and walked to the counter. "Hello, again, Miss Caruthers," he said with a smile, but she didn't respond. She moved to one of the desks, retrieved Matt's paperwork and returned to the counter.

"Everything was in order," she said in a very businesslike voice. "I've had the deed papers prepared, which you'll need to have notarized. I can do that for you, for an additional fee, if you like."

"That will be fine," Matt replied, and signed the papers. Amanda stamped the papers, folded them and placed them in a large envelope. "These are your copies. You should keep them in a safe place. That comes to eight dollars."

Matt reached inside his jacket, removed his wallet, and pulled out a twenty. Amanda took the bill and walked to the rear of the office, where she made change from a small box. Matt saw that she moved very gracefully. She returned and laid the change on the counter.

"Thank you," she said, and was about to turn away again when Matt spoke up. He wanted to talk with her some more, so he said, "Say, can you tell me where I can get some…provisions? I got to my house late last night and realized that there was no food there."

Amanda glanced at the clock on the wall. "The General Store should have what you need," she replied. "They're still open for another hour." This time she turned away, apparently dismissing him, and Matt saw that she was getting ready to close the office. He saw that it was nearly four o'clock.

"Thank you again," he said, but when there was no reply he turned and went out the door. As he went down the steps he shrugged it off. She was very beautiful, but she was also pretty cold and very private, Matt decided. *I guess Mrs. Higby was right,* he thought, and remembered that people of this era reacted to things differently than what he was used to. In his own time, a woman whose fiancé had run out on her would most likely go out and find herself someone new. But, this wasn't his own time. He'd have to be careful not to react inappropriately, or to say the wrong thing, in his dealings with these people.

He walked outside and saw that the sun was already far down in the western sky. Another couple of hours and it would be getting dark. He crossed the street to the barbershop and entered long enough to get directions to one of the local stables. He planned to rent or purchase a horse and buggy within a couple of days so he'd be able to get around.

He crossed the street again and walked toward the General Store. He saw with delight that Amanda was also headed in that general direction, several yards ahead of him. He watched her as he walked along the street.

Amanda stopped from time to time to look into the store windows, waving occasionally through the glass to people that she knew. At one such window she stopped and looked back in Matt's direction, having seen his reflection in the glass. Matt threw a hand in the air and waved, but Amanda turned and continued on her way without acknowledging him.

Matt smiled to himself. *There is no way,* he thought, *no way* that anyone that beautiful can be that cold. He decided that, should their paths cross again, he would either get her to smile or get a slap in the face for his trouble. With that in mind, he followed her and saw that she entered the General Store.

Matt came in a minute or so behind her, and saw that she had her back to him and was speaking to Mrs. Caruthers. Over Amanda's shoulder, Mrs. Caruthers saw him enter and gave him a nod and a smile. Matt walked up beside Amanda and, leaning on the counter with his elbow, said, "Well, if it isn't Miss Caruthers. And this would be your sister?" he said, looking at Mrs. Caruthers.

An old line, he thought, something that would have fallen flat in his own time; but Mrs. Caruthers gave a twittering laugh and said, "Oh, Mr. Collins!" He saw that she was flattered.

But, if the mother was flattered, he saw that Amanda gave little notice. She simply turned and said, "This is my mother, Mr. Collins."

"We met earlier today, dear," Mrs. Caruthers explained to Amanda. She turned to Matt. "How are you doing, Mr. Collins?"

"Fine, fine," Matt replied. "I was told that I could pick up some supplies here, so I thought I'd stop in before closing time."

Amanda turned back to her mother and said, "I'll be going home now. See you and Father at six?"

"Of course, dear," Mrs. Caruthers said, and Amanda turned to leave. Matt tipped his hat to her but Amanda walked out without comment.

"I met Amanda at the Assessor's Office earlier today," Matt said to Mrs. Caruthers by way of explanation. He paused, then said, "I hope I didn't offend your daughter just now. She didn't look too happy."

"No, Mr. Collins," Mrs. Caruthers said. "She's just a very serious young lady. Now, what can I get for you?"

Matt went through the store with Mrs. Caruthers, picking out items here and there—canned goods mostly, and some fresh vegetables from the local farms. He also picked up a few jars of preserved items, to stock the pantry. No telling how long he'd be here, and if he left them behind when he returned to his own time, no harm done.

As she helped him with the items, Mrs. Caruthers said to Matt, "So, what is your line of work, Mr. Collins?"

"At the moment, I'm working for my uncle. Taking care of some of his affairs, and of course trying to locate my cousin."

"I recall a Mr. Barrett some months ago."

"Yes, he was my uncle's business manager. Unfortunately, he died a while back."

"Oh, I'm so sorry," Mrs. Caruthers said. "He was such a nice man."

"I actually never met him," Matt said, "but after he passed on my uncle contacted me and asked me to step in for a while. Before that, I was a teacher."

"A teacher! I never would have guessed that. What did you teach?"

"I was an assistant history professor at...a university." This seemed to impress Mrs. Caruthers.

"You hardly seem old enough," she said. In that era, most university professors were much older men who had been teaching for decades.

"I was lucky to have that opportunity, I guess," Matt said, "but once I got involved with it I found that it really didn't appeal to me. Not nearly exciting enough. When my uncle contacted me, I gave it up on the spot."

"Are you married, Mr. Collins?"

"No," Matt said. He judged that Mrs. Caruthers wouldn't think that he knew about Amanda's former fiancé, so he decided to confide in her. "I was engaged once, but she died in...an accident."

"Oh, Mr. Collins, I'm so sorry! What happened?"

"A, uh, train accident," he said, knowing that he couldn't give her the real version of the event. "Several people died. But, that was some years ago."

Mrs. Caruthers changed the subject. "You know, we're having a big town picnic after harvest time. It would be nice if you could attend."

"Yes, Mrs. Higby down at County Courthouse told me about that. I'll do my best to make it, if my uncle's affairs don't intrude. I just hope I don't stick out like a sore thumb. I don't have anyone to bring with me yet. I don't really know anyone here in town."

"Don't you worry about that," Mrs. Caruthers said. "If you find yourself alone you can join our family for the picnic, if you like."

"Thank you, Mrs. Caruthers," Matt said. "I'll try to do that."

Matt brought the items to the counter and Mrs. Caruthers added up the total. "That'll be six dollars and forty cents," she said, and Matt pulled a fifty-dollar bill out of his wallet. "How about setting me up an account with this," Matt said. "That way, when I need more supplies you can deduct it from this."

"Of course," she said, again impressed. Most of the local families kept a running total and would pay it off at harvest time, or sooner if they came into some money in some other way. Only the wealthier families paid in advance.

Matt looked at the collection of items, then said, "I don't think I can carry all of this back to the house. If you'll give me a few minutes, I was going to get a horse and buggy to get around in. Maybe I can still get one today."

Mrs. Caruthers looked out the front window, down the street. "It looks like Mr. McCallum is still over at his stable. Go see what you can do; if not, I can have Jack bring these out to your house later."

McCallum was indeed still at the stable, and after sizing up Matt he quoted a price for a horse and buggy that was more than a little on the expensive side. McCallum was used to customers dickering with him, but Matt didn't bat an eye as he laid out the cash. McCallum hitched the horse to a small four-seater buggy, and as an afterthought threw a saddle and blanket in the back. "In case you just want to use the horse," he explained. "Can't be hitching up the buggy every time you want to go somewhere. Just tie him to a tree and let him graze in your yard. Bring him in every couple of days and I'll make sure he gets fed proper and brushed."

"Thanks, Mr. McCallum," Matt said, and he climbed into the buggy. He grabbed the reins and, trying to look like he knew what he was doing, successfully guided the horse and buggy to the front of the General Store where Mrs. Caruthers had his purchases waiting out in front. He loaded the supplies into the buggy and climbed back in.

"Thanks for your help, Mrs. Caruthers," Matt said as he snapped the reins. She waved at Matt as the horse trotted up the street and headed for the farm.

CHAPTER 12

▼

At dinner that night at the Caruthers house, the family was gathered around the large dining room table. As usual, they discussed the day's events. Mrs. Caruthers turned to her husband and said, "That Mr. Collins seems to be such a nice man, don't you think?"

Mr. Caruthers shrugged. "He seemed well-mannered, I guess," he said off-handedly.

Mrs. Caruthers turned to Amanda. "I understand you met him this morning, dear," she said, and Amanda nodded. "What was that about?"

"At the office. His uncle deeded him a half-interest in his farm," Amanda said.

Mr. Caruthers spoke up. "Mayor Higby came in to the store this afternoon," he said, "and you know how secretive he is about bank customers. Even so, he let me know that this Mr. Collins is pretty well off, or at least his uncle is. Says his uncle is wanting to buy property here, which is what the old man's son was doing here."

"I wouldn't think there'd be much left around here, what with Josiah Green buying it up," Mrs. Caruthers said.

"Well, Green can't buy *everything*," Mr. Caruthers replied. "Might not be a bad thing for him to get some competition. Might bring in a better price for the sellers."

"Oh, I felt so bad," Mrs. Caruthers said. "When we were talking in the store this afternoon, I asked Mr. Collins if he was married. Seems he was engaged some years ago, but his fiancé was killed in some sort of a horrible accident. I was sorry that I brought the subject up. The poor man."

The conversation turned to other topics, but Amanda was startled to hear this bit of information. She had almost made up her mind that Mr. Collins was something of a 'ladies man', flirting with whoever came along; but having experienced her own similar situation of loss, decided that he was probably trying to compensate for the loss by being overly friendly with those he met.

"Surely he's found someone else by now," Amanda said offhandedly.

Mrs. Caruthers shook her head. "No, according to him he's got no one. Just him and his work."

The family conversation continued but Amanda was oblivious. For some reason, she couldn't get Matt Collins out of her mind that evening. Later, as she sat at her dresser and brushed out her long, flowing hair, Matt's face kept intruding on her thoughts; and as she fell asleep that night, his face was still there.

CHAPTER 13

▼

Around ten the following morning, Matt saddled the horse and headed back into town, this time heading for the Western Union office near the train station. He spent some time composing and then had the agent send a dozen telegrams to various towns within a several mile radius of Montrose.

"If you get any replies, just hold them here. I'll be in town every two or three days to check," he told the agent, and paid for the telegrams along with an extra five dollars for the agent's trouble. The manager picked up the note, snapped it, and said with a smile, "Thanks, Mr. Collins!"

Matt walked over to the train station ticket master's office and introduced himself. "I'm trying to locate my cousin, Ben Parkwood. The last time we heard from him was three weeks ago last Saturday. I just wanted to check and see if maybe he'd purchased a ticket."

"Well, we can sure check," the ticket master, a man named Blevins, told Matt, "but they don't always put the name down in the register." Blevins looked back through a few pages but presently shook his head. "Nope, nothing here. We don't get too many passengers through this station, though; mostly freight and the like."

Matt nodded and said, "Thanks for checking." He walked back to where the horse was tied and, taking the reins, climbed up into the saddle and guided the horse back into town.

Reaching the main thoroughfare, Matt looked up at the clock above the County Courthouse. Eleven forty, and he nodded to himself. He'd try lunch again at the hotel a little later. Matt rode the length of the town, up one street and down the other, becoming familiar with the layout. Nearly an hour later he rode back to the main thoroughfare and up to the hotel, where he tied the horse out front and went inside.

The restaurant was fairly busy, and Matt waited for Mrs. Wharton to notice him. She soon came over and said, "Mr. Collins, good to see you again. Need a table?" Matt nodded and Mrs. Wharton, looking around at the crowded restaurant, said, "I'll have one for you in just a few minutes. You can have a seat at the bar while you wait if you like." Matt nodded again and sat on one of the stools. As he looked in the mirror, he saw Amanda Caruthers and the same two girls from lunch yesterday, sitting across the room behind him. Matt was still impressed at how beautiful this girl was.

Matt watched the three girls talk amongst themselves for a few minutes and on an impulse, he got off the stool and made his way through the tables toward them. The girls were still talking animatedly as Matt walked up and said, "Excuse me for interrupting. Miss Caruthers, it's a pleasure to see you again. I wanted to thank you again for your help yesterday."

The other two girls, startled at the intrusion of this good-looking man, stopped talking and stared in open-mouthed awe at Matt, then looked at Amanda. She had said nothing to them about this handsome stranger, and they were understandably curious.

"You're welcome, Mr. Collins." She said nothing further, and under the table one of the girls lightly kicked Amanda's shoe with her own shoe.

"Mr. Collins, this is Lucy Metcalf," she said, indicating the girl to her left, "and this is Sarah Miller," indicating the redhead across the table.

"Lucy, Sarah, pleased to meet you both," he said with a smile. He turned back to Amanda. "Do you dine here often?"

Amanda made no reply, and Lucy spoke up. "Oh, we eat here almost every day, Mr. Collins," she said with a giggle, and Sarah nodded in agreement.

"Well, then, perhaps I'll need to start doing the same," he said, still looking at Amanda. She said nothing, instead taking a sip of her tea. It was obvious that she didn't want to prolong the conversation. Mrs. Wharton came up beside him and said, "I have your table ready, Mr. Collins."

"Ladies, I hope to see you again," he said, but he looked at Amanda as he said it. He turned and followed Mrs. Wharton across the room.

The two girls watched him leave, and as soon as he was out of earshot they turned to face Amanda, who was looking down at her plate as if nothing had happened.

"Mandy, who *was* that?" Sarah said excitedly in a low voice. "He's so handsome! Why didn't you say anything about him?"

"I met him at the office yesterday, for business. That's all."

"That's *all?*" Lucy said. "He sure went out of his way to come and talk to you. What's he doing here in town?"

"He moved into his uncle's farm, the old Wyatt place outside of town; you know, the one they were fixing up a while back."

"I wonder if he's married," Sarah said, then, ruefully, "he probably is. All the good looking men are married."

"In fact he's not," Amanda replied, and Sarah and Lucy looked at each other, thinking that for some reason Amanda had been keeping this information to herself.

"You think he'll be at the town picnic and dance?" Lucy asked. Sarah chimed in with, "I hope he likes to dance!" The two girls giggled some more as they continued their conversation, speculating about Matt.

Amanda glanced sideways across the room and saw that Matt was looking around the room at the patrons. His gaze stopped on her and he gave her a slight nod. Amanda lowered her eyes and turned back to the table, seemingly indifferent. Still, something about him had piqued her interest. His reaction to her the first time they met; his conversation with her mother at the store; his coming to her table today. Well, he was new in town; she couldn't avoid seeing the man. She put it down to coincidence. She had to admit that he was handsome, and seemed to be very personable.

Some time later, the girls finished up their lunch and Amanda glanced around the restaurant again, only to see that Matt was gone. Sarah was saying, "Mandy, come on. I've got to get back to the store."

"Me, too," Lucy said, and they all got up and walked to the door together. "I'll see you both later," Amanda said, and headed back to the County Courthouse.

CHAPTER 14

▼

It was a week later and Matt had made no progress in his search for Ben Park-wood. None of the telegrams had elicited a response, and although he casually brought up the subject to some of the regional travelers, no one had seen or heard anything of Ben. Matt admitted to himself that he'd need to start scouring the surrounding towns and try to pick up a clue. He had hoped that he would have been able to locate Ben from here.

Matt was walking today, having taken the horse to McCallum's early that morning. As he trudged toward the downtown business area from the train station, he saw the dark clouds approaching. There was a heaviness in the air, and he could tell that a major downpour was imminent.

He had just reached the end of the board sidewalk on Maple Street when the first large drops began to fall. Looking around, he saw the townspeople scatter for shelter as a large bolt of lightning suddenly struck the spire of the Catholic Church nearby. A tremendous thunderclap shook the air and the downpour liter-ally burst from the sky as Matt began running toward the nearest store with an awning, three buildings away. He did his best to keep his footing on the slippery surface as he half walked and half ran toward the store.

From under the brim of his hat he saw several figures racing across the already quickly flooding street, making for various cover from the deluge. Aside from the rain, the lightning was dancing everywhere, striking the ground with regularity. He made it to the entrance of the store and was grateful when the doors opened and he was motioned inside.

"Lord, look at you, Mr. Collins!" a voice said, and he removed his hat and saw that it was the confectioner's shop. Mrs. Morris and a handful of the townspeople were inside. "Here, give me that hat and coat," Mrs. Morris continued, "I'll hang them up in back to dry."

"I doubt if these will dry too quickly," Matt replied as he peeled off the sodden jacket. He felt as if someone had turned a hose on him; even the sleeves of his shirt were wet. The rain had come with a suddenness he had seldom seen; if this kept up, there could be major flooding in no time. He handed the jacket to Mrs. Morris and nodded a greeting to the other townspeople as he walked back to the entrance to watch the storm.

The rain was coming down in sheets and he could hear the pounding of the raindrops on the roofs, a constant drumming sound that indicated just how powerful this storm was. The thunder was almost continuous, accompanying the lightning. It was then that he heard someone say, "Look out there!"

Across the street, a figure in a long dress was trying to hold up the bottom of that dress, balance a small and ineffective umbrella, and navigate the running water in the street in an attempt to get over to the store. Between the rain and the flooding water, she was having a difficult time of it. Another flash of lightning striking just yards away galvanized the figure into a faster pace—a mistake, since within a few steps she suddenly slipped and fell heavily to the street.

Matt instantly dashed out the door and into the downpour, splashing through the ankle-deep water to the figure's side where he bent down. "Are you all right?"

He was surprised to see that it was Amanda, a grimace on her face as she reached down to one ankle. She sucked in her breath in pain as she touched it.

"Can you walk on it?" Matt asked, but Amanda shook her head.

"I don't think so."

"Well, we can't stay here." Quickly, Matt reached down, scooped her up and turned back toward the store, expecting them to be struck by lightning any second. But their luck held as he reached the sidewalk and then the relative safety of the confectioner's shop. Mrs. Morris again held the door open for him.

Mrs. Morris looked at Amanda's ankle. "That doesn't look good. Here, put her down over here."

Matt gently set Amanda down in a chair and watched as Mrs. Morris removed Amanda's shoes and set them nearby. He followed Mrs. Morris to the rear of the store where she brought out a couple of folded blankets and handed them to him. Matt went back out into the store and saw about a half dozen people gathered around Amanda.

He made his way through the knot of people and shook out one of the blankets, which he then threw around Amanda's shoulders. Amanda pulled the blanket up over her head. Her hair was soaked from the downpour and hung down around her face in tendrils. Her dress was soaked as well. She looked up at him briefly, nodded her thanks and then shrunk away from him. Matt leaned down to her.

"Oh, come on, Miss Caruthers, I'm not all that bad, am I?" he said in a low voice.

"It's not that, Mr. Collins," Amanda replied from under the blanket. "It's just that…I know I must look a mess. And I feel so clumsy."

"You look a little wet, that's all. So do I." Matt pulled up a chair. "Mind if I sit with you?" The others had returned to the front of the store to watch the storm.

Amanda didn't answer, so Matt sat down next to her and leaned back. "I guess the storm moved quicker than we did. What were you doing out there?"

Amanda nodded and said, "I was headed back to work after running an errand when the rain came. I thought I could make it in here but I was soaked before I knew it."

Mrs. Morris walked up with a couple of cups of hot tea. "Here, you two, take some of this or you're liable to catch your death." Matt and Amanda gratefully took the steaming cups and sipped sparingly. Mrs. Morris said, "I'm afraid your shoes are ruined, Amanda. How's your foot?"

Amanda held out one dainty foot and grimaced as she wiggled it. The ankle looked slightly swollen. "I think it's just a small sprain," Amanda said, looking up at Mrs. Morris. She turned to Matt. "Thank you again for helping me."

"You won't be able to walk on that," Matt said. Then, "I'll get you to your parents' store after the storm." Amanda nodded hesitantly. Matt peered out the front door at the sky.

"It looks like we're going to be here for a while. I don't think this storm is going to let up anytime soon." He turned back to Amanda. "So, how have you been?"

"Fine," she said noncommittally, then after a slight pause, "and you?"

"Keeping busy," he said. "Still no word on my cousin. Otherwise, just getting familiar with the area. I'll be making some short trips pretty soon to some of the larger towns nearby. I'm sure someone must have at least a little bit of information."

She nodded silently and sipped at the tea. Although she was glad that it was Matt that had come to her rescue, she felt like an idiot for falling and twisting her ankle. On top of that, she was halfway soaked and felt as though she must look horrible.

Matt, on the other hand, was still amazed at how beautiful this woman was, even under these circumstances. Although he had interacted with her at most a half dozen times, he found himself thinking about her quite often.

After a short while, the rain eased up and the sun even tried to peep out from behind the clouds. The water that had flooded the streets had dissipated but it had left behind a muddy mess. The other citizens, seemingly undeterred by this, one by one made their way out the front door and headed for their respective destinations. Finally it was just Matt, Amanda and Mrs. Morris left in the store.

"The General Store is what, two or three doors down?" Matt asked.

Mrs. Morris nodded. "She won't be walking on that foot, though. We'll have to go over to Doc Ramsey's and find her a crutch."

"He's not in today," Matt said. "I heard at the train station that he had to go over to the logging camp for an emergency." Matt thought for a minute. "It's not that far. I can carry her over to the General Store."

"Oh, no, Mr. Collins, I couldn't..." Amanda said, but he bent down and scooped her up before she could say anything else. This was as close as he'd ever been to her, only inches from that lovely face, and he said, "Put your arms around my neck. It'll help me balance better." She said nothing, but slipped her arms around him. Matt turned to Mrs. Morris and said, "I'll be back for my jacket in a jiffy."

As he walked the short distance, Matt thought to himself, I could definitely get to like this.

Amanda was saying nothing, so Matt said, "I just hope *I* don't fall. We'd really be a sight then."

Amanda's face broke into a smile at the thought of that. She turned to him briefly and said, "Well, let's hope that doesn't happen."

Matt noticed the curious stares from a few of the townspeople as he made his way to the General Store without incident and walked through the doorway. Mrs. Caruthers looked up from behind the counter and shouted, "Jack!"

"I'm all right, Mother," Amanda said quickly, "it's just my ankle." Matt carried her behind the counter and back to the office. He set her gently into a chair and stood up. Mrs. Caruthers immediately examined the ankle as Mr. Caruthers came in.

Amanda looked up. "I slipped and fell in the street during the storm. Mr. Collins came to my rescue, and we waited out the storm in Mrs. Morris' shop. Then Mr. Collins was kind enough to bring me here."

Mrs. Caruthers looked up. "I don't think it's very bad. She'll have to stay off of it for a couple of days, though."

Matt said, "Let me show you something I learned. Bring me some bandages."

Mr. Caruthers nodded and left, returning shortly with the remnants of a sheet which he began tearing into strips. Matt remembered that ready-made bandages did not exist here. Matt took a long strip and began wrapping Amanda's ankle with it, making sure not to get the bandages too tight. When he was finished, he tied it off and said, "Take that off in a few hours, soak her ankle in cold water, and re-bandage it for another few hours. That should keep the swelling to a minimum and help it to heal quicker, too."

Mrs. Caruthers nodded and said, "Thank you, Mr. Collins."

"Yes, Mr. Collins," Mr. Caruthers said. "We're indebted to you."

"I think Doc Ramsey will be back by tonight," Matt said. "He should look at it, of course. If it's all right, I'll stop by to check on her tomorrow."

"Of course, Mr. Collins," Mr. Caruthers said as he and Matt walked back out into the store. With a wave, Matt was out the door.

Mr. Caruthers returned to the office where his wife was trying to make Amanda as comfortable as possible. "I don't think it's too bad," Mrs. Caruthers said. "Still, why don't you go over to Doc Ramsey's office and leave a note. Amanda can stay here for a while."

Mr. Caruthers nodded. "I'll let them know down at the Assessor's Office as well." Mrs. Caruthers turned to Amanda as her husband left. "You gave us quite a scare at first. When I saw Mr. Collins carrying you in here, I thought the worst."

Amanda nodded. "Sorry, Mother. It was awfully nice of him. If he hadn't come to help me when I fell I don't know what would have happened. I'd probably still be sitting out there."

"Well, I'm sure someone would have helped," her mother said.

Amanda thought for a moment, then said, "Mother, you seem to know him a lot better than I do. What do you think of him?"

"He's a gentleman, no doubt about that. Apparently rich, but not spoiled. Level headed, obviously family oriented—why do you ask?"

"Just…curious," Amanda said in a distracted voice. Her mother gave her a questioning look but Amanda was staring at the ceiling.

Mrs. Caruthers thought to herself, "I wonder…" but said nothing.

CHAPTER 15

▼

August turned into September and then into October, and Matt was still no closer to his goal. He knew that it wasn't for a lack of trying, though. He had just never realized how inaccessible practically anyone could be in this time period. Why, Ben could have been right across town from him, or even at a nearby neighbor's, and he'd never know it unless someone made the connection and told him.

He maintained weekly contact with Professor Parkwood, and they had even sent him additional topographical maps that were far more detailed than anything available in the current time period. Despite these advantages, Ben Parkwood was nowhere to be found. Since Matt's projected stay in this era had already doubled, Professor Parkwood had increasingly pressed to have Matt return to his own time and cancel the rescue mission. But Matt had pleaded for additional time and Stinnett had given the okay. Stinnett monitored the equipment almost constantly and felt that the anomaly was remaining stable enough to allow Matt to take the risk.

Matt had also gotten to know Mr. and Mrs. Caruthers much better, along with several of the other townspeople. He was really beginning to like this place, even though nearly everything he was used to in the way of conveniences didn't exist here. Despite his knowledge of this era, it was a daily learning experience as he adjusted. Matt also made a mental note to visit the contemporary Montrose when he returned to his own time, to see what kind of changes had taken place over the span of a century plus. He had taken dozens of photos with the digital camera and probably had the entire town cataloged already.

Although disheartened by his failure to locate Ben Parkwood, Matt found himself looking forward to those times when he ran into Amanda. He found himself thinking about this girl more and more, and took every opportunity to talk to her when he could. She was civil toward him, but her cold exterior showed no sign of wavering.

Matt's own demeanor had changed considerably since his arrival here. He felt alive again, and although he still thought about Carolyn from time to time, it was Amanda's face that he carried in his mind most often. He considered her cold attitude a challenge, and thought of various ways that he might be able to break through the wall that she had put up around herself.

This particular afternoon had found him headed for the General Store once again. As he entered, he saw that there were hardly any customers inside. Mr. Caruthers was nowhere to be seen, and Mrs. Caruthers stood behind the long counter cataloging some newly arrived supplies.

"Good afternoon, Mrs. Caruthers," Matt said as he came up to the counter.

"Well, Mr. Collins, it's good to see you again," she said. "How have you been?"

"Busy," Matt replied. "I'll be off again for a few days, so I thought I'd stop in and pick up a few items I'll need for the trip." He pulled a small list from his pocket and slid it across the counter.

Mrs. Caruthers picked up the list and examined it. "No problem," she said as she began going around the store, picking up the items on the list.

"You know, the big town picnic and dance is next Saturday," she said over her shoulder. "I hope you remembered that you can join us."

Perfect!, Matt thought. With most of the townspeople gathered in one place, he might be able to more easily pick up a clue to Ben's whereabouts—and it would give him another chance to see Amanda, he hoped, in a more social setting. "Is your whole family going to be there?" Matt asked.

Mrs. Caruthers nodded. "Of course," she replied. "Even my two sons and their wives are planning to come in. They live in Harrisburg now." She paused, then said, "Just be sure to say something about Amanda's new dress. She's very proud of it, and can hardly wait to wear it." Mrs. Caruthers sensed that Matt had more than a passing interest in her oldest daughter, but had refrained from saying anything to either of them, instead waiting to see if anything developed. She had a very good opinion of Matt and knew that he, or at least his uncle, was very well off. However, he didn't seem to act like most of the other privileged young men around the area. Most of them were either content to live off of their family's wealth or intent on squandering it. Matt seemed to be very level headed.

She was also curious about Matt's lack of lady friends. Most of the eligible bachelors spent a great deal of their time "shopping around" for a suitable spouse, and spent an inordinate amount of their lives attending socials, dances, and the like. As far as she could tell, Matt socialized little and certainly didn't flirt with the ladies. He appeared to be a gentleman of the first caliber.

"Will you be bringing anyone with you to the picnic, Mr. Collins?" she asked offhandedly, wondering if perhaps Matt had made some other female acquaintances recently of which she was unaware.

"No, if I am able to make it, it'll just be me." He picked up the box full of supplies and tucked it under one arm. "Well, thank you again. And," he said as he prepared to leave, "please tell Miss Caruthers that I said hello."

"I will, Mr. Collins. You have a good trip."

Later that day, Amanda stopped at the General Store after work as she did nearly every day. She spoke to her mother about a few things and was about to leave when Mrs. Caruthers said, "By the way, that nice Mr. Collins was in earlier today."

Amanda was instantly interested but outwardly showed nothing. "And…?"

"He mentioned that he'd be at the picnic and dance next Saturday, if he was back in town."

"That's nice," Amanda said neutrally. "I'm sure he and his date will have a good time."

"He's not bringing a date," Mrs. Caruthers said. "Said he was coming alone. I invited him to spend part of the evening with us if he wanted."

"That's nice of you," Amanda replied. "Well, I'll be heading home now. See you and Father later."

As she walked toward her house, Amanda's thoughts were on Matt. She thought back over the previous weeks since he had arrived in Montrose. She realized that he had tried his best to get to know her better, and she had tried her best to keep that from happening. Her fear of humiliation had overcome her desire to get to know this man, and deep down she regretted what she had done. She vowed that she would have a better attitude toward Matt the next time they met—if there was a next time. He might have given up on her by now, for all she knew.

CHAPTER 16

▼

Matt had finally been able to return to Montrose around two o'clock the following Saturday, and after dropping off the horse at McCallum's stable he walked tiredly toward his house. The streets seemed strangely deserted, until he suddenly remembered that the big picnic and dance were taking place today. Immediately he thought of Amanda, and knew that she'd be there. He wondered if he'd be able to finally break through that cold exterior of hers. No harm in finding out, he said to himself. He so much wanted to see her, to talk to her again. Breaking into a jog, he reached his house a short while later. Going inside, he locked the door behind him and descended to the cellar.

He stripped off his clothing, shaved, and stepped into the shower. Twenty minutes later he stepped out, feeling like a new man. He rummaged through the wardrobe and found a proper suit, and spent the next thirty minutes getting dressed. White shirt, separate collar, proper tie, followed by pants, suspenders, and a vest. The suit jacket felt long, but a look in the mirror satisfied him that he was properly dressed for this era and for the celebration.

Matt disliked hats, and was about to leave the bowler behind when he put it on and took another look in the mirror. Although he thought it looked odd on him, he knew that the fashion of the day dictated that he wear it. It was important that he fit in with these people, and not create any unusual speculation.

He walked to the computer but found no messages from Professor Parkwood. He'd been here for several weeks now with nothing to show. He was about to send another message telling Parkwood that his search had so far been unsuccessful, but decided to wait. He might just pick up a clue from someone at the picnic, and be able to send more optimistic news by tomorrow. For all Professor Parkwood knew, Matt was still out and about the countryside looking for Ben.

He walked up the steps to the kitchen, secured the door to the cellar, and made a sweep of the house before leaving. Even if someone were to get in, they wouldn't be able to get down to the cellar—and there was little of value on the upper floors. He locked the front door behind him and walked toward the center of town.

The weather had already turned, and Fall was in the air. It was decidedly cooler than it had been just a week earlier. As he walked along Main Street in the late afternoon, he saw that nearly all of the businesses were closed, with signs that said "Gone to Picnic" pasted inside the windows. The saloon was open, but Matt saw that it was nearly deserted as he walked past. He was sure that it would fill up after the festivities.

From a distance he could hear music, the oom-pah-pah of the tuba carrying quite a distance. As he got closer he could hear what sounded like trumpets playing a tune. As he reached the end of the street he was unprepared for the throng of people gathered in and around the Town Square. There must have been over a thousand people, and then he remembered that many of these were farm families, and only came into town for church or special occasions. The smell of various foods filled the air, and the atmosphere was festive.

Matt headed for one of the tables that had been set up for refreshments. He saw that each table had one or two specialties, depending on which local family's table it was. Pies from one family, cakes from another, fried chicken, beer supplied by the saloon, all free and served with a smile. He also saw at least a half-dozen men cranking away on old-fashioned ice cream machines. The ice cream would be served later, after the dance, and it was obvious that they wanted to make sure that there was enough to go around. Matt quickly ate a light meal and then wandered about the plaza.

As he sauntered about the festivities he could feel the carefree atmosphere of the place. So serene and bucolic, like nothing he'd experienced before. Everyone smiled at him and nodded in greeting, as if he'd lived here all his life. He realized that he felt at home here, more so than anywhere he'd lived since he was a small boy.

He paused to watch several couples dancing. A large dance floor had been built in the middle of the plaza and was a good sixty feet across. The town band played, mostly waltzes. Then through the dancers, he caught his breath as he saw Amanda sitting on the opposite side of the dance floor. The late afternoon sun glinted through the trees, highlighting the new blue dress that accentuated her gorgeous figure. She was a vision of beauty, and it was difficult for Matt to take his gaze off of her. With her were her mother and her two younger sisters, and as he watched he noticed that the sisters were harmlessly flirting with several of the local boys who were grouped together nearby. He saw that a few of the young teen boys were trying to talk one of their number into asking Amanda's youngest sister Rebecca to dance, pushing him forward gently, but he was too embarrassed and kept shaking his head. Matt thought he'd have some fun with them, at the same time giving himself an excuse to get close to Amanda.

Walking toward the group, Matt walked up to the boy and said, "What's wrong, son? She's a girl. She *wants* you to ask her to dance, can't you tell?" Speechless, the boy shook his head and shrank back further, his friends giggling. Matt leaned toward the boy and said softly, "How about if I show you how it's done? Would that help?"

"Maybe," the boy said, and nodded slightly. Matt pulled the boy to one side. "You're Stevie McDonald, aren't you?" Matt asked, and the boy nodded.

In a low confidential voice, Matt said, "Well, first, Stevie, don't be afraid. And don't be concerned about your friends. They may be teasing you now, but once you start dancing with Rebecca they'll be jealous and envious of you. Trust me, once you take the first step, they'll follow your lead. And tomorrow, you'll be the one they all look up to, because you were the first. That wouldn't be so bad, would it?"

"No," Stevie said in a quivering voice, "I guess it wouldn't."

"Then come with me," Matt said, and walked toward Amanda and her family.

"Mrs. Caruthers, you look lovely," Matt said to Amanda's mother, and Mrs. Caruthers smiled at him. "Good evening, Mr. Collins, it's good to see you. We weren't sure if you'd be able to make it."

"Oh, I got back into town a little later than I planned, but I wouldn't have missed this for anything." He turned to Amanda. "Hello, Miss Caruthers," he said, smiling at her.

"Hello, Mr. Collins," Amanda replied impassively, looking away and busying herself with her fan. Inside, though, she was thrilled that Matt had come to the dance after all. She had seen him arrive earlier and had been occasionally watching him through the crowd, and she was elated that he had come over when he saw her.

Matt turned to the other two girls. "Hello, Sallie. And, Rebecca, there's someone here I want you to meet." He reached behind him and pulled Stevie McDonald around. "Rebecca, this is Stevie."

"I know, Mr. Collins. We go to school together."

"Oh, right. You know, Rebecca, Stevie here was just telling me how pleased he'd be if you would do him the honor of dancing with him. Right, Stevie?"

Stevie nodded nervously, sure that she would turn him down. Instead, Rebecca jumped up and took Stevie's hand. "Just don't step on my new shoes," she said as she led him toward the dance floor. Stevie's face broke into a smile and he beamed at Matt as he was pulled along behind Rebecca. Mrs. Caruthers laughed to herself.

The scene was not lost on Stevie's friends. There was some hurried whispering, and then the tallest of the remaining boys walked purposefully toward them.

"Mrs. Caruthers, would it be alright if Sallie danced with me?"

"Well, Charles, why don't you ask her?" Quick as a flash, Sallie nodded, took Charles' hand, and they were gone. The other boys, amazed at the ease with which this scene had transpired, scattered to find their own partners for the dance.

Matt turned back to the women. Mrs. Caruthers looked at him bemusedly. "Mr. Collins, I didn't think those boys would ever work up enough backbone to do that."

"Well, the right word at the right time…may I join you?"

"Of course," Mrs. Caruthers said, and Matt took the chair that was angled to Amanda's right. Mrs. Caruthers was happy that Matt was showing some interest in Amanda, but she was concerned at what Amanda's reaction might be. So far, no man had been able to break through the barrier that Amanda had put up around herself after William Reed.

"So, Miss Caruthers, how have you been?"

"Fine, Mr. Collins," Amanda said, her face still impassive.

"Enjoying the festivities?"

"Yes, Mr. Collins."

"That's a beautiful dress, by the way," Matt said.

"Thank you for noticing, Mr. Collins." Matt leaned back and sneaked a bemused look at Mrs. Caruthers, one eyebrow raised and a half-grin on his face as if to say, she's a tough one. Mrs. Caruthers understood immediately. She had figured that, if Matt did come to the dance, he'd be making some sort of advance toward Amanda. Her motherly instinct had not been wrong, either. She smiled at Matt, then turned to her daughter.

"Amanda, dear," Mrs. Caruthers said, "I'm going to look for your father. Can you keep an eye on the girls?"

"Of course, Mother," Amanda said, and Mrs. Caruthers got up. Matt did likewise and touched the brim of his hat. As Mrs. Caruthers moved off, Matt sat back down, happy to be more or less alone with Amanda. He turned to her and saw that she was leaning forward, her attention centered on watching her younger sisters on the dance floor. She had been watching the clumsiness of the two young couples, but saw that they seemed to be getting the hang of dancing properly. Presently she relaxed and sat back in her chair.

Matt studied her profile. He was astounded at her beauty, and just as puzzled at her demeanor. He had always had a disarming way of making people feel at ease, but it didn't seem to be working on this girl regardless of his best efforts.

"So, there's quite a few people here," he said. "I didn't realize that so many people lived around here."

Silence.

"I'd guess about a thousand people, maybe two thousand."

More silence.

Matt said, "By the way, how's your ankle?"

"It's fine."

Undeterred, Matt decided to take the direct approach. "Miss Caruthers, do you dance?"

A sigh, then, "I've been known to."

"No, what I mean is…would you dance with me?"

"I have to watch the girls," Amanda replied.

"Well, you could watch them a lot better from the dance floor, don't you think?"

She hesitated, still not looking at him.

"It's going to be dark before long," he said, noticing that the gaslights around the square were being lit. "There can't be too many songs left, and I'd hate to miss out on an opportunity to dance—especially with someone so lovely."

Amanda turned to face him, slightly embarrassed at his straightforwardness. "You're very direct, Mr. Collins. Almost impudent, like a…like a schoolboy," she said admonishingly.

Matt stood up and held out his hand to her. "Well…I promise not to step on your shoes," he said with a grin.

A slight smile involuntarily crossed her face, and Matt could feel her softening a bit. "But, I've got to lose this hat," he said. He put the hat on the empty chair and turned back to her, his hand still extended.

With another sigh, she rose and laid her fan on her chair. Then, taking Matt's hand but not looking at him, she followed him to the dance floor. For some reason she didn't understand, inside she was thrilled with the opportunity to be near this man. But, it wouldn't do to show that. She remembered that she had decided to make an effort at being less aloof with Matt, but being in the midst of practically the entire town population held her back. On the outside, she maintained her cool composure.

The band began playing a half-time waltz, and Matt did his best to remember all the moves. It had been years since he had danced like this, but he wanted so much to be close to her. Still, there was a good foot and a half between them, one hand at her elbow, the other holding her other hand away. Proper etiquette at this point. As they moved around the dance floor, she stared off into the distance, not looking at him. Matt, on the other hand, looked straight into that lovely face and felt elated. He noticed that most of the other couples on the dance floor were watching them, and whispering to their partners. Whenever he caught a glimpse of them, they nodded and smiled.

Amanda could feel him looking at her but kept her eyes off to one side. She didn't want anyone thinking that this was anything more than a courtesy dance with a new resident of the town. Even so, the townspeople were astonished that she had even consented to dance at all. Her reticence around others was well known by this time, which is why none of the other young gentlemen had even bothered to ask her for a dance.

Matt, though, didn't care. He had accomplished his goal and reveled in the time he was spending with her. Something inside of him made him feel electrified whenever he was around this girl, and as they waltzed around the dance floor he was lost in the moment.

Before he knew it, the song ended—much too soon, he thought—and she walked ahead of him back to the chairs and sat down. Undaunted, Matt moved his hat to one side and sat down next to her.

"Thank you, that was delightful," Matt said, but she gave him no response.

"Ladies and gentlemen," the bandmaster said, and everyone stopped talking and turned toward the bandstand. "In just a short while, we'll have a presentation by the mayor and town council, commemorating this year's festivities and our new Village Hall." There was applause, and then the bandmaster continued. "We'll be playing our last few songs for a while so that the band can also enjoy the festivities. Have you enjoyed yourselves so far?" There was a roar of approval from the crowd, and the bandmaster turned to the band, raised his baton, and a lively number ensued.

Off to one side, a commotion caught Matt's attention. Someone was pushing through the throng of dancers, and suddenly a huge hulk of a man about thirty years old with a dark and scowling face was standing in front of them. Matt could smell the whisky on the man's breath as the man looked at Amanda, and saw that

Amanda was apprehensive and uncomfortable as she did her best to ignore the man.

"Amanda Caruthers, I'd like to have the next dance with you." It was more of a demand than a request. The man reeled slightly, and it was obvious to Matt that he had been drinking heavily.

"No, thank you, Mr. Green," Amanda said firmly, still not looking at him.

"But I insist," Green said in a loud voice, grabbing Amanda's arm in an attempt to pull her up from the chair. Matt jumped up, grabbed the man's arm and jerked it away. "Say, fella, she said no," Matt said good-naturedly. Green jerked away and stared at Matt, venom shooting from his eyes. The man was a good six inches taller than Matt, and his bulk made him seem all the larger to Matt.

"And who might you be, mister?," Green said.

"Matt Collins," Matt replied with a smile, and put out his hand.

Green slapped Matt's hand away. "She your girl?"

"Well, no, but...."

Suddenly one of Green's huge hands was on Matt's chest, pushing him back. "Then this don't concern you." Green gave a shove and Matt stumbled backward, lost his balance and sat down heavily in the chair.

Once again, Green grabbed for Amanda's arm. Some of the townspeople had noticed what was happening and had stopped to watch the scene. A few of the men from the crowd began moving toward them, sensing that something was wrong.

Green grabbed her above the elbow, and Amanda slapped at his hand with her free arm. "Stop it!", she hissed, but Green held on effortlessly. He grabbed her sleeve, roughly pulled her to her feet and was about to pull her close when Matt suddenly appeared at Green's side. Reacting quickly, Matt threw a short but powerful swift punch into Green's side, the sudden shock from the blow to the ribs knocking the wind out of Green and causing Green to let go of Amanda's arm. Before Green knew what was happening, in one movement Matt grabbed one of Green's arms, spun him around, and held the arm high up in the middle of Green's back. Green struggled to get loose but found that he could not.

Using the twisted arm as leverage, Matt walked Green toward the outer edge of the plaza as some of the other townspeople followed. They all wanted to see how this would turn out.

Matt whispered into Green's ear, "Listen, friend, I think you've had a little too much to drink. Why not call it a night and go home, okay?"

Green struggled for a bit but found that he could not get out of Matt's grip. He sensed that Matt had the upper hand and stopped struggling. Matt pushed him away, prepared in case Green decided to fight.

And Matt was right. Green turned to face Matt, brought up his fists and began circling toward Matt like an old-time boxer. Some of the younger boys shouted, "Fight! Fight!" and before long there was a good-sized crowd around the two men.

Matt just stood there, warily eyeing Green as he circled. Suddenly Green threw a punch that would have knocked Matt out cold had it connected, but Matt easily ducked out of reach.

"Listen, Green. I don't want to fight you," Matt said conversationally.

"I don't imagine you do," Green replied in a low menacing voice, a wicked look on his face. He was sizing up this smaller opponent and decided to finish this quickly. He swung again and was surprised as Matt easily ducked back out of reach a second time. This infuriated Green even more. "Sticking your nose where it don't belong. Come and get what's due you," Green said.

Matt thought furiously about how to handle this. Green was probably close to two hundred and fifty pounds, nearly a good hundred pounds heavier than Matt, and it looked to be all muscle. Matt glanced around at the spectators and saw that they were mesmerized by the scene, but no one was moving toward them. Oh, well, so much for any help, Matt thought.

Green rushed in, surprisingly fast for someone so drunk, and threw another punch. The fist just missed Matt's jaw as he jerked his head to one side but the blow landed high up on one side of his chest just below the collarbone. Rolling with the punch, Matt sprang to his feet, but his chest felt like it was on fire. It felt like he had been hit with a board. Green was coming in again but Matt ducked under the blow, at the same time instinctively landing his own fist low in Green's stomach. It was like hitting the side of a building, but incredibly Green doubled over for a second. Time enough, Matt thought as he spun around and, locking his hands together, brought his two-fisted blow down into the middle of Green's back with all his strength.

Green sprawled in the dirt face first, pushed himself up, shook his head and got unsteadily back to his feet. Matt still wondered why no one was coming to help him, but his attention was centered on Green, who was charging once again. Matt leaped to one side, dropping to a crouch and bringing one of his legs into Green's shins with a sweeping motion. With a bellow, Green once again tripped and fell painfully into the dirt. Green got up, his eyes red with fury. He began circling Matt again.

Matt knew that Green was waiting for the opportunity to land a haymaker to the side of Matt's head. Even in Green's drunken state, the blow would definitely knock Matt out and might even give him a concussion, or worse. Matt knew that he could ill afford to take another punch. He knew he had to outthink this opponent, instead of playing Green's game. He knew he had one chance, and waited for it as Green circled.

Once again Green got close enough and threw a swing, but Matt was prepared. He jerked back and, as Green's arm whistled past, grabbed the beefy wrist with both hands and twisted with all his might. He spun around and, jerking Green's arm behind him and up toward the middle of Green's back, shoved the man forward. Green's momentum from the punch still propelled him forward and, with one arm behind him, he was off balance. Matt fell with him this time, landing on top of Green and keeping the arm high up in Green's back. Green's face had again buried itself in the dirt, and Green bellowed like a mad bull as he spat dust out of his mouth. Green tried to twist away but Matt increased the pressure.

Matt leaned toward Green's ear and said in a low voice, "If you don't give up now, I'll break it." Matt gave the arm another jerk, and Green hissed in pain. Green struggled but couldn't get loose, although it was taking all of Matt's strength just to hold one of the man's arms. Finally Green said, "Let go." Matt jumped up and stepped away, ready for another charge. Green got to his feet and faced Matt. Matt put up his fists, but Green slowly turned, rubbing his arm. He squinted at Matt, his eyes trying to focus. He pointed at Matt and growled, "No one in this town treats me like that." Matt thought to himself, here we go again, and watched Green closely to see how he would continue the fight. But, to Matt's surprise, Green simply said, "I think we'll meet again," then turned around and pushed his way through the crowd. Matt watched as Green crossed the plaza and headed down the street, finally being swallowed up by the darkness.

Mr. Caruthers came up beside Matt. "Thank you, Mr. Collins, for helping Amanda. But I thought sure that you were in for it."

"Yes, so did I. Who *was* that guy?" Matt asked, frowning as he straightened his clothing.

"That's Harland Green," Mr. Caruthers replied. "His father is Josiah Green, the county's largest landholder, among other things. Harland's not quite...right. He's a bully and most of us just stay out of his way, but occasionally he causes some real trouble. His father has so far been able to keep him out of jail by buying off the victims, but we all figure that sooner or later Harland's going to do something really bad. I'm afraid that in protecting Amanda you might have created a problem for yourself."

Several of the men had gathered around Matt, dusting him off and shaking his hand. Apparently Matt had done something that no one else in town had thought of doing or would dare to do—confront Green directly—which Matt thought odd. Matt nodded to each of them and then turned back to Mr. Caruthers. "Yeah, I've heard about Josiah Green. So that's his son? Seems with all that money he could have someone teach his son how to act around ladies." He looked around. "Is Amanda all right?"

"She's over there with her mother," Mr. Caruthers said, and Matt followed him.

"Such a brute," Mrs. Caruthers was saying, shaking her head as she stood over Amanda, who was seated in her chair. She turned to Mr. Caruthers and Matt. "Her arm may bruise, and the sleeve on her new dress is torn, but she's all right. Thank you so much, Mr. Collins. Are you all right?"

"I think I may have a bruise as well," Matt said, rubbing his chest where Green's blow had connected, and then with feeling, "The man is strong." He turned to Amanda. "Miss Caruthers, are you sure you're all right?"

Amanda nodded, her eyes flashing. "The only thing worse than Harland Green's manners is his smell." The people within earshot laughed at the comment as they slowly filtered back to the dance floor.

Matt straightened his clothing. Satisfied that he was still presentable, he looked at Amanda and said, "I'd still like to have another dance, if you're up to it."

"Oh, I don't think so," Amanda said apprehensively, looking around the crowd.

Matt knew what she was thinking. "He's gone," Matt said casually. "Forget about him. Let's enjoy ourselves while there's still some of the evening left."

This time she looked up at him but her face was solemn. "All right. Mother?"

"I'll watch the girls. You two go ahead."

Matt led Amanda to the dance floor as a slow waltz began. This time, he held her a little closer, one arm partly around her waist, and was pleased to see that she was at least looking at him from time to time. He smiled at her and said jokingly, "You know, just being around you is quite an experience. Does your presence always cause this much commotion? Lightning storms, fights...I can't wait to see what's next."

She actually laughed, and smiled at Matt. "What is it about you, Mr. Collins? Is everything humorous to you?"

"Well, no, not everything," Matt replied, "but some things are." And some things are puzzling, too, Matt thought to himself. For instance, Amanda was without a doubt the most beautiful woman here tonight, and yet none of the other young gentlemen were even trying to get her to dance. Matt practically had to beg her himself. If what Mrs. Higby had told him was true, she must have really been traumatized by her former fiancé.

After the dance, Matt escorted Amanda back to her seat where the rest of the Caruthers family had gathered. He was about to sit down when he noticed his bowler hat in the chair. It was crushed flat from Green pushing him into the chair.

"Oh, Mr. Collins, your hat," Amanda said sadly. "I'm afraid it's ruined."

Matt actually laughed as he looked at it. "I honestly never liked that hat. Looks like Green might have done me a favor." Amanda looked at him oddly for a moment, then smiled as she realized he was serious. Mr. Caruthers looked at the hat and shook his head. "Mr. Collins, you stop by the store on Monday and I'll fix you up with a new one. It's the least we can do after what you did."

"No," Matt said, "thank you anyway, but I meant it about the hat."

Mrs. Caruthers spoke up. "Well, at least come to our house for dinner on Monday. We can offer you a good home cooked meal."

"Now that would be great," Matt said, "and I could sure use one, but I'm afraid I'll be out of town for a few days early next week. I should be back by Wednesday or Thursday." He paused, not wanting to lose this opportunity. "Would Friday be all right?"

"Of course," Mr. Caruthers said. "Next Friday it is. Now, come on everyone, the ceremony is about to start."

The townspeople were slowly moving toward the temporary platform that had been erected at one end of the plaza. Amanda took her father's arm, followed by Rebecca and Sallie and their new young escorts. Matt and Mrs. Caruthers brought up the rear. Mrs. Caruthers slowed a bit and put her hand on Matt's arm.

In a low voice, she said, "Mr. Collins, may I speak with you?"

"Why, sure, Mrs. Caruthers. What is it?"

Mrs. Caruthers waited until the others were out of earshot. "I've noticed that you seem to have taken a fancy to Amanda. I need to explain to you why she seems so…distant."

"I already know, Mrs. Caruthers. I heard that her fiancé ran off with another girl. That must have hurt her terribly."

"Oh, I don't know about that," Mrs. Caruthers replied. "I doubt that her father would have given his permission for her to marry that William Reed anyway. Mr. Caruthers and I both knew what kind of person young William was. Not too stable, although we all thought he would change eventually." She paused. "And I think Amanda wasn't so broken up by losing him, as she was by how it was done. She's certainly not carrying a torch for him, or anything like that. It's just that the poor girl was so embarrassed, and in front of the whole town. Some of them knew what was going on, but no one bothered to tell her, or couldn't bring themselves to tell her. Afterwards, we tried to tell her that it didn't make any difference, that the fault was William's and not hers, but you know how gossip is. She felt that she was the laughing stock of the town because she was too trusting. Now, she doesn't trust hardly anyone outside of our family. And in the meantime, while she was involved with William, practically all of the other eligible young men of her age ended up marrying and starting families. I think Amanda felt that she had missed her opportunity. Now, the only men left are the likes of Harland Green and his friends, and she'll have none of that. And neither will her father and I."

Mrs. Caruthers stopped and faced Matt. "You're a very nice young man, Mr. Collins, very personable. I think you're sincere. But I'm asking you, if you're not serious about Amanda, don't play with her emotions. Just in your brief encounter with her tonight, and over the past few weeks, I can see that if anyone can break through her reserve it's you. Please don't break her heart. I don't think she could take it."

Matt was stunned. Mrs. Caruthers was very insightful, and obviously could tell how he felt about Amanda. "Mrs. Caruthers, if you think I'm being too forward, or acting improperly…"

"No, no, it's just that…a mother can tell—she's starting to *feel* again. And it's because of the interest that you're showing in her. Just don't hurt my daughter, please."

Matt understood exactly what she was saying. And yet, he hadn't planned on this relationship getting as far as it had. He only knew that he was inexplicably drawn to this girl, and couldn't help his feelings. And carrying around the knowledge of what was to happen to this girl, he had wanted to give her brief remaining life…something. Or was he just being selfish?

"Mrs. Caruthers, I would never do anything like that. Even though we've known each other for just a short time, I find that I care for Amanda—very much." He paused, then said, "Thank you for being honest with me. You've given me something to think about." They started walking again and caught up with the rest of the Caruthers family.

Following the speeches, everyone returned to the plaza for the ice cream and other refreshments. Although the festivities were in full swing again, Matt was subdued and somewhat reserved. He had really looked forward to spending some time with Amanda on this special evening, but now he had to seriously consider what that might mean. Amanda noticed that Matt wasn't his usual self, and wondered what had caused the change in him. Inside, she was concerned, although outwardly she retained her composure. Finally, Matt rubbed his temples and said, "I apologize, but you'll all need to excuse me. I'm very tired and should be getting some sleep. I've been burning the candle at both ends over the last few days, and that tussle with Green didn't help. Mr. Caruthers, Mrs. Caruthers," he said, shaking their hands, and adding, "Amanda, Sallie, Rebecca, thank you all for letting me join your family for a short while. I've had a wonderful time."

"Of course, Mr. Collins. Will we see you at church tomorrow?" Mr. Caruthers said, and Matt nodded.

"Yes, of course you will. I think I'll feel better after a good night's sleep," he said, and turned away, walking slowly toward his house.

Watching Matt leave, Mrs. Caruthers said to her family, "The poor man. He must be all tired out, and yet he came to the dance anyway. I wonder why he even made the effort?" She looked at Amanda as she said this, but Amanda was looking away, crestfallen. Mrs. Caruthers could tell that she was disappointed that Matt had left. Despite her demeanor on the outside, on the inside Amanda had felt elated at the attention Matt had shown her.

As for Mrs. Caruthers, she felt that she had done the right thing in speaking to Matt. She knew that her conversation with him would lead to one of two things: either Matt would lose interest in Amanda, in which case it would show that his feelings for her weren't too deep; or, if he was sincere, he would continue his attempts at courtship. If the former, then Amanda wouldn't get hurt again. If the latter, perhaps it was just what Amanda needed to bring her out of her self-imposed exile from life. Either way, Mrs. Caruthers would know, and soon.

*   *   *   *

In the shadow of one of the buildings, two pairs of beady eyes watched Matt walk slowly along Depot Street. Green pointed and in a low voice said, "That's him."

One of Green's friends, a thin reed of a man with a squint, nodded and whispered, "Yeah, I've seen him here in town from time to time. Doesn't look too big. He actually got the best of you?"

"Shut up," Green growled, still rubbing his arm. "He must know how to wrestle or something. Nearly broke my arm or I would have made short work of him. Anyway, see what you can find out about him. I've got to go to Reading tomorrow on business and I'll be gone for a few days." He paused. "Meet me in the saloon next Wednesday. Bring the other boys, too." The other man nodded and the two turned and melted away into the shadows.

CHAPTER 17

▼

The following morning found Matt once again walking toward town from his house. He had awakened shortly after daybreak, and the first thing he noticed was the large dark bruise just below his collarbone. He flexed his arm. Painful, but not too bad. He'd have to watch out for Green. If Matt was any judge, he knew that an angry Green would be like a wounded rhino.

Matt had showered and shaved in the small bathroom in the cellar, and afterwards had checked the equipment. Everything seemed normal. He was due to contact Professor Parkwood later that evening and report his progress—or actually his lack of progress, as it turned out. Matt knew he'd have to redouble his efforts to find Ben Parkwood.

As he walked along the tree-lined streets, he saw many families coming into town, riding horses or in wagons. The town had at least a half-dozen churches, and the incoming families made beelines for their respective buildings. He remembered that the Caruthers family attended the Montrose Methodist Episcopal Church on, what else, Church Street, where most of the places of worship were located.

Matt liked walking, but he made a mental note to get the horse back from McCallum's stable as soon as possible.

He reached the building and saw that there was what appeared to be a greeter's line at the top of the steps. Everyone smiled and nodded to each other as they entered. He went up the steps and was about to introduce himself when Mrs. Higby appeared at his side. "Mr. Collins, it's so good to see you. I've been wondering when you were going to come to church. Let me introduce you." Mrs. Higby led Matt to where the pastor, Reverend Shipman, was greeting the arriving parishioners and introduced Matt to the Reverend. Then, approaching several people in turn, Mrs. Higby continued the introductions. Matt saw that he quickly became the center of attention. Mrs. Higby obviously had a lot of influence with the parishioners, and her evident interest in him made him someone special to them. They responded in kind, and once inside Mrs. Higby said, "Since you're new here, please join our family for the service."

"I'd be delighted," Matt replied, and followed her to the third pew from the front. Mayor Higby, his wife and children were there, and they dutifully moved across to make room. Matt took a few seconds to look around at the crowd, and saw that the Caruthers family was seated directly across the central aisle. He nodded a greeting to Mr. and Mrs. Caruthers, who responded with a nod and a smile. Mrs. Caruthers whispered something to Amanda, seated next to her, and Amanda looked at Matt and tilted her head. Her face was impassive.

The singing was beautiful, the organist expertly manipulating the instrument. When it came time for the sermon, Reverend Shipman held everyone's attention as he recounted a story of sin and redemption. From time to time Matt would steal a glance across at Amanda, but she sat staring forward or following the sermon in her Bible. After the sermon, church was dismissed, and as he made his way toward the door Matt could feel the eyes on him from some of the congregation and saw people whispering to each other. He knew that he was the subject of their conversation, and figured that his fight with Green the previous night at the dance had something to do with this. He was still puzzled at the circumstances of the fight, with no one coming to his aid. Oh, well, no harm done. He had no idea that he was the first man to ever best Green in a fight.

After the sermon, Matt was about to leave when Mrs. Higby said, "Of course you'll be staying for the lunch, won't you, Mr. Collins?"

Matt had forgotten that most families of this era made a day of going to church, having lunch after the morning service and socializing well into the afternoon hours. As if on cue, his stomach reminded him that he had not eaten since the previous evening.

"Of course, Mrs. Higby, I'd love to." She led him outside to the large grassy area adjacent to the church, where tables had been set up. A line had already formed. There appeared to be enough food to feed twice as many people as were here, and he filled up a plate and headed for a large tree nearby where the Higby family had already taken possession of a portion of the shady area beneath. He sat down with his back to the trunk and watched the congregation.

Mr. Higby leaned over and said, "You know that was one brave thing you did last evening, taking on Harland Green like that. Even more amazing that you beat him."

"It wasn't bravery as much as trying to avoid getting my head caved in once everything started," Matt replied. "The man is strong as an ox." Matt lowered his voice and leaned toward Mr. Higby. "I've been meaning to ask about that. Don't take this the wrong way, but no one seemed too eager to help me out. Why is that?"

Mr. Higby frowned slightly. "It's not what it seems," he said. "Green is a bully, make no mistake. But everything happened so fast, and then it looked as though you had the best of him. Several years ago a couple of men in town decided to challenge Harland, and although he backed down at the time, inside of a week the windows in their businesses were broken out in the dead of night and the premises torched. Of course everyone knew who did it, but the case never made it to court. Green's father hired a lawyer from Philadelphia who had the case thrown out. No witnesses, so no case. Any time anyone has stood up to Green, they've had something happen to their property. It's odd, though," he continued. "You do something to Green, he retaliates, but that's it. Nothing further. Makes it all that much harder to prove he did it. You'd think he'd keep at it, but he doesn't. 'An eye for an eye', if you know what I mean."

Matt said, "So obviously he's still planning on getting even with me."

Mr. Higby nodded, then said, "Oh, you can count on that. You really made him look bad. No one's ever gotten the better of him in a fight before. He's nearly crippled a couple of men, but again, his father always gets him out of it somehow. Pays off the victim, usually, or has one of his lawyers get the son out of it. In your case, though, I'd bet Green will be wanting a rematch. Could be now, could be in a few weeks. Whatever he's planning, he'll make sure it's on his own terms, and that he'll win."

"Well, I'll keep my eyes open," Matt said. "Thanks for explaining."

As the afternoon progressed, Matt found himself watching the Caruthers family across the way. After the meal, many of the men, women and children gathered in their respective groups, the men and women talking amongst themselves and the children playing. For many of these families, especially the women, this was one day a week when they could get together and talk. For the rest of the week, their chores at home or at the family business kept them busy and they rarely had time to socialize.

Matt noticed that Amanda had made her way alone to the bank of a small stream nearby. She had removed her shoes, sat down on a small blanket, wrapped her arms around her knees, and rested her chin on them, watching the water as it flowed. Her sisters frolicked nearby but no one else approached her.

Matt stood up. "If you folks will excuse me, there's someone I'd like to talk to." The Higby family nodded and watched as Matt headed for the stream. Mrs. Higby leaned toward her son and said, "Word is he's taken quite a fancy to Amanda." Mr. Higby shook his head. "A lot of good that'll do him," he said matter-of-factly.

But Matt was not so pessimistic. Coming up on her silently from behind, he took the opportunity to study her for a few moments. The sun glinted off of the lustrous black hair. He was about to say something when Amanda said, "Care to sit down, Mr. Collins?"

"How did you know I was behind you?," Matt asked as he sat down beside her.

"You have a unique after-shave. I noticed it last night at the dance."

"Not too strong, I hope?"

"No, not at all, it's quite nice. It's just…different." She turned to look at him. "There's something different about you, too, but I can't quite decide what it is." Her face remained impassive. "Are you feeling better today?"

"Yes, and again I apologize for leaving so early last night. You have a very nice family. It was great to spend some time with you…I mean with all of you." He had deliberately misspoken, hoping for a response, but there was none. Matt decided to press on. "I had a wonderful time with you at the dance last night," he said. "Thank you again for dancing with me." He paused. "How's the arm?"

"Bruised," she replied. "He's a filthy brute," she added with disgust. But then she smiled and said, "Thank you for coming to my rescue. He's never tried anything like that before. Must have been the whisky."

They sat there in silence for a short while, the only sounds the water in the stream and the distant voices from the congregation carrying to them on the wind. Before long Amanda turned to face him, her face serious. "Mr. Collins, I need to ask you something."

"Sure, go ahead."

"Why were you so persistent with me at the dance last night?"

"Well, why not? I didn't have a date for the dance, and neither did you, so I figured we could enjoy each other's company. It would be a shame for both of us to waste a whole evening alone, don't you think?"

"Surely you could have danced with any of a dozen other girls that were there."

Matt looked at her quizzically. "I didn't *want* to dance with any of the other girls. You were by far the most beautiful girl at the dance. I just thought it fortunate that things finally worked out the way they did."

She looked at him silently for a few moments. "I don't like to be used, Mr. Collins." She turned back to watching the stream.

"Used? No, no, I would never..." His voice trailed off. Although he couldn't imagine how, he realized that he must have given her the wrong impression with his remark. He knew he had to correct this misunderstanding, and fast.

"Listen, Amanda, I like you. I like you a lot. Ever since the first day I met you, I realized that there was something special about you. I just wanted to get to know you better." He paused, then said wryly, "You know, you're not making it very easy, either."

She looked at him and said, "I suppose you're right. But I have my reasons."

Matt didn't act as if he knew anything about her past. He leaned back on one elbow and looked around. "You know, everything here is so serene, so restful. Not at all what I'm used to." After a pause he asked, "How long do these gatherings last?"

"Oh, it's still got a while to go. Everyone goes home around four, usually."

Matt pulled out his watch and saw that it was half past one. "Care to take a walk with me?"

"That would be nice," she said noncommittally, then hesitated. "But we'll need a chaperone."

Matt again remembered that social protocol here was very different from his own time. He looked around and said, "Wait here, I've got an idea."

He got up and walked over to where Stevie McDonald was talking to Rebecca. "Stevie, can I talk to you for a minute?" Stevie nodded and came over to Matt.

"How's everything going with Rebecca?"

"Great!", Stevie replied. "Thanks, Mr. Collins. You were right last night. I really think she likes me."

"Good," Matt said. "Listen, Stevie, how'd you like to do me a favor?"

"Sure, Mr. Collins, what is it?"

"Well, I need to have a private talk with Miss Amanda, take a walk around the area, but we need someone to go along with us. How about asking Rebecca to go for a walk? That way, you two can chaperone Miss Amanda and me."

"Yeah, that sounds great!" Matt could tell that Stevie wanted to get Rebecca away from the other children, even for a little while. Stevie turned and walked over to where Mrs. Caruthers was sitting, talking to some of the other ladies from the congregation. Matt followed closely behind.

"Excuse me, Mrs. Caruthers. Would it be all right if Rebecca went for a walk with me?"

"Oh, I don't know, Stevie," Mrs. Caruthers began, as if to decline, when Matt stepped up. "Hello, again, Mrs. Caruthers. I wouldn't mind tagging along with Stevie and Rebecca. I was thinking of asking Amanda to join us as well."

Mrs. Caruthers smiled. "Well, in that case…of course, Stevie. And, thank you, Mr. Collins." In a flash, Stevie was gone, off to find Rebecca.

"My pleasure, Mrs. Caruthers. Ladies," he said, bowing slightly as he turned to leave.

Mrs. Caruthers watched him leave, then turned back to her conversation. "I think Mr. Collins has taken a liking to Amanda."

The other ladies smiled and nodded, and their conversation turned to matters of romance.

Matt walked over to Amanda, who was now standing next to the stream. "I found us a chaperone. Two, actually. Stevie McDonald and Rebecca."

Amanda looked at Matt with a puzzled look and said, "They can't chaperone us. They're children."

Matt explained. "Well, the way it worked out, we're going to chaperone each other, sort of. Stevie asked your mother if he could take Rebecca for a walk, and I told your mother that we'd tag along with them."

Amanda smiled. She understood how he had engineered the scenario, and was impressed. Otherwise, she and Matt would need to find one of the older ladies from the church who would be willing to go along, and *that* wouldn't be very pleasant for them.

The two couples headed up the street, and it wasn't long before Stevie and Rebecca were far enough ahead to be out of earshot. Matt and Amanda walked slowly, enjoying the day. Here and there they could see other couples at a distance, enjoying the day much the same as they were.

Matt said, "You know, you really have a nice town here. Very different from where I'm from. Back at home, it's like there's never enough time to just slow down and enjoy life."

"You're from Pittsburgh, aren't you?" Amanda asked, and Matt nodded. She continued. "Do you have family there?"

"No, I live the bachelor life."

"No lady friend?"

"Well, Amanda, I wouldn't be here with you if I did." He looked over at her and said in a reassuring tone, "No, no lady friend. I haven't been involved with anyone for a long, long time. Just me and my work."

"What kind of work is that?" Amanda asked. She knew, from the bits and pieces of information that she had picked up about him from Mrs. Higby and others, that he was apparently well educated, relatively well off financially, and single. She of course said nothing about the story that her mother had told her about Matt's late fiancé.

Matt thought quickly. "I've been involved in...a few different things. But, right now, I've taken some time off from all of that and I'm working exclusively for my uncle."

"Yes, and you're still trying to find your cousin. Are you having any success?"

"No, not yet," Matt replied. "But it's just a matter of time." He looked at her and, making up his mind, decided to change the subject. "You know, when I first met you, that day at your office, I thought that you were the most beautiful girl I had ever seen."

Amanda didn't know what to say. She felt somewhat embarrassed at hearing this from Matt.

Matt, sensing from her silence that he may have said something wrong, and seeing her uneasiness, said, "I'm sorry. Am I making you uncomfortable?"

"No...well, yes. I hardly know you, Mr. Collins. Are you like this with all the girls?"

Matt laughed. "Of course not. It's just that...ever since I met you, I've thought about you—a lot. There's something different about you. I just wanted to get to know you better, and I think it's important that I be honest with you." He paused. "I know I'm not following proper etiquette, but I try to be logical about things. If that's the way I feel about you, I thought you should know."

They walked in silence for a while. Presently Amanda said, "You know, you really don't know very much about me."

"That's something I hope to change, and soon," Matt said. "But, do you think you could do me a favor?"

"What's that?"

"I'd really appreciate it if you'd call me Matt. 'Mr. Collins' is a little too formal for me. I know, I know, maybe it's not proper, but at least on the rare occasion when it's just us alone together?" He stopped and faced her. "Please, Amanda?"

"Mandy. Call me Mandy. All right, Matt."

They continued walking. Here and there they could see other couples walking about, enjoying the beautiful day. Ahead, Stevie and Rebecca had stopped at the water's edge and were throwing stones across the stream, trying to skip them across the water.

"So, Mandy, tell me about yourself."

"Oh, I don't suppose I'm a very exciting person. I've lived here all my life. I've been working at the Assessor's Office for about three years. Father is a good friend of Mr. Milhouse, which is how I got the job in the first place."

"Your father's a very influential man in town, isn't he?"

"Father's often said that his family was very lucky to have found this place, and been able to grow with the town. Yes, you could say that he has influence with many of the town's principal citizens, but they all respect him. He's always been a man of his word."

Matt nodded in agreement. "Well, after all, that's the most important thing for any man to have—his word. More important than money, power, fame, or just about anything else." They stopped and leaned up against a fence railing. Matt continued. "But I'm getting away from the point. I already know what you *do*. I want to know, what do you *like*?"

Amanda shrugged. "I try not to get too passionate about anything; I've found that it can lead to disappointment sometimes."

Matt pressed on. "But what excites you, makes you happy? What makes you laugh?"

Amanda shrugged again. "Not much of anything, not for a long time." There was resignation in her voice.

Matt looked at her and sighed. "Mandy, you can't live like that. You're letting the fun part of life become extinguished, I'd guess because of some unfortunate things that may have happened to you. You know as well as I do that everyone has to live with disappointments."

Amanda looked down and shook her head. Almost to herself, she said in a low voice, "I'm not letting that happen to me again."

Matt said, "Not let *what* happen to you?" There was no reply. Matt slowly reached out and took one of Amanda's hands between his own hands, and held it gently. "Mandy, do you feel this?" Amanda nodded, not saying anything.

Matt said, "This is what life's all about. The warmth of someone else; the feeling that two people have for each other." He squeezed her hand gently. "I meant what I said earlier: I like you, a lot. I'm hoping that there's something, some similar feeling, inside of you as well about me." He leaned down and, with one hand under her chin, slowly lifted her head to face him. His other hand intertwined with the fingers of her hand.

To her credit, she did her best to keep her composure on the outside; but as she looked up at Matt, inside she felt emotions coming to the surface that she hadn't felt in months. Just the touch of his hand was electric to her. Still, she looked at him passively, trying to fathom whether she could believe what he was saying. As she looked deep into his eyes, she knew that he was sincere.

But, she knew that this was not the time or place to continue this—in broad daylight, where a hundred pairs of eyes could be watching them at any time. She squeezed his hand briefly, then said, "We should get back."

Matt sighed and nodded, and waved at Stevie and Rebecca to return. The two younger children soon came running up, and the four of them retraced their steps toward the church. Except, on the return walk, Amanda slid her hand into Matt's as they walked.

This small gesture wasn't lost on Matt, who knew that he had made some headway and was satisfied to leave it at that for the present. He felt that if he pressed any further at this juncture, he might lose everything that he had accomplished with this girl.

As they neared Church Street and began coming upon more people, Amanda let go of Matt's hand and widened the distance between them slightly. She too understood that something was happening between them, and didn't want to jeopardize it by starting any rumors or speculation among the townspeople. If this did turn into something more, well, there was plenty of time, she thought to herself.

Matt, too, was hoping that this might turn into something more, but his thoughts were driven by just the opposite—the realization of the *lack* of time the two of them had. He knew that he only had weeks, maybe days, to find Ben Parkwood and get back to his own era. And, there was the specter of Amanda's demise hovering in the background. But even as he thought about this, he wondered at what had brought he and Amanda together. True, he had been infatuated with her from the first time they met, but he admitted to himself that he had pressed the relationship at every opportunity—seemingly prompted by an inner force. It was as if something else took over when he was around this girl, guiding his actions.

Well, he'd think about that later. Matt had learned not to worry about 'what ifs', and had always tried to concentrate on the here and now.

As they returned to the church grounds, Matt saw that it was already half past three. He couldn't believe that their time together had passed so quickly. He followed Amanda down to the edge of the stream and helped her gather up the blanket and other items she had left there. He then escorted her back to her family.

"How was your walk, Amanda?" Mrs. Caruthers said.

"Very nice, Mother. It's a beautiful day."

Mrs. Caruthers was amazed. She hadn't heard Amanda describe anything positively for some time. "And how about you, Mr. Collins?"

"Amanda is right. I haven't been this relaxed for weeks. It's really beautiful here."

Mr. Caruthers spoke up. "Enjoy it while you can. First frost is due any time now."

Matt realized again that things he took for granted simply didn't exist here. For instance, that these people had little or no advance warning of weather changes, as he did in his own time. They just took what came and lived with it.

Matt was about to leave when Mrs. Caruthers said, "Now, Mr. Collins, don't you forget about that dinner on Friday."

Behind her, Amanda looked at Matt and, with her eyebrows arched, nodded slightly with a questioning glance as if to say, you will be there, right?

"Not a chance I'd forget about that, Mrs. Caruthers. I'm looking forward to it. My cooking skills aren't that great anyway. I make do when I'm on my own, but just barely." Matt grinned as he said this.

Mrs. Caruthers passed a basket to Matt. "Here, take this. Fried chicken, biscuits, potatoes—something for later tonight."

Matt wasn't about to refuse. "Why, thank you so much." He turned to Amanda. "Maybe I'll see you in town sometime this week?" he said, and Amanda nodded. Matt headed for the street and turned toward his own house.

Mrs. Caruthers could tell that Amanda's demeanor was brighter than she'd seen it for a long time, and she was pleased.

CHAPTER 18

▼

Matt arrived at the hotel restaurant at a little after twelve the following day. He looked around the room but failed to find Amanda among the patrons. Mrs. Wharton came up to him and said, "Table, Mr. Collins?"

"Not today, thanks. I've got to catch the train to Scranton in a bit." He looked around again. "But," he said, taking a seat at the bar, "I will have a glass of tea." Mrs. Wharton nodded and moved off.

She returned and set the glass of tea down on the bar. Noticing Matt looking around, she said, "What are you looking for?"

"Not what, but who," Matt said. "A young lady," he explained. "Amanda Caruthers." Mrs. Wharton nodded. She had seen the couple at the dance on Saturday night, and had heard about the church outing as well. News of that type traveled fast in a small town.

As if on cue, Amanda, accompanied by Lucy and Sarah, appeared in the doorway. The girls headed for their usual table, not noticing Matt at the bar.

He waited until they were seated and then made his way over to them.

"Hello, again, ladies," he said. "Excuse me for interrupting, but I've only got a few minutes to spare." He looked at Amanda. "Miss Caruthers, could I have a word with you in private, please?"

Amanda said nothing, simply nodding and rose from the table to follow Matt to a more or less empty portion of the restaurant. They sat down at a table, Amanda's back to the other patrons.

Amanda looked at him. "The gossip will really start now," she said with a slight smile. "I'll be lucky to get back to work without Lucy and Sarah worrying me to death with their questions. They heard about our outing yesterday."

"Just tell them you're trying to be nice to a lonely old man."

Amanda giggled. "Believe me, if it wasn't me here with you they'd be trying to take my place in an instant."

"Not a chance of that happening," Matt said. "You know, I knew you had it in you."

"Had what?"

"That sweet disposition. Your mood, it's different today. Something happen?"

"I just spent some time last night thinking about what you said. You were right. Life is too short to go through it without being happy. We might as well take advantage of what comes our way."

"Well, I'm glad you took it to heart." He finally felt as if he was connecting with her on the same level. The atmosphere was much more relaxed. Sitting here with this beautiful girl, he felt as if he was on top of the world. They chatted for a few more minutes, and Matt explained that he would be out of town for a few days.

Matt stood up and took one of Amanda's hands in his. This was not lost on Lucy and Sarah, who along with most of the patrons had been surreptitiously watching the couple the whole time. Matt said, "I'll see you Friday night, if not sooner."

"Take care, Matt," she said, standing. He gave her a wink and they turned and walked back across the room. Matt saw her to her seat and then, touching his hat, said, "Goodbye, ladies," and headed out the door.

CHAPTER 19

▼

The preceding weeks had brought Matt no luck. Although he had traveled as far as Binghamton to the north, Mansfield to the west, and Milford to the east over the last few weeks, he had nothing to show for it. He hoped that Ben Parkwood had at least remained in the more populated areas. This time he had headed south, toward Scranton, and found himself there on Tuesday morning.

As he had done in the other towns, he first went to the local constable's office and filed a report on his missing "cousin". Then, he decided to check the hospital. He had a photo of Ben Parkwood that Professor Parkwood had provided, and he had shown this to everyone he questioned. Nothing so far.

As Matt went up the steps of the Scranton Hospital, he expected to get the same result. He had promised Professor Parkwood that he would do his best, and when he began this strange journey his confidence was high that he would succeed. But, in contrast to his own time, he had found that it could be very difficult to locate someone in this era, especially a stranger who hopefully wouldn't be calling attention to himself.

The hospitals of this era were far different from his own time. They depended in large part upon charitable donations from wealthy citizens, and had only recently added nursing staffs. The various wards were privately funded, and there was much infighting among the doctors as to who would receive treatment. The doctors spent nearly as much time looking for donations as they did treating the patients, and in many cases most patients were given a fatalistic outlook by the doctors: "If they live, they live. If not..." In many cases, it depended upon the general health and recuperative powers of the patient as to whether they survived or not.

Matt entered the main doors and walked down the hallway toward the nurse's station. The building was huge, rivaling the size of any hospital from his own time, but the care available here was archaic in comparison.

He stopped at the nurse's station, deserted for the moment, and waited. He knew that the nurses were constantly looking after the patients and spent little time here.

After some delay, he heard footsteps behind him and turned to see a matronly woman walking toward him. She smiled and said, "Can I help you, sir?"

"I hope so," Matt replied. "I'm looking for my cousin, Ben Parkwood. Our family hasn't heard from him in some time and thought that he might have gotten hurt or something." Matt brought out the photo and showed it to her.

"Ben Parkwood," she repeated, and looked at the list of patients. She shook her head. "No, not in this ward. You might try upstairs, though."

Matt thanked her and walked to the stairs. He remembered that each hospital ward was separate here, and each one kept its own patient records.

The second floor held a long corridor with different wards leading off to each side. As Matt walked along the corridor, he read the hand-written signs on each door. This one said "Scarlet Fever", the next said "Diphtheria", and so on. Matt was glad he had received the inoculations prior to his journey. He reached the nurse's station at the end where he found a plain-looking girl writing in a notebook. She looked up. "Can I help you?"

"I hope so," Matt replied. "I'm trying to locate my cousin. His name is Ben Parkwood. Our family hasn't heard from him in some time and thought that he might have gotten hurt or something."

"Ben Parkwood," she repeated, and looked at the list of patients. "No, I don't see his name here. However, we do have a few patients whose identity we don't know."

"Why is that?" Matt asked.

"Well, some are brought in unconscious, or too weak or injured to speak to us. We do our best to get them comfortable until the doctors can see them."

"My cousin's been missing for some time." Matt reached inside his jacket and pulled out the small oval photograph. "Here's his picture, it's fairly recent."

The nurse took the photo and looked at it closely, her eyes widening. "I think this is…I mean, there is a resemblance…" She stood up and motioned Matt to follow her. They walked down the corridor to the room at the end and entered quietly. The nurse held her finger to her mouth, indicating to Matt that he should be quiet. The room was dimly lit, and she led the way down a row of beds until she came to one near a window.

Matt leaned across and looked at the man lying on the bed. He drew his breath in sharply. Although the man was pale and thin, he recognized Ben Parkwood's face on the pillow. Parkwood's breathing was shallow but regular. Matt noticed scars and bruises that were healing. He nodded to the nurse and motioned her back out into the hallway.

"That's him," Matt said. "Can you tell me what's wrong with him?"

"He was brought in several weeks ago. I think he was the victim of an awful railroad injury of some sort, but no one from the railroad knew who he was. His left leg was crushed, and he had other injuries as well. He was too well dressed for a railroad worker, but he had no papers or anything to indicate who he was. He's in a bad way with that leg, which is why we kept him in here. We've asked him what his name is, but he can't tell us—says he doesn't remember."

"What have they been doing for him?" Matt asked.

"As much as they can," she replied. "We can't operate on his leg until he gets stronger, and some of his other injuries heal."

"He must be in tremendous pain," Matt said. "Are they giving him anything for it?"

"No, nothing."

"Why not?" Matt said.

You'd have to ask the doctor about that. Doctor Greevely. He'll be back in town next Tuesday."

"That's another week. Can he be moved?" Matt asked, and the girl shook her head.

"Absolutely not. The doctor was quite specific on that. He's afraid any movement would cause even more problems with that leg."

"When can I speak to Ben?" Matt asked, and the nurse shrugged her shoulders.

"You can try now if you like, if he'll wake up," she replied.

Matt followed her back into the ward and to Ben Parkwood's bed. The nurse leaned over him and gently shook his shoulder. "Sir? Sir? Can you hear me?"

Ben Parkwood, his face almost as white as the pillow, moved his head from side to side slightly and opened his eyes. He tried to focus on the nurse but then squinted in obvious pain. "What is it?" he said weakly.

"There's someone here to see you." She moved out of the way and Matt pulled a chair next to the bed and sat down. "Ben, it's me, Matt Collins."

"Who?" Ben said weakly.

"Your cousin, Matt Collins. Uncle Henry, your father, sent me to find you."

"My father? But he's..."

"Very worried about you," Matt said quickly. "It's all right now. We'll get you home soon. Back to Sandra and your father."

Ben looked up at Matt. "Your name is Collins? But I don't recognize you. You're not from the project. How…?"

"Don't worry about that now," Matt said, then turned to the nurse. "He sounds delirious. Is it all right if I sit here for a while?"

"Of course, just try not to disturb the other patients," the nurse said, and moved off.

Matt turned back to Ben. "Listen, Ben, your wife and father are very worried about you. I knew your father from the university. It's a long story, but I've come back to take you home." He looked at Ben's leg. "What happened, anyway?"

"It was Green."

"Harland Green?"

"Yes," Ben said, trying to move but wincing in pain. "The farm we bought in Montrose. Green wanted it. I told him I wasn't going to sell. A few weeks later he came back with a couple of his friends and roughed me up a bit. Told me he needed to have the farm. Something to do with part of his father's businesses. I told him no again. He left. I figured I'd be gone before anything else happened. Then, as luck would have it, the equipment in the cellar just shut off, and nothing I could do would get it operating again.

"I took three of the cylinders, put in as much information as I could, and took them to Philadelphia. I knew where there was a building under construction, and I also knew from our time that it would be razed soon. I took a chance and planted the cylinder in the dirt where the new foundation was going to be poured the next day. I did the same with the other two cylinders at two other locations. A couple of days later I was making my way back to Montrose. I was in Scranton when I got jumped and bundled into a railroad boxcar and knocked out cold. That's all I remember. The next thing I know, I'm in this hospital with my leg shattered. But it must have been Green. He must have followed me and made his move when he had the opportunity. Took all of my money and identification as well. Left me for dead."

Ben tried to push himself upright a little more but a stab of pain shot through him. He choked back a scream and lay back down. "Damn doctors, won't give me anything for this pain. I think my leg is gone."

"You've got a couple of splintered bones, as near as they can tell," Matt replied. "They said they won't operate until you're better."

"Operate? Don't let them operate on me!" Ben said, grabbing Matt's arm and straining to raise his head. "My God, if they can't fix it they'll like as not cut off my leg." Ben sank back into the pillow. "You've got to get me back. They can fix me, back in my own time."

Matt leaned forward. "Quiet! Listen, I've got the portal operational again. Just hang in there. Have you said anything to these people?"

"Of course not. At least I don't think so. I couldn't tell them who I am, or where I came from. Green must think I'm dead, or else he would've come here and finished the job. He's ruthless."

"Yeah, I've had a run-in with him myself."

"Listen, Matt, if he thinks you're standing in the way of him getting that farm, he's likely to try the same thing with you."

"Well, if I can get you out of here and back to Montrose, he'll have a hard time finding either one of us," Matt said with a grin. "Like I said, the portal is operational again. I've been in contact with your father." Matt looked at Ben closely. "Listen, do you think you've got a concussion or anything?" Ben shook his head. "No, no, it's just my leg," he replied. "God, it hurts. I think the bones are scraping together."

Matt grimaced, then said, "I've got a small first aid kit with me. Not much, but there's some painkillers in it. Give me a couple of days and I'll figure out how to get you out of here and back to Montrose. I've got till next Tuesday before Dr. Greevely gets back here."

Ben held onto Matt's arm. "Thanks, Matt, for coming to help me. I didn't think anyone was ever going to come."

Matt grinned again. "When your father asked me to come, at first I said no way. Now, I wouldn't have traded this experience for anything. It's been a real eye-opener. I'll explain everything to you later." He sat down on the bed and counted out a handful of the pills. "Listen, hide these in the mattress. Take one every twelve hours, or longer if you can stand it. I should be back by next Monday at the latest to get you out of here."

"Matt, I don't even know what day it is, and there's no clocks in here."

Matt reached down and pulled out the pocketwatch. "Here, take this. It's about ten in the morning on Wednesday, October 28." He gave the watch to Ben and then poured a glass of water. "Here, take one of these now. It should help the pain." He watched as Ben swallowed the pill, then eased him back onto the pillow. "Remember, by Monday, maybe sooner. And remember not to say anything to these people!" Ben nodded and closed his eyes.

Matt stopped at the nurse's station on his way out. "Thank God he's okay," Matt said to the nurse. "My family's been worried sick about him. Listen, I'm going to make arrangements with our family doctor to come here and visit Ben within the next few days and consult with Dr. Greevely. In the meantime, please don't let anyone else know he's here." Matt counted out several bills and passed them to the nurse. "This should cover his care. Just let me know if you need more."

"I'll leave a note for Dr. Greevely," the nurse said, making a note of Ben's name on the patient roster. "Otherwise, no one's been asking for him. I'm so glad you found your cousin, Mr. Collins."

"So am I. Thank you for your help," Matt said, and turned to leave.

Outside, Matt looked around and saw a few buggies for hire across the street. He climbed into one and told the driver to take him to the train station at the edge of town. Once there, he found that the next train in the direction of Montrose would be leaving in an hour.

"But, I can't get you all the way to Montrose," the stationmaster said. "Closest stop is Towanda, about, oh, thirty miles away. Or, you can wait till Thursday for the next Montrose run."

"Towanda will be fine," Matt said, and bought a seat for himself.

CHAPTER 20

▼

It was Wednesday, and Amanda had finished her lunch at the hotel. Her two friends had been unable to join her, so Amanda had come alone.

She had taken a booth off to one side of the room, wanting to spend some time by herself. The lunch crowd had thinned out and she was about to leave when she overheard a gruff voice coming from behind her. She peeked around slowly and saw that Harland Green and two of his henchmen were seated a few tables away. They hadn't noticed her behind the partition. Amanda hunched down and listened.

"One more piece of property. One more and my daddy will own that whole area," Green was saying. "But he wouldn't sell. Now the other one's in there." Green slammed his hand down onto the table. "I'll make him sell, or make him wish he had."

"Listen, Green," one of the other men said. "You saw what he did to you at the dance."

Quick as a flash, Green had the man by the throat. "I told you not to bring that up, ever again!"

The man's hands pawed at Green's fingers as they tightened around his throat. The other man shifted uncomfortably in his chair. "C'mon, Green," he said, "let him go."

Green let go and the man began gasping for air and coughing. Green glared at him and said, "Don't make me do that to you again."

Still trying to breathe, the man nodded. As if nothing had happened, Green spoke again. "My daddy's already told me that I have just one more chance to get that piece of property, and that I'd better be quick about it. Well, I got rid of the other fellow, I can get rid of this one, too."

Amanda's eyes widened. She knew that Green was talking about Matt, and that she had to get to Matt and warn him about Green and his cronies. She knew Green to be an evil person, sadistic and cruel, and that he would stop at little to get what he wanted. She slipped out of the booth and was heading for the front door when the trailing end of her dress caught on something. She turned around to find Green standing on the hem of her dress.

"Well, if it isn't *Miss Caruthers*," Green said, standing there with his arms crossed. His foot still rested on the dress, preventing Amanda from leaving.

"Mr. Green, will you please get off of my dress?"

Green smiled and shook his head. "Not until you promise to go out with me some time. Besides, you still owe me a dance."

"I'd rather catch pneumonia," Amanda said with a sneer, and the smile left Green's face.

"You think you're so much better than everyone else, don't you?" Green said as he stepped closer. In a low voice that only Amanda could hear, he said, "Maybe I'll bring you down a notch or two before long."

The contempt on Amanda's face was obvious. "You are disgusting, Harland Green," she said. "Now get off my dress!" She pulled at the material as Green suddenly lifted his foot. Amanda stumbled back a few steps, almost losing her balance. Green laughed loudly.

"I'd say that you and I will be getting together, and soon," he said, and there was no mistaking the meaning in his words. Amanda shuddered involuntarily and whirled around, darting out the door. Seeing that she wasn't followed, she ducked through a passageway between two buildings, and headed toward Matt's house.

When she got there, she knocked on the door rapidly. Nothing. She tried the door but, oddly, found that it was locked. She peered into the windows but saw nothing, no movement. Then she remembered that Matt had said he might be delayed on his trip. He had told her that he would be back today, Wednesday, but she had not yet seen him. He had always returned on time before, and Mrs. Higby had always let her know as soon as he was in town. Well, at least if Green was here in town he was away from Matt. She only hoped that she was able to get to Matt before Harland Green did.

*   *   *   *

Later that evening at the Caruthers house, Amanda bustled about the kitchen with her mother, saying nothing but keeping a serious face. Her mother noticed and decided to give Amanda a few more minutes to bring up whatever it was that was bothering her, or else Mrs. Caruthers would.

The minutes passed with not a word from Amanda. Mrs. Caruthers set down the tray that she was holding and turned to her daughter.

"Amanda, dear, what's bothering you?"

"Nothing, Mother, I'm fine." But Amanda didn't look at her mother as she said this. Mrs. Caruthers took Amanda's hands and led her to the walk-in pantry in the back of the kitchen.

"This should be private enough for a few minutes," Mrs. Caruthers said. "Now, are you going to tell me what's wrong?"

"Mother, I'm so confused," Amanda blurted out. "I think that Matt cares for me, but he's become so…private, lately, and he won't tell me what it is. I'm sure it has something to do with his cousin."

"Well, Mandy, you can't expect the man to confide everything to you. That's family, and it must be important to him." She paused. "Has Mr. Collins said anything to you, I mean about the two of you?"

"I think he cares about me, Mother. And I do care about him. I'm just so…afraid. I don't think I could bear it if he were to leave me now, or if something were to happen to him."

Amanda was surprised at her mother's reaction. "Amanda Caruthers! Don't you think you're being a bit selfish? I've gotten to know Mr. Collins fairly well these past few weeks. If he's the man for you, then let it work itself out. If he's not, then—well, I'd be surprised if he were to treat you poorly. I think he's a good man—and I know he cares about you, too."

"So do I, Mother, but that's not what I mean. I overheard Harland Green planning some of his deviltry today, and I think Matt is going to be on the receiving end of it, and soon."

Mrs. Caruthers looked concerned. "Did you tell your father about this?"

"No, not yet. I was going to warn Matt but he's not back in town yet."

"Go, tell your father this instant! That Harland Green is a demon. Your father needs to know about this."

Amanda walked toward the parlor where her father was sitting. "Father, I need to talk to you."

A short while later, Mr. Caruthers put on his coat and walked to the kitchen. "Mandy told you about Harland Green?" he asked, and his wife nodded. "I'm going down to the saloon to let some of the other men know. We can at least try to warn Mr. Collins the minute he gets back."

"I'll keep the dinner warm," she said as he turned and left.

CHAPTER 21

▼

Matt felt excited as he rode into Montrose late Thursday morning. He had rented a horse in Towanda and had ridden all morning. After all this time, and on the verge of giving up, he had nearly accomplished his task here. Ben was in bad shape, and Matt didn't know how he was going to get Ben moved here to the farm, but Matt would think of something. The only chance Ben had was to get him through the portal, return him to his own time.

At the back of his mind, Matt also knew that time was running out. The portal had already experienced two blackouts since he'd been in this time period. If it was getting ready to collapse, he'd have to move fast. Besides that, he kept thinking about Amanda's fate. Although he didn't know the exact time, or date, or where it was supposed to occur, he knew that her death was coming soon. He felt torn between his obligation to the Parkwoods—the whole reason he was here—and this girl that had come into his life.

Matt had only experienced a few times in his life where his decision made the difference to someone else's life, or safety. Usually, he was presented with two options: do this, or this will happen, or do that, and that will happen. He didn't like being in that position, and if he didn't like the choices he had more often than not come up with a third option, trusting his instinct. He had never been wrong yet.

And here it was Thursday already. His dinner with the Caruthers family was tomorrow night, and he had a lot to do before then. He spurred the horse with his heels and rode through town at a fast trot. Passing the stable, he headed for his own house. He'd bring the horse back to the stable later and board it for the night.

As he rode through town, he failed to notice Amanda on the balcony outside of her office. She had stepped out for some air before lunch and had seen Matt ride through town. She held up an arm to wave but slowly lowered it when she saw that Matt hadn't noticed her. The look on his face was serious, and she could tell that he had something important on his mind. Could it be that he had found his cousin? Was his cousin all right? Or had something happened to him?

Besides all that, she remembered the conversation she had overheard at lunch the day before. Harland Green would be looking for an excuse to start something with Matt. She had seen Green and his gang entering the saloon earlier that morning and knew that they would already be drinking and plotting their deviltry. She had seen it happen before, and she knew she had to warn Matt as soon as possible.

Her intuition made her return to the office. She gathered her things and turned to one of the girls. "Martha, I'm leaving a bit early today. See that the office is locked up properly if I'm not back."

"Of course, Mandy. Is everything all right?" Martha said, seeing the look on Amanda's face.

But Amanda had already gone through the door and was heading down the stairs. Outside, she turned and began walking in the direction of Matt's house on the outskirts of town.

From the saloon, Harland Green and four of his gang were seated around a table, drinking as usual, and even though it was early afternoon they all had a pretty good start with the liquor. They had also seen Matt ride through town. "There goes that son of a bitch," Green growled, and turned back to his drink. "I think a week from Saturday would be a good day to deal with him." The others at the table nodded. They had never seen Green so fixated on someone before, and knew that it was mainly because Matt had embarrassed Green in front of the whole town at the picnic. In addition, Green wanted the Parkwood farm, and both Ben and Matt had refused to sell to him. Green's father had told him, in no uncertain terms, for him to get that farm.

Matt jumped from the horse, tied it to the fence, and ran up the steps to the door. Entering, he closed the door behind him but in his excitement failed to lock it. At the cellar door, he punched in the code and descended the stairs, leaving the cellar door ajar. He strode to the computer but saw that another power fluctuation must have occurred, which had shut down the system again. He rebooted it and, knowing that it would take several minutes to load, stripped off his clothes and headed for the shower.

Twenty minutes later, Amanda walked up the street at a fast pace. She had quickly walked the distance to the house and saw with relief that Matt's horse was tied up out front. She was concerned that he might have gone off again before she got there. She walked up the front steps and was about to knock on the door when she saw that it was slightly ajar. She immediately became wary, knowing that Green and his bunch were out for Matt, but she cautiously reconnoitered the area and was relieved to find nothing out of the ordinary. Besides, she had glanced into a side window of the saloon on her way here and had seen Green and his men still grouped around a table, drinking. She knew that they couldn't have gotten here ahead of her. She listened at the door for a moment, but hearing nothing from inside, raised a hand and gently pushed the door open silently.

CHAPTER 22

▼

She listened again for a few moments. Nothing.

"Matt?" Amanda called out as the door swung inward. She cautiously peered inside. "Matt?"

No answer. Amanda cautiously entered the foyer and closed the door behind her. She looked around. It was her first time inside Matt's house. She noticed that the furniture, although new, was somewhat plain, as were the other furnishings. The ticking of the grandfather clock that sat against the wall was loud against the silence of the house.

She continued into the dining room, then went through to the kitchen. Oddly, there was nothing on the shelves, nothing to indicate that anyone lived here. She went from room to room, all the while wondering why the house felt so empty when she knew that Matt obviously lived here.

She was about to climb the stairs to the second floor when she heard a strange noise coming from the kitchen area. Curious, she went to the kitchen and found the door to the cellar slightly ajar at the back of the kitchen. Cautiously, she opened the door and peered down the stairs, expecting to see nothing but gloom and darkness below. She heard the odd noise again coming from the open doorway.

She was surprised to see what appeared to be daylight filtering up the staircase. From her vantage point she could see little of the cellar, but what she could see was sharply defined from the bright light. A low hum seemed to be in the air as she slowly made her way down the stairs.

She was about to call out for Matt again when what she saw made her catch her breath. The cellars in houses of that time were dark, musty places, used more for storage than anything else. This was totally different. The cellar in this house was brightly lit, with finished walls and an unusually high ceiling, and gleaming metal tables and strange boxes atop the tables, some of them the like of which she had never seen before. She surveyed the expanse of the cellar, and saw the brightly polished metal of the portal sitting in the center of the room. She stared at it for a few minutes and then resumed her inspection of the cellar. She then looked up to find recessed boxes in the ceiling, the source of the light that illuminated the expanse. It appeared to her to be indirect sunlight filtering through the boxes, but she hadn't seen any openings in the floor above. Everything was sharply defined, not what she expected or imagined in a cellar. She walked forward and stopped in the center of the room, marveling at the sight.

Atop one of the tables, one box in particular again made the strange sound that she had heard from upstairs, and she quietly approached the table on which it sat. The strange flat box was open, and the inside of the lid looked like a picture, although like no picture she had ever seen before. The picture seemed to glow, and she reached out a hand to touch it. As soon as her fingers had touched the surface, the box made a soft whirring noise and suddenly the picture changed. She gasped and instinctively snatched her hand away, watching in awe as the picture changed to several lines of printing. She leaned toward the picture to read the writing.

"Mandy."

She whirled around, her hand coming to her mouth to stifle her scream. Matt was standing behind her, clean shaven, his hair wet, a long robe wrapped around him and a look of concern on his face. He had come from the shower tucked away on one side of the cellar.

"What are you doing down here?" he asked, as he reached around her to close the lid of the laptop. "How did you get in here?"

"I was looking for you, Matt," she said in a bewildered voice. "Your front door was open, and I…Matt, what is all of this?"

Matt thought for a second. He had been so wrapped up in his thoughts that he had completely forgotten to secure the doors behind him when he entered the house. Damn! Now, how was he going to explain this to her?

"It's…equipment. Very delicate equipment. Did you touch anything?"

"Nothing except the picture in that box. Matt, it *changed*. I've never seen anything like that." She looked around the room again, and her voice was shaking. "This isn't right. Matt, what is all this?"

"It's some of my uncle's equipment. He's a…researcher, a sort of scientist, among other things. This equipment helps him with his work."

Amanda looked up at him, a look of confusion on her face, and then her gaze swept past him to the ceiling. "And the light? Where does it come from? I didn't see any openings upstairs, and yet it's like sunlight."

Matt took her hand and walked her to the stairs. "Come upstairs," he said, and led her up to the kitchen. At the top of the flight, he reached for the light switch and flicked off the florescent lights that were recessed into the cellar ceiling. The cellar was plunged into darkness.

Amanda's mind was whirling as she came to the top of the stairs. Matt led her to a kitchen chair and sat her down. Reaching into the icebox, he pulled out a pitcher of tea and filled two glasses. Placing these on the table, he sat down across from her.

"How long were you down there?"

She looked across at him with something akin to fear in her eyes. "Only a few minutes. Matt, I know that I don't know you very well, and I don't want to pry into your affairs, but…but even though I haven't seen much of the world, I know that things like that just don't exist."

"Sure they do…after all, you saw them," Matt said in an offhand manner, trying to diminish what was obviously to her a frightening experience.

"Yes, I saw them, but…" She closed her eyes and put her hands up to her face, shaking her head. "No. Something is just not right with all of this."

Matt thought furiously. Because of his absent-mindedness, he had seriously jeopardized the entire mission, the very reason he was here. He had given her a glimpse of the future, and unless he could somehow make her think that the things she had seen were nothing special, he could have a real problem on his hands.

Matt took a sip of his drink and sighed. "I'd like to be able to tell you all about it, but I don't have the time to do that right now. It would be best if you just forgot about what you saw and left it at that for the time being."

"*Forget* about it? I *can't* forget about it! And you said those things help your uncle with his work. What *is* that work? I thought you were here just to manage your uncle's affairs, and find your cousin."

"I am", Matt replied. "And I have a very short time to accomplish that."

"*Why* don't you have time? Matt, I can help you, if you'll let me."

Matt got up and gazed out the kitchen window. He so much wanted to tell her everything, but Professor Parkwood's warnings kept coming to the fore. He knew that it was not his decision to make.

He turned to her. "Mandy, it's no secret that I've grown very…fond of you. Against my better judgement, it's grown into something more." He saw the hurt look on her face and hurriedly said, "No, I said that wrong. I'm sorry." He took a deep breath and continued. "In the grand scheme of things, I should never have let my feelings for you become an issue. If I hadn't been so selfish, and had kept my mind on my task…" His voice trailed off. "I said that wrong, too," he said. "Look." He sat down again and faced her. "More than anything else, I have to finish the job that I was sent here to do. Much more than you can ever realize depends on it." He was surprised at the tears that sprang into her eyes.

"You're telling me that your work here is finished, and you're leaving, is that it?" she asked in a shaky voice.

"You're jumping to the wrong conclusion." He paused, then continued. "Listen, I've heard what happened with you and William Reed. I know what it's like to lose someone, too, maybe not in the same way as you. But because of that, back when I felt myself falling for you, I promised myself that I wouldn't let 'us' happen. I didn't want to get hurt again, or to hurt anyone else."

"And I know how you lost your fiancé," Amanda said. "Mother told me the story. Oh, Matt," she said, choking back a sob, "that must have been awful for you."

Matt winced inside at the memory of Carolyn. "It was," he replied. "The worst thing that's ever happened to me. But," he said, "some things can't be changed. She's gone, and that's it." He stood up, took both of her hands, and pulled her up from the chair. He held both of her hands in his, looked into her eyes, and said, "For the longest time I thought that there could never be anyone else that I could care about in that same way. Then I met you. In the short time that we've known each other, you're all I can think about. I've come to realize that I care more about you than anyone else in the world. But, and you must understand this, the work that I came here to do has to be completed. I can't allow anything to stop that. I made a promise to some people, gave them my word, and it's a promise that I have to keep. I'm sorry that all of this has happened between us."

"Are you?" Amanda said. "Are you really sorry?" The tears kept flowing. Just seeing her like that was tearing him up inside.

"Mandy, I…" His voice trailed off. He couldn't lie to this girl. "No, I'm not sorry."

Amanda looked up at him, the tears still in her eyes. "Matt, I love you," she said simply.

"Mandy, don't," Matt said. "I…I can't, not now."

"Then tell me that you don't love me, too," she said. Her hands went up and grabbed his arms near the shoulder, and she looked up into his face. The tears continued to streak down her face.

Matt put his arms around her and held her close. "I can't do that, either, Mandy," he said resignedly. Her arms went around him and they stood there, holding each other tightly, feeling the bond between them that was stronger than any embrace. But, even as they stood there, Matt was kicking himself for letting this happen.

How could he tell her the truth about himself? How could he tell her the truth about her own future, what little there was left of it? And yet in that moment he knew that, despite Professor Parkwood's warnings, he could not stand idly by and let this girl die. On top of all that he had been sent here to do, he had fallen in love with Amanda Caruthers. He had lost Carolyn; he would not lose Mandy, too. To hell with Professor Parkwood and his warnings, Matt thought to himself. He had to think this through, and figure out another solution. But what? What if there *was* no solution?

She held him tightly, but Matt grabbed her shoulders and held her away from him. "Mandy, I hope to be able to explain all this to you, at the right time. Just not now. You're going to have to trust me." Even as he was saying these things to her, he looked deep into her eyes. His proximity to this beautiful woman made his emotions take over. "But...*I do love you*," he said with feeling. He paused for a second, then bent down and kissed her softly on the lips. He closed his eyes, put his arms around her, and kissed her deeply—one hand at the small of her back, the other entwined in the hair at the back of her head, holding her close to him. She responded in kind, and he could feel her heart beating as he held her close.

The kiss ended but they held each other close, neither wanting to let go. In that moment they both knew that they were destined for each other, and that nothing could change that.

Amanda reached up and put her hands at the back of Matt's head, pulling him down for another kiss. As she held him, Amanda was swept up in the passion of the moment. She had never felt anything like this before. The years of pent-up emotion, of the need to love and be loved, came flooding into her. She knew without doubt that she had found her soulmate, and that she loved him with all of her heart.

As for Matt, he could feel the warmth of her breasts through her clothing, and when he looked down at her again he saw that her eyes were closed, her cheeks were flushed and her mouth was half-open. His own body was responding in kind, but the weight of his mission pushed itself to the fore once again. He knew that it could be disastrous to continue this.

With great reluctance and a lot of self-control, he took her arms and gently pushed her away. "Mandy, I want you very much—but not here, not like this. It wouldn't be right." He sighed, then said, "Listen to me. Maybe you can help me after all. But first, I have some things that I have to take care of. I want you to go back to town now, and if I don't see you sooner, I'll be at your house for dinner tomorrow night. Don't say anything about any of what you saw downstairs to anyone—that's very important. Okay?"

Amanda nodded slightly. "I'll be waiting for you. And, Matt," she said, "please don't disappoint me."

He knew what she was thinking—the fear in the back of her mind that he would never come, that he would leave her the same way William Reed had left her. And the uncertainty that she must be feeling after seeing the equipment below.

He smiled at her, looked steadily into her eyes, and said very deliberately, "Mandy, I do love you." He could feel the relief in her. "And I would never do anything to hurt you," he said with feeling. "Never." He kissed her again, softly this time.

Amanda's face burst into a smile. God, she was beautiful, Matt thought to himself. She grabbed him, hugged him tight, and said, "You promise?" Matt nodded, and she turned toward the door.

She was about to leave when Matt said, "You be careful." She stopped, a look of concern crossing her face. "Oh, Matt, the reason I came here. I have to warn you. Harland Green is planning on starting some trouble with you, very soon I think. I overheard him talking to a couple of his friends yesterday. I don't know what they're planning, but I know him well enough to know that you're the one that needs to be careful. He's a snake, so watch your back."

"I will," Matt promised. "Now, on your way. What will people think if they know we've been alone in here for all this time?" he teased.

"They can keep their opinions to themselves," she said, her eyes flashing angrily. "I've been the subject of enough gossip in this town already, and I don't care *what* they think!" But, he noticed that she looked up and down the street before she went down the porch steps. He smiled to himself as he watched her walk toward town, and then made sure to lock the door from the inside.

As Matt turned back toward the cellar, he frowned. Too much was happening too fast. He certainly didn't need the added problem of Harland Green, and having to be constantly on his guard. But if he could find a way to get Ben Parkwood back here, and quickly, then he could at least send Ben through the portal to safety. In the meantime, he'd need to figure out what to do about Amanda, and about Green.

Matt spent the remainder of the day working out a plan to get Ben out of the Scranton hospital and back to the farmhouse in Montrose.

CHAPTER 23

▼

Early on Friday morning, Matt rode into town and headed for the train station. The stationmaster, Mr. Blevins, was glad to see Matt.

"How are you today, Mr. Collins?" Blevins said.

"Fine, fine," Matt replied. "Listen, I need to ask you about something. Is it possible for someone to rent a train for an excursion to Scranton and back, say for two or three days?"

"Sure," Blevins replied. "We have the occasional private excursion for visitors in from the big city. Of course, it depends on where and when they want to run it. Freight and mining trains take priority on the lines. Weekends are best."

"That would be perfect," Matt said. "I'd like to see if a train is available to take me to Scranton and back, either tomorrow or Sunday. I'll need one passenger car and one freight car."

"Short notice, but let's see," Blevins said, pulling out a ledger book and opening it to study the schedules. Before long he said, "We've got one available that can pull out of here Saturday about noon. One layover in Tunkhannock for a couple of hours, then into Scranton." He turned the page. "You'd have to stay in Scranton until the lines open back up Sunday afternoon. The return trip on Sunday would get you back in here that night around ten." He looked up. "Provided, that is, that I can find a crew willing to work over the weekend. It being at the last minute and all, it's probably not going to be cheap."

"Don't worry about that. This is very important, and I'm even willing to pay a bonus. Just two things, though. On this end, as few people as possible need to know about this. And, I need a crew that'll keep this to themselves. No gossip."

"These are hard working men, Mr. Collins. They do an honest day's work and expect to get paid for it. That's all they care about."

"Good," Matt said. "See what you can set up and I'll stop back in later this afternoon to check with you."

Blevins nodded. As Matt left the office, he reached for his watch—and remembered that he had given it to Ben. Matt got back on his horse and rode into town, stopping off at the jeweler's shop to pick out a new watch. He then headed for the bank.

Mr. Higby looked from the check, to Matt, and back to the check. "You sure you want this in cash, Mr. Collins?" Higby said, and Matt nodded.

"Small bills, twenties and fifties, if you can," Matt said.

Higby said, "Of course we can. Would you like this in a satchel or in sacks?"

Matt thought for a moment. "A satchel, I think. Less conspicuous, wouldn't you say?"

Higby nodded and moved off toward the safe. The check was drawn to "Cash", on Matt's account, and was in the amount of ten thousand dollars. Higby procured a satchel and began filling it up with stacks of currency. When he finished, the satchel was nearly full. He snapped it shut and brought it out to his desk, where Matt sat waiting.

"You can use one of the private offices to count it," Higby said.

Matt looked at Higby. "Mr. Higby. I wouldn't think of it. If you say it's all there, then it's all there."

Higby puffed with pride. "Why, thank you, Mr. Collins. Will you be at church Sunday?"

"I'm afraid not. I'll be out of town again on business. But, just keep that between us if you would. I should be back by Monday."

"Of course. Have a good trip," Higby said, extending his hand. Matt shook it and walked out of the bank, satchel in hand.

Later that afternoon, Matt rode back to the train station. Inside, he saw Mr. Blevins wave at him through the window. Matt tied up the horse and went inside.

"Got what you needed, Mr. Collins," Blevins said. "One of the best engines on the local line, and four crew to run her. They'll meet you here Saturday morning about eleven." He dropped his voice. "They agreed to do it for double time pay, if that's all right with you."

Matt nodded appreciatively. "You've done a great job, Mr. Blevins. Tell the men I'll have their pay with me on Saturday. And thank you for being so efficient." Matt slid a twenty across the counter, which Blevins picked up with glee.

"Thank you, sir!" Blevins said.

Returning outside, Matt heaved a sigh of relief as he mounted the horse. One more obstacle out of the way. If all went well, he and Ben Parkwood would be out of here within a week.

As he thought this, a vision of Amanda popped into his mind. He hadn't figured it all out yet, but once Ben was back here in Montrose, Matt planned to keep a very close eye on Amanda.

But then what? She was already a part of history, dead in a fire. Even if he could stop that from happening, the risks in doing so were enormous. He would be changing a specific historical occurrence.

It then occurred to him that maybe the fire had occurred *after* he and Ben had left this time period, in which case there would have been nothing that he could have done anyway. But could he leave her to such a fate? Of course not. Could he possibly warn her in some way? But how? Or would he be powerless to stop it anyway? Just thinking about it, trying to make sense of it all, made his head swim.

He shook his head to clear it. Be practical, Matt! he said to himself. First things first. Ben Parkwood is the whole reason you're here; he deserves your undivided attention. And Professor Parkwood, and Sandra—they're counting on you to pull this off. Just because you've gone and fallen for this girl is no fault of theirs. Don't jeopardize the mission for your own selfish reasons. Besides, they're the reason you had this fantastic opportunity anyway. If nothing else, you've had one of the greatest adventures in all of history.

Once they returned from Scranton, maybe Ben could furnish some advice.

He rode to his house, tying the horse out in front to graze. He ran up the steps and deactivated the locks. The door popped open and he made sure to secure it behind him. Then, he did the same with the cellar door and descended to the room below.

CHAPTER 24

▼

Seven o'clock on Friday evening found Matt walking up the steps to the front door of the Caruthers house. He grabbed the ornate knocker on the door and gave it a few sharp taps. The door opened almost immediately and he smiled when he saw Sallie.

"Hello, Sallie," he said.

"Mr. Collins, won't you please come in?" she said, acting very proper as she had been taught, and Matt removed his hat and entered the foyer. Sallie took his hat and placed it on the hat rack next to her father's. She turned and said, "Come with me, please."

He was surprised at the size of the house as they walked through. The rooms were very large, the ceilings high and the furnishings warm; the place had a good feel to it.

Sallie ushered Matt into the large bookshelf-lined den, where Mr. Caruthers was sitting behind a huge desk in a leather chair, smoking a pipe and reading a letter. Mr. Caruthers immediately put down the pipe and letter, arose and came around the desk with his hand extended. "Welcome, Mr. Collins. We're so glad you could join us."

"Thank you," Matt replied, shaking the hand. "I must say you have a beautiful house, Mr. Caruthers."

"Be sure and say something to Mrs. Caruthers about that," Mr. Caruthers said with a grin. "She did almost all of the decorating. It's her 'showplace' and she's very proud of it."

Matt nodded and said, "I will." Mr. Caruthers walked to the small bar at the side and said, "Care for a drink, Mr. Collins?" as he held up a bottle of Scotch whisky.

"Please, call me Matt. Actually, I'm not much of a drinker. Maybe a little gin and tonic if you have it."

"Of course." Mr. Caruthers mixed the drinks and brought the gin and tonic to Matt. He held up his own glass. "I prefer whisky myself, but in moderation. To your health, Matt."

Matt held up his own glass. "And to yours." As he sipped the drink, Matt walked to one wall that held several photos.

"Family?" he asked, and Mr. Caruthers nodded. "Yes, that's my mother and father. My father was in the war, of course, and luckily came through without a scratch. I was just a lad then. After he came home, he sold the farm we had in upstate New York and moved us here. He wanted to find a small town to grow with but didn't want to go "out West". We started the General Store and it passed to me when he died."

"And this one?" Matt said, pointing to another photo. It showed a young couple and three small children.

"Oh, that's me and Mrs. Caruthers, and our two boys and Amanda. Sallie and Rebecca hadn't come along yet when we took that. That was, oh, twenty years or so ago."

He was interrupted by Mrs. Caruthers at the doorway. "Hello, Mr. Collins. We're so glad you could make it. Amanda will be down presently." Matt smiled at the protocol. In this time period, it was proper behavior for young ladies to have their guests wait a few minutes before joining the group.

The two men were chatting for a few more minutes when Matt felt another presence in the room. He turned to the doorway to find Amanda standing there, radiant in a muted red dress.

"Ah, Amanda," Mr. Caruthers said. "Come in and say hello to Mr. Collins."

She walked into the room and offered her hand, which Matt took as he bowed slightly. Again, protocol demanded that he behave properly for her family. She sat down on the sofa and gestured for Matt to sit across from her in an armchair.

"You two talk for a while," Mr. Caruthers said. "I'll go see if Mother needs any help in the dining room."

Matt and Amanda watched him leave, then turned to face each other. They'd at least have a few minutes of privacy. "I'm so glad you came, Matt," Amanda said, breathing a sigh. "I wasn't sure if you would."

"How can you say that, Mandy?" Matt asked. "I wouldn't have missed this for anything." He reached across and took both of her hands in his, looking steadily into her eyes. "And I meant everything I said to you yesterday." He smiled. "It's good to see you again. As usual, you look beautiful. I missed you." He lifted her hands to his face and kissed them.

In the kitchen, Mrs. Caruthers bustled about as she spoke to her husband. "You've probably noticed that Mr. Collins has taken quite a fancy to Amanda," she said, and Mr. Caruthers nodded. "Any thoughts on that?"

"He's a nice young man. She could do a lot worse," he said noncommittally.

"Oh, Jack," Mrs. Caruthers said in an exasperated tone, "haven't you seen the change in her? She's coming alive again. It's hurt me so this past year to see her so withdrawn. Nothing at all like the girl she used to be, so happy."

"She does seem to be in a lot better spirits lately," he admitted.

"I think he really cares about her. I know that she cares about him. What I'm trying to say, Jack, is that maybe you should have a talk with Mr. Collins; find out how he feels about her."

"You mean find out what his intentions are," Mr. Caruthers said in a rueful voice. "But they haven't known each other all that long. Do you think it's too soon to be talking to him about this?"

"No I don't," she said, "not this time. I can tell this is different. Trust my intuition on this, Jack."

"I always do, on everything," he replied matter-of-factly.

CHAPTER 25

▼

The dinner went smoothly, and Matt was surprised at how delicious the food was. The past few years for Matt had been a combination of restaurants and microwave dinners, and it was rare when he could enjoy a home-cooked meal.

"Mrs. Caruthers, that was simply the best meal I can remember having for, well, years. Thank you all for inviting me."

Mrs. Caruthers beamed. "You're very welcome, Mr. Collins. Perhaps you and Mr. Caruthers would like to spend some time in the den to relax."

"Not the den, Mother. I thought Mr. Collins might like to sit out on the porch. It's a beautiful night. Not too many of these left before it turns cold. Maybe you and Amanda can join us in a little while."

Mr. Caruthers led Matt out to the wide front porch, where they found rocking chairs and two porch swings. Mr. Caruthers took one of the chairs while Matt sat in the porch swing next to him.

"So, Mr. Collins, how are things going?"

"Very well. I meant to tell you, I found my cousin. He's in a hospital in Scranton."

"Hospital? What happened?"

"He was in some kind of accident. No one knows exactly what happened, and he doesn't remember specifically. He did recall, though, that Harland Green had something to do with it. Green's been after Ben for some time, pressuring him to sell our farm. I don't know why that farm is so important to Green."

Mr. Caruthers snorted. "I don't either, but I might have guessed Green would be involved," he said with a sneer in his voice. "Much as I hate to say this, though, I'd bet your cousin will never be able to prove that Green had anything to do with his accident."

"You're right; that's what Ben said," Matt replied. "But that's not my main concern. I'm trying to make arrangements to get Ben out of that hospital and back to my uncle's place in Philadelphia. We all feel that he'll get better care there."

Mr. Caruthers nodded. "Of course he would. I understand that they have some of the finest doctors in Philadelphia."

"You know how Green is," Matt said. "Apparently Green thinks Ben is dead, or gone back to where he came from. Ben is concerned that Green might find out where he is and try to finish the job. And his uncle and I are concerned that Green might make another attempt on Ben's life if Green finds out that Ben's still around. In the interests of Ben's safety, please don't say anything to anyone about this."

"Of course I won't," Mr. Caruthers said. "And if you need any help, just ask."

"Thanks, I will," Matt replied.

They sat in silence for a few minutes, and Mr. Caruthers leaned forward. "Listen, Mr. Collins…Matt," he said. "Mrs. Caruthers asked me to have a talk with you about something."

Matt could tell that Mr. Caruthers had grown serious. "Sure," he said, "what is it?"

"It's about Amanda. We've noticed that you two have been seeing a lot of each other lately, and we feel that there might be something developing—something a little more serious than just a casual friendship."

That was an understatement, Matt thought, especially if Amanda's parents could have known about yesterday. What if they *did* know about yesterday? Matt said nothing, waiting on Mr. Caruthers to continue.

"She's been through a lot these past couple of years. Her emotions have taken a beating. Her mother and I of course want to protect her as much as we can, but she's an adult now and can do what she pleases. It's just that…as a parent, you never really let go of your children. Amanda's always confided in us, asked us for counsel when she's troubled about something. But this is different. She seems to be coming out of her shell, and it's all been since you've been seeing her. I know it's only been a short while that you two have known each other, but under the circumstances I need to know how you feel about Amanda."

Matt liked Mr. Caruthers, and respected him. To tell this man half-truths, or to avoid the issue, just wouldn't be fair. He looked at Mr. Caruthers and spoke.

"Emotionally, I figure we've all got to face unpleasant situations in our lives," Matt said. He turned to stare off into the distance. "I had a girl once, grew to love her, but she died." Mr. Caruthers, having heard the story of Matt's fiancé, nodded in understanding. Matt continued. "That's been a few years ago. Since then, I've seen other girls briefly, even had some of them become very serious about me. But none of them created any feelings inside of me.

"The very first day I came to this town, one of the first people I met was Amanda. I have to be honest with you—I was awestruck. She is without a doubt the most beautiful woman I have ever met. But it wasn't just that. Despite her cold exterior, something about her just fascinated me. I knew that I had to get to know her better. I found myself thinking about her more and more, every day. So I pursued the opportunity. I wasn't trying to be selfish, and I even had doubts myself about the propriety of what I was doing.

"But the more I got to know her, the more I knew that it was more than just a passing fancy. I've grown to care for her, very much." Matt looked at Mr. Caruthers again. "What I'm trying to say, Mr. Caruthers, is that I've fallen in love with your daughter."

Mr. Caruthers frowned briefly. Mrs. Caruthers was right—this *was* serious, he thought. He was silent for a few moments, then said, "And Amanda? How does she feel about this? Have you told her how you feel?"

"Yes I have, and she loves me, too." Matt waited, thinking that he may have said the wrong thing. "Is there a problem, Mr. Caruthers?"

Mr. Caruthers, deep in thought, shook his head and leaned back in the chair. "No, there's no problem," he said slowly. "Mrs. Caruthers thought as much, but me being Amanda's father, she wanted me to talk to you about it. When I met Mrs. Caruthers the first time, I knew that she was the woman I wanted to marry. But, we had a two-year courtship, and it was nearly a year into that before I declared my feelings to her. This is awfully fast, awfully soon."

"Not if you know in your heart that it's right," Matt said. "I know this is right. Amanda knows, too." Matt leaned forward. "After what we've both been through, I think—no, I *know*—that we can tell the difference. What I feel for your daughter is real."

"I believe you, Matt," Mr. Caruthers said. "Her mother and I just don't want her to be hurt again, especially not like before."

"I would never do that, Mr. Caruthers," Matt said with feeling. "Not in a million years."

Mr. Caruthers made up his mind. He held out a hand and said, "No, I can tell you wouldn't. Thank you for being honest with me."

The sound of the front door opening made them both look around. Mrs. Caruthers, followed by Amanda, brought out a pitcher of tea and some glasses, which she sat on the small round table nearby. "I thought we could use some refreshment," she said. She poured the glasses and handed them around, then sat down next to Mr. Caruthers. Matt dutifully moved to one side of the swing and Amanda sat down next to him.

They all sat there, enjoying the evening and engaging in small talk, when after a while Mrs. Caruthers said, "Jack, why don't we go inside for a while? There's a couple of things about the store I wanted to talk to you about." But Mr. Caruthers knew that she wanted to know the results of his talk with Matt, and to give the two younger people a little privacy. After they left, Matt and Amanda sat in silence, the swing slowly gliding back and forth.

Amanda's hand found Matt's, and she squeezed it tightly. "So, what did you and Father talk about?"

"We talked about you," Matt said. "And we talked about the two of us. Your parents care about you very much."

"Of course they do," Amanda replied in a matter of fact voice, turning to face him. "What did you tell him?"

"I told him the truth—that I've fallen in love with you."

"You told him *that*?" she said, slightly shocked. "What did he say?"

"He accepted it. I think they knew, your parents. I think your mother has suspected as much for a while." He looked at her with an impish smile. "I've done it now, you know—declared my feelings for you, and to your father no less. I'm in it up to here."

Her eyes sparkled as she looked at him. "And you have no regrets?"

"Only that I hadn't met you sooner," he said, and he put his arm around her. "I want to spend the rest of my life with you."

"Oh, Matt," she said, and threw her arms around his neck and held him tight. "And I want to spend the rest of my life with you, too."

The words hit Matt like a rock, bringing him back to earth. Good God, he thought, what about what was to happen to her? She had only days left to live. She *would* be spending the rest of her life with him. But that didn't change his feelings. At this moment, holding her close and feeling her warmth, he was as content as he'd ever been in his life. He just hoped that he could find a solution.

*   *   *   *

Inside the house, Mr. and Mrs. Caruthers had gone into the den, closed the door behind them, and sat down.

Mrs. Caruthers was anxious. "Well? What did he say?"

Mr. Caruthers looked at her and nodded. "Oh, it's serious. It's *really* serious, at least for Mr. Collins. What exactly has Amanda told you?"

"Well, Jack, I think she was waiting for Mr. Collins to make the first move, to say something to us about the relationship. She's not about to precipitate anything, especially anything dealing with love or romance. Did he say anything along those lines?"

"I'll say he did," Mr. Caruthers replied. "Apparently they haven't been letting the grass grow under their feet. He just told me flat out that he's fallen in love with her, and that she feels the same. That's a pretty strong statement. I approached it from a couple of angles, but I can tell he's sincere about his feelings for her. And Amanda?"

"Oh, she's very certain of her feelings for him. She's just…apprehensive. She doesn't doubt Mr. Collins, she's just afraid of being hurt again in some way."

"He won't do that to her, I'm sure," Mr. Caruthers said. "But he did tell me that he's finally located his cousin." Mr. Caruthers relayed the information Matt had told him about Ben Parkwood to his wife, who listened silently. "So," he continued, "if he can get his cousin back to Philadelphia, he'll have that burden off of him. Until then, though, I think he'll be concentrating on that. After that's taken care of, I think we'll be able to let everyone in town know what's going on. I think a lot of them know already, or at least suspect." Mrs. Caruthers nodded, happy at last that her eldest daughter was finally going to be back to some semblance of normalcy in her life.

CHAPTER 26

▼

Saturday morning found Matt at the train station at ten o'clock. Mr. Blevins had also come in to introduce Matt to the engineer, a short stocky man named Vincent.

"Vincent here is one of the best drivers on the line," Blevins was saying. "His crew will get you to Scranton and back safely."

"I appreciate that," Matt replied, nodding at Vincent. "By the way," Matt said, reaching inside his jacket, "here's half the pay for you and the crew." Vincent took the envelope and his eyes widened as he saw the amount of money inside.

"Mr. Collins, that's five hundred dollars in there," he said in a low voice.

"Yes," Matt said, as if it was the most obvious thing in the world, "and you'll get the other five hundred when we get back here tomorrow night."

Vincent looked at Blevins, who nodded. "It's all right, Vincent," Blevins said. "You just take good care of Mr. Collins here."

Vincent's face broke into a huge smile, and he held out a hand to Matt and shook it vigorously. "Thank you, sir!" he said with feeling, and headed off toward the huge steam engine idling nearby.

Blevins turned to Matt. "That's a few months' worth of pay to those men," he said.

Matt shrugged. "Well, as long as they keep where they got it to themselves."

He followed Blevins back into the office and checked the map. "You said we had a layover in Tunkhannock, right?"

Blevins nodded. "Yes, there's a passenger train coming through in the other direction, headed for Binghamton. Your train will wait on the siding. If the other train's on time, shouldn't be more than an hour or two layover."

"Is there a telegraph office at the Tuckhannock station?"

"Sure," Blevins said. "Operator goes off duty at seven, but you'll be there before that." He paused. "If you need to send a telegram, we can do it from here."

"No, no," Matt said, "I was just asking, just in case. How about a place to eat?"

"No, afraid not," Blevins said.

Matt pulled a twenty out of his pocket. "Listen, could you run over to the hotel restaurant and pick up something for me to take along? I completely forgot to bring anything. And bring something for the crew as well."

Blevins nodded, took the twenty and scurried off. Matt looked at his watch. Ten forty. He climbed onto the train and stepped into the passenger car, noticing that the rows of benches so prevalent on standard passenger cars were missing. Instead, he saw the ornate furnishings more reminiscent of a stateroom than a rail car. At least he'd be traveling in comfort. He spent some minutes inspecting the interior of the rail car, then walked through and stepped onto the rear platform. He saw the caboose slowly coming up behind. Two of the crew would be riding in the engine, and the remaining two would be in the caboose. He had already looked at the freight car ahead and noted that it was newly cleaned, with fresh hay scattered about the floor. It was still customary for many travelers to ride their horses for a portion of their journey, and utilize the railway system when possible. Therefore, the freight cars were usually readied for just such a situation.

Matt looked around the station and saw that the few people in the vicinity weren't paying any attention to the preparations with the train. Obviously Blevins had kept his word and had not mentioned the excursion to anyone, as had the train crew. This was just another anonymous train taking a trip on the line.

He felt the slight bump as the caboose connected to the rear of the train, and heard the hiss of steam as the lines were connected. There was a knock at the door.

"Here you go, Mr. Collins," Blevins said, handing over a large sack. "I've already taken care of the crew. You'll find enough food in there to get you there and back, and then some."

Matt nodded. "Thanks. I'll try to check in with you when we return. By the way, I'll need to have a horse and wagon here when I get back tomorrow."

"No problem," Blevins said. "I'll make sure there's one at the siding for you. If there's no one here, just take it. You can bring it back later."

"I appreciate that," Matt replied. Blevins tipped his cap and left. Matt looked in the sack and found two chickens, a pie, various side dishes and a couple of bottles of wine, along with plates and silverware.

Twenty minutes later, Vincent rapped at the door. Matt opened the door and looked out.

"We can leave any time you're ready, Mr. Collins," Vincent said. "The line's clear for now."

"Then let's get going," Matt said with a grin. "And, by the way, I'm going to be doing some work in here and maybe try to get some rest. Any problem with locking the doors?"

"Not at all; just throw the bolts," Vincent replied. "I'll let the caboose crew know. Only way we'll need to disturb you is if there's an emergency of some sort."

"Fair enough," Matt replied. "I'll see you in Tunkhannock."

Minutes later, Matt heard the steam whistle and felt the jolt as the train began moving. He sat down at one of the window seats and watched as the outline of Montrose dwindled away behind the train. With luck he'd be back here tomorrow night, with Ben Parkwood, and they'd both be back in their own era within the week. Matt was anxious to return, but not a little saddened at leaving this beautiful place. He'd really grown to like it here. And what about Amanda? He still hadn't come to any conclusions about that situation. He'd have to get Ben's advice on that as well.

The trip to Tunkhannock was uneventful. When they arrived, the train was backed onto a siding and Matt watched through one of the windows as the crew sauntered off toward town. Vincent had told him that they'd have at least a two-hour stopover.

Matt waited until they were out of sight and then exited the train and walked over to the stationmaster's office. He was relieved to see that the only employee on duty was the telegraph operator, who was dozing in his chair.

Matt walked up to the counter and cleared his throat. The telegraph operator stirred and, seeing a well-dressed gentleman standing there, jumped up and came to the counter.

"Yes, sir?"

"I need to send a telegraph message to Scranton. Is there someone at that end who can deliver it? It needs to get to the recipient immediately."

"Yes, sir," the man replied.

"Send this to the Scranton Hospital, Third Floor ward. "Relatives of Ben Parkwood arriving in Scranton tonight. Authorizing release of patient to relatives. Arrange assistance at daybreak Sunday for transport of patient to private train." Sign the telegram "Dr. Greevely". Got that?"

The telegraph operator read the message back to Matt, and then tapped out the message with the telegraph key. "Should take about an hour or so for the reply."

Matt nodded. "I'll be back in an hour, then." He paid the operator and left.

There was always the chance that the hospital would try to verify the telegram with Greevely, but that was unlikely. With an 'official' notification from the doctor, there would be no reason to refuse the request—and Matt hoped that the hospital would have no way of knowing that the telegram wasn't from the real Dr. Greevely. Matt would get to the hospital, oversee Ben's transfer to the train, and they'd be back in Montrose well before Greevely's scheduled return to the hospital on Tuesday. Even if anyone tried to trace them after that, they'd have a hard time doing so.

Matt returned to the telegraph office an hour later. The operator waved a piece of paper in Matt's direction. "Delivered and verified, Doctor," the man said, obviously thinking that Matt was Dr. Greevely. "They said they'd have everything ready."

"Good. Thank you so much," Matt said, and retraced his steps to the train. A short while later they were on their way again.

It was already dark when the train rolled into Scranton that evening. Matt gave each of the crew a fifty-dollar bonus and made arrangements to meet them at the train the following morning at 7:00 am sharp.

"Just have her ready to go," Matt said, and Vincent nodded.

"She'll have a head of steam, don't you worry," the stocky engineer said, and with the rest of the crew melted away into the darkness. Matt brought along a small bag of toiletries, a fresh shirt, and the valise with the cash, and made his way into town to find a hotel.

Matt booked a room for the night and, after freshening up, headed downstairs to the restaurant. He ate a leisurely dinner and returned to his room, going over his plans one more time before turning in for the night. With a little luck and a lot of bravado, he'd be able to pull this off.

Bright and early Sunday morning, Matt gathered his belongings and again descended the stairs at the hotel, paying his remaining bill at the counter. He walked out into the clear crisp morning and, pausing on the portico, took a deep breath. This is it, he thought, and walked down the steps to the street.

He wakened a driver in a wagon and told the man to take him to the hospital, instructing the man to park the wagon near the rear entrance and wait for him. He walked into the deserted hospital and made his way to the third floor. The nurse, thankfully, was not someone he had met during his previous visit.

"I'm Doctor Sampson," Matt said to the woman. "I believe you had a telegram from Dr. Greevely concerning my patient, Ben Parkwood." He waited for the reaction from the nurse.

"Yes, Doctor, we did," she replied. She rummaged in the desk and removed a clipboard. "Hospital rules; you'll need to sign him out and take full responsibility. Dr. Greevely wasn't available but I asked Dr. Pfaff to authorize the release." She handed Matt the clipboard, and he scribbled an illegible signature at the bottom of the page.

"Do you have some men available to help me move him?"

"Yes, we do," she replied. "We didn't expect you quite so early. Wait here and I'll go get them." She rose and walked down the hallway.

Matt walked down the hall to the wardroom and looked in. Ben was lying on a cot near the door, his clothing in a small bag on the floor, ready to go. Ben stirred and opened his eyes, focusing on Matt.

"Collins, you made it! Thank God!" he said in a weak voice.

"Shhh!" Matt said in a low voice. "My name is Dr. Sampson for the moment. Don't forget that. I've got a private train waiting to take us back to Montrose. How are you feeling?"

"Better," Ben replied. "Those pills you gave me work well; they take a lot of the edge off of the pain. But, I'm hungry."

"There's food on the train," Matt replied. "We'll get you there and get you as comfortable as possible."

He was interrupted by the arrival of the nurse and four men dressed in working clothes. "These men will help you," the nurse said, then in a lower voice, "you'll need to pay them directly."

Matt nodded. "I understand," he said, and watched as each man took a corner of the cot and lifted it easily. Matt directed them down the stairs and out the back entrance to the wagon, where they gently lifted Ben's cot to the bed of the wagon. They climbed onto the big wagon and settled themselves.

Matt climbed up front with the driver and nodded. The driver cracked his whip and the horse moved off slowly toward the train station.

At the station, Matt instructed the men to bring the cot containing Ben onto the passenger car, where they deposited it in the center of the room. Matt followed the men outside and handed each of them a twenty. Smiling, the men moved off and were soon out of sight. Matt gave the wagon driver a fifty and thanked him for his help, and then walked to the engine.

"Whenever you're ready, Vincent," Matt said, and Vincent waved to the rest of the crew. Matt returned to the passenger car and heard the steam whistle, then felt a jolt as the train began its journey.

Once inside, Matt heaved a sigh of relief. "Well, that wasn't so bad," he said to Ben as he reached into his vest pocket for his watch. "Right on time. You still doing OK?"

Ben nodded. "How about some of that food?" Matt moved to the sideboard and returned with two plates of food.

They ate in silence for a while, and Matt removed the plates when they were finished. He walked to the end of the rail car and came back, bringing two short boards with him, and he placed these on either side of Ben's injured leg. From the kit he pulled out a large roll of cloth bandage and began wrapping the cloth around Ben's leg. "This should keep that leg from moving too much," he explained. He pulled a chair up next to Ben's cot and said, "Listen, Ben, there are several things I need to discuss with you.

"First, the portal has experienced two blackouts since I've been here. Your father had originally planned on me being here for about three weeks. Well, it's been a couple of months now. According to what they told me, the portal will cease to operate within the next few weeks, so we don't have much time."

Ben sat in thought for a few minutes. "The blackouts, what's happened? Were you able to reinitialize the system each time?"

"Yeah, no problem with that," Matt replied. "I found that your original laptop was totally dead when I arrived. I replaced it with one of the spares I brought with me and it initialized right away. Everything comes back up, and I've been able to reestablish contact within a few hours each time."

"Well, that's positive," Ben said. "That's a good sign. The other portals, the ones that collapsed, became very unstable prior to collapse. I think this portal will remain operational until it finally just goes out all at once. On the one hand, that's good, but on the other hand we won't have much warning."

"From what I can tell," Matt replied, "the power levels should be at maximum in about three days, maybe a little more. We can try for a transfer then." He hesitated, then said, "There's something else I need to discuss with you."

For the next hour, Matt gave Ben a condensed version of all that had happened to him since his arrival in August. He explained how he had integrated himself into the town's life, of his fight with Green, and of his search for Ben; and throughout, he explained about his growing relationship with Amanda. He also explained about Amanda's coming fate.

"So, I need your advice," Matt finally said. "I just can't leave her to die."

"You might have to, Matt," Ben said in a serious voice, shaking his head. "One of our primary concerns in visiting this era, or of visiting any era, was to take special care not to deliberately change anything. This is a little different— you're wanting to prevent an occurrence from happening, but that could set off a chain of events as well."

"Maybe I could stay here," Matt said, but Ben frowned.

"Definitely not," Ben said emphatically. "That could be even more disastrous. With the knowledge that you have, you could make changes that you weren't even aware of, with terrible consequences." He leaned back onto the cot. "Let me think about this," he said. "We've still got a few days anyway." He looked up at Matt. "I don't think I've thanked you for all you've done. You took quite a risk coming for me, and I appreciate it. Otherwise I would never have made it back."

"We're not back yet," Matt said. For some reason he felt somewhat depressed and helpless. To Ben, Amanda was just another faceless person, but to Matt, she had become the center of everything. He could not, he would not, let her die.

CHAPTER 27

▼

The return trip to Montrose was uneventful, and they pulled into the station just after dark. The air was chilly, and Matt found a couple of blankets that he threw over Ben. He exited the car and found the horse and wagon just as he had requested, waiting nearby. He pulled the wagon next to the train car and, instructing the crew, had them carry Ben and the cot onto the bed of the wagon.

"I'll need some help unloading Ben at my house," he said, and Vincent nodded, motioning the men to climb onto the wagon. The streets were deserted as they made their way through town. The short trip to the farmhouse took very little time, and the men carried Ben and the cot into the front foyer of the house.

"That will do," Matt said as the men lowered Ben to the floor. He walked back onto the porch with the men and pulled out an envelope. "Here's the rest of your pay," he said, handing the envelope to Vincent, "and I really appreciate all your help. Please return the horse and wagon to the train station. Mr. Blevins will take care of it first thing in the morning."

The crew waved their good-byes and, boarding the wagon, drove off into the darkness. Matt returned to the house and made sure that the door was locked behind him. He spent the next half-hour gently maneuvering Ben and the cot down the stairs to the cellar.

CHAPTER 28

During the following week, Matt and Ben were able to relay their status to Professor Parkwood. A solid link was established between the computers at either end, and after a few days it was determined that the transfer could take place the following Monday evening. That gave Matt a scant five days to figure out what, if anything, could be done for Amanda.

Although the medicines were helping, Ben still lost consciousness from time to time due to his weakened state. Matt knew that it was imperative that he get Ben back through the portal and to the complex. Matt worried that Ben might develop an infection, something that was beyond his capabilities to handle.

That Saturday afternoon, Matt saw that Ben was resting comfortably. He dressed quietly and was about to leave when he saw that Ben had come around again.

"What are you up to?" Ben asked.

"One final thing to take care of," Matt replied. "There's a church social later this afternoon and several of the townspeople have asked me to attend. It's my last chance to interact with these people before you and I go back. That is, if you think you'll be all right here alone for a few hours."

"Of course," Ben replied. "If I run into a problem, I've got this." He held up a small signaling device, the companion one of which he had given to Matt. "But, I'm pretty comfortable."

Matt nodded. "Thanks, Ben," he said.

Ben knew that Matt was becoming increasingly worried about Amanda's fate. He had imagined if he had been in that position and it had been Sandra in the same situation, he knew that he too would have tried to think of a way to prevent it.

Ben spoke up. "Matt, I know this dilemma concerning Amanda is on your mind. The truth is, we just don't know what kind of consequences could ensue, which is why we try to play it safe and not change anything. But, if Amanda's fate is already a part of what happened here in 1896, or soon will be, then it stands to reason that we can't change it no matter what we try."

Matt shook his head. He turned to Ben and said, "I've thought this through a hundred times, and still don't have an answer. But, I love her—I can't just do *nothing.*"

Ben nodded. "I know, Matt," he said. "I'll try to think of something."

Without another word, Matt trudged up the stairs and through the door.

CHAPTER 29

▼

The social was already in full swing when Matt arrived. He walked around the large meeting hall, speaking to all of the people that he had come to know these past few months, and was saddened as he realized that he would never again be seeing them. He had grown to love this town, with its peaceful lifestyle and serene existence.

As he spoke to the various people, he let it be known that he would be returning to Philadelphia in the near future and did not know how soon he'd be able to return to Montrose. He let them think that it might be as much as six months. Mrs. Higby in particular was saddened by this, as she had come to like this nice young man very much and was used to seeing him every few days.

After a while he had made his way around to where most of the Caruthers family was gathered. Mr. Caruthers smiled broadly at Matt and pulled him to one side. In a low voice, he said, "I thought we'd make an announcement about you and Amanda before long. You just let me know when you think the time is right." Matt nodded but said nothing. His inability to come up with a solution to Amanda's imminent fate vexed him, but he could do nothing about it.

Mrs. Caruthers came up beside him and took his arm. "Amanda will be back in a few minutes," she said. "I think she's with a group of her friends." Matt looked across the room and saw Amanda laughing and smiling, and surmised that she was telling her friends the news about her and Matt. She saw him through the crowd and waved happily.

On an impulse, Matt turned to Mrs. Caruthers and suddenly gave her a hug. "Thanks, Mrs. Caruthers, for everything you've done for me."

Mrs. Caruthers was surprised at this gesture from Matt. She sensed that something was amiss with him and said, "What was that for?" Matt said nothing. She shrugged and squeezed his arm.

Amanda appeared at Matt's side a short while later and took his hand. As the afternoon wore on, the couple remained together. If not official, it was very clear that the two young people were now 'an item', and this provided plenty of talk for the people at the social.

Finally Mr. Caruthers said to his family, "It's time we were heading home." He soon learned that Rebecca and Sallie had invited their boyfriends to ride home in the Caruthers wagon, which created a problem. There weren't enough seats to go around.

Matt spoke up. "I can bring Amanda in my wagon, if that's all right." Again, a chaperone would be required but before anyone could say anything, Mrs. Higby came up and said, "If Mr. Collins wouldn't mind giving me a ride home also, I wouldn't mind riding along with them."

"Sure," Matt said. They went out and saw that it was after sunset. The air was chilly and Matt handed blankets to Amanda and Mrs. Higby.

Matt drove the buggy through the darkening twilight, Amanda beside him and Mrs. Higby in the back. Matt was glad that Mrs. Higby had offered to chaperone the couple. She would see to it that Amanda arrived home safely. After that, Matt would take Mrs. Higby home on the way back to his own house.

Matt looked at his new watch and became concerned. He had taken too much time at the social, and Ben was in no shape to be left alone this long. Taking the ladies home and returning to his house would take at least another hour, maybe more. He slowed the buggy and turned to Mrs. Higby.

"Mrs. Higby, would it be all right if I stopped by my house for just a few minutes? I need to check on something. I'll be as quick as I can."

"Of course, Mr. Collins," Mrs. Higby said. "I'm enjoying the ride."

Matt turned the buggy toward his own house and was there inside of fifteen minutes. He jumped to the ground and cinched the horse to the post. He looked up at Amanda. "Back in a few minutes," he said, and went up the steps to the front door. He was about to move the false brick to one side and punch in the code when he looked to his right. There, coming out of the shadows, Harland Green and one of his cronies were advancing slowly. They both carried wooden ax handles. Matt instinctively backed away and was about to make for the opposite side of the house when another of Green's men appeared from around that corner, blocking his exit.

"So, we meet again," Green said, his voice low and menacing. Green stopped about ten paces away from Matt and stood there, glaring.

Matt sighed, then said in an authoritative, dismissive voice, "Listen, Green, I don't have time for this tonight. You want to fight like a man, man to man, then name your place and I'll be there."

Green's cronies were taken aback. They had never heard anyone speak to Green like this before. Usually Green's adversaries, or victims, would beg for mercy or be reduced to driveling idiots when Green advanced on them. This man was different—they sensed no fear in him.

Matt, though not afraid, was very wary and watchful. He didn't like these odds at all and thought furiously, looking for whatever choices or actions might be available to him.

"But where's the fun in that?" Green said. Suddenly Matt heard a commotion from the buggy and saw Amanda and Mrs. Higby being forcibly brought up to the porch by a fourth man.

Amanda said nothing, the loathing on her face evidence enough of her contempt for these ruffians. But Mrs. Higby was more vocal. "Harland Green, how *dare* you? Do you have any idea what you're doing?"

"Shut up, you old biddy," Green said with a snarl. He looked at the two women. "Too bad you two had to come along. But I've waited long enough for this."

Mrs. Higby began to pull away when the man behind her pushed her hard, knocking her to the floor of the porch. Amanda rushed to her and knelt down at her side.

"Keep 'em there," Green said to the man, and turned back to Matt. "You may think you got the best of me at the dance, but you just postponed what you had coming. I don't like people telling me what to do, and I don't like what you did to me. On top of that, you refused to sell me this place. I always get what I want, one way or the other."

"Is that why you tried to kill Ben Parkwood?" Matt asked, and Green frowned.

"How do you know about that?" Green asked.

"Because Ben told me all about it. He confirmed what I've suspected all along—you're a coward, Green, and you get what you want through fear and intimidation. There's only one problem: I'm not afraid of you, or your lackeys."

Green's eyes blazed. "So, he's still alive. Is he here?" Matt said nothing, and Green continued. "No matter. Well, you may say you're not afraid, but that's not very smart since there's four of us to deal with one of you."

"Let the women go, Green," Matt said.

"NO!" Amanda screamed. "Matt, I'm not leaving you here."

'Amanda, do as I say. Take Mrs. Higby and get back to town. I can deal with this trash.'

Green screamed in rage and swung the ax handle viciously, shattering a window. 'Nobody's going anywhere,' he said. 'Like I said, it's just too bad that the three of you were trapped in here when the fire broke out.'

Matt realized instantly what was about to happen. Green planned to kill them all, put their bodies inside the house and set the place on fire—all just to get even with Matt. This must be it, he thought as he looked at Amanda. This is the fire that ended her life. But, unless he could come up with a plan, and fast, there would be three more victims to join her as well.

'They'll hang you, Green, you and your friends. You might be crazy enough to think that you can get away with it, but your friends don't look that stupid.' Matt was deliberately baiting Green, hoping to goad him into a frenzy and watch for him to make a mistake. But, Green didn't go for it.

'They do what I say, Collins,' Green said complacently. 'And they'll say what I tell 'em to say. We were nowhere near this place when it caught fire, right, boys?' The three men looked at each other and nodded, but Matt could see their uncertainty. Green had so cowed them that they dared not disagree with him, but they knew he was capable of murder if he was angered enough.

'A terrible accident, but one that will take care of you *and* let me get this place into the bargain,' Green continued. 'And,' he said, looking at Amanda, 'maybe I will get to know you better before this is all over.'

The look of revulsion on Amanda's face was clear. 'You'll have to kill me first,' she said.

'Well, we'll see about that. Boys, hold Mr. Collins there. I'll be back in a while.'

Two of the men advanced toward Matt while Green stepped over and grabbed Amanda by both arms, lifting her off the porch. Green swung her over one broad shoulder and turned to the front door of the house. He gave the door three tremendous kicks and the door sprang from its hinges and fell inward. Amanda was kicking and screaming but Green said, "Scream your head off if you want. There's no one around for miles."

As Green and Amanda disappeared through the doorway, Matt suddenly lunged for the nearest man, grabbed him by the lapels of his jacket and quickly swung him around, using him as a shield as the other man came at him with the ax handle. The wood make a dull clonk as it hit the man he was holding in the back of the head, splitting the man's scalp, and the man fell senseless in a heap as Matt grabbed the ax handle from his falling hand.

The fourth man shoved Mrs. Higby out of the way and came at Matt swinging. It was all Matt could do to fend off the attack by the two men. He got in a few blows but failed to slow them down much, intent instead on keeping them at bay. Mrs. Higby, showing surprising agility for someone of her age, leaped to her feet and ran to the buggy. Jumping into it, she whipped the horse and sped toward town.

On the porch, Matt swung the ax handle as best he could, maneuvering around until he had both of the men in front of him. At least this way he didn't have to worry about his back.

Inside, Green dropped his weapon near the door and threw Amanda to the floor. Moving quickly, he threw himself on top of her, his hands grabbing for her breasts through the dress.

Amanda was disgusted, a look of scorn on her face as she fought back feebly— but she was scared, too. She knew that there was no way that she could get out of this predicament without help, and it didn't look like any was coming. She slapped at his face but the blows seemed to have no effect whatsoever. One of Green's hands groped at her breasts, at the same time pushing her down onto the floor. His other hand reached down and pulled her dress up, reaching between her thighs as she kicked and screamed.

Outside, Matt was tiring quickly. So far, he had been able to fend off his opponents' blows, but it was just a matter of time before one of them got to him. One good blow and he'd be done for.

Gathering his strength, Matt made a series of short, swift swings, one of which connected with one of his opponent's wrists. Matt actually heard the sound of the bones cracking in the man's wrist and the man dropped to his knees in agony, the ax handle clattering to the ground.

Matt turned his attention to the remaining man, who knew he was in trouble. "Green!" the man screamed, doing his best to keep Matt at bay as Matt advanced on him.

Inside, the shout pierced through Green's lustful frenzy. He pushed himself to one knee and heard the man shout again. He turned to the doorway and saw his man moving backward across the porch, doing his best to deflect the blows from Matt's weapon. His other men were nowhere in sight. With a grunt and a frown, he got to his feet and, picking up the ax handle near the door, turned to go out when Amanda came at him, kicking and scratching. He spun around and, as if he was swatting a fly, backhanded her and sent her sprawling. Amanda landed heavily on the floor and lay there moaning, half-conscious.

As Green went out onto the porch, he saw that Mrs. Higby and the buggy were gone. Green knew that it wouldn't take long for the townspeople to get back here. He looked to his left and saw Matt's back not three feet away. His man paused and backed away when he saw Green, and instantly Matt realized that something was wrong. He was about to turn when Green landed a crushing blow meant for Matt's skull. Anticipating what was about to happen, Matt ducked and turned just in time so that the blow landed across his middle back. Matt was knocked to the floor, in searing pain and nearly unconscious from the blow, the wind knocked out of him.

Green raised his arm and was about to land another blow when his man spoke. "Green, listen, we've got to get out of here! They'll be back with the sheriff in no time!" Green looked around and saw one of his men unconscious, blood seeping from the back of his head. The other man walked up, holding his broken wrist. Green looked down and saw that Matt was still breathing. "Not till we finish this," Green said.

Matt was barely able to move. He had never felt pain like this in his life, and knew that he was helpless to stop what was coming. He had no doubt that Green was getting ready to kill him. He tried to crawl away but had covered only a couple of feet when he felt a huge hand grab the clothing on his back and pick him up like a sack of grain. He felt himself being shaken and then saw Green's face close to his, and through the pain he heard Green say, "It would be too easy to kill you with my bare hands." Green turned his head away and shouted, "Get the kerosene!"

Matt felt himself being swung in an arc, then a sensation of weightlessness as Green threw him bodily through the air and into the house. He landed heavily near Amanda, who was still semi-conscious and moaning. It was all Matt could do to crawl to her side before he passed out.

Green stepped away from the house as his henchman went around the outside perimeter, dousing the wide porch completely with the cans of kerosene. The first man had regained consciousness and was holding a handkerchief to the back of his head, while the second man had fashioned a sling for his broken arm. The three men then joined Green as he struck a match and tossed it toward the house. Almost immediately, the kerosene caught fire and in a matter of a few seconds the entire outside of the house was engulfed in flames.

"C'mon, boys, that should do for them," Green said, and the four made their way to the nearby woods to watch.

Inside, Matt and Amanda lay nearly senseless on the floor. A strong odor brought Matt to his senses, however briefly, and through his blurred eyes he could make out shadowy forms through the windows, moving about outside. He got to his hands and knees and shook his head to clear it, but it didn't help much. He was about to try and stand up when a loud whoosh knocked him flat again as the kerosene ignited outside. Looking up, he saw through the open doorway and through the windows that every opening to the outside was covered in sheets of flame.

Matt crawled to the kitchen but saw through the window that the back of the house was also on fire. No exit that way, he thought as he put his hands up and grabbed the edge of the table, trying to raise himself. His hands found the pitcher of water on the table and he knocked it over toward him, the water drenching his face as it poured out. The water helped clear his brain as he staggered to his feet. Taking the pitcher, he shuffled to Amanda's side and poured the remaining water on her face.

Amanda gasped a couple of times and then opened her eyes. She looked around dazedly, trying to comprehend what was happening. There was a large welt down one of her cheeks. Matt said, "Mandy, listen to me. You've got to find a way out of here. Go upstairs; see if you can make it out one of the windows."

"Not without you."

"Listen, I've got to get Ben. He's down in the cellar. Please, do as I say. I'll be right behind you."

The flames were higher now, and the heat from the fire was becoming almost unbearable. Outside, they heard shouting. Amanda ran up the stairs to the second story and checked each room. The flames were already up to the second floor windows, and as she looked out the window she saw her parents standing below with Mrs. Higby. Many of the townspeople had arrived, alerted by the ringing of one of the church bells in town, and they had seen the glow and the occasional tongue of flame reaching above the trees beyond the town. The men ran up breathlessly, eager to help, but it was obvious that there was little they could do.

"Father, help us!" Amanda screamed from one of the upper windows. Mr. Caruthers, looking up and seeing his daughter, made a dash toward the house. Several of the townspeople grabbed him and held him back. "Jack, you can't! You'd kill yourself! The fire's too big!"

"That's my daughter in there!" Mr. Caruthers said in a strangled voice. Mrs. Caruthers looked up again to see Amanda looking through the window, then being forced back as the flames shot higher. Mrs. Caruthers screamed and fainted. The fire brigade arrived and began pumping water furiously, but the fire had taken hold and the water did nothing to slow its progress.

*   *   *   *

Inside, Amanda staggered back down the stairs, choking from the black smoke that was now billowing from the outer walls. She coughed as the smoke burned her eyes, and she could only feel her way toward the kitchen.

"Mandy, drop to the floor," she heard Matt say, and she found a small pocket of more or less breathable air near the floor. Through the haze, she reached out and grabbed Matt's outstretched hand. "The cellar," she heard him say, "we've got to get into the cellar."

"Matt, we'll never get out if we do that!"

"Trust me. Come on!" he said, pulling her as he crawled toward the kitchen. He somehow found the cellar door and reached up to the hidden panel, hoping that the wiring for the switch hadn't burned through. He punched in the combination and the cellar door clicked open. "Quick, down the stairs!"

They half crawled, half fell down the stairs, the door closing behind them. Below, everything was calm and quiet, just as he had left it. He dragged Amanda into the shower and turned it on, flooding them both with water. After a few minutes they were able to breathe and see again.

Amanda dropped to the floor outside the shower, wiping the water from her face and pushing her hair back. Matt staggered out of the small room and went over to Ben, who was lying on the bed. "Matt, what's going on?" Ben asked.

"The whole house is on fire, Ben. There's no way out up there. I figure we've got less than an hour before the flames eat through the cellar ceiling. Unless the people outside can get the fire under control we've had it. I'm sorry."

"Green's work?" Ben asked, and Matt nodded. Ben propped himself up on one elbow, grimacing in pain, and pointed toward the far wall at the end of the cellar. "Take something, whatever you can find, and cut open the fiberglass panel on that wall."

"The wall?" Matt asked in a confused voice, and Ben said, "Do it, quick! It's where the passageway goes to the barn. Remember the power cables from the solar cells? They run through there. It might be big enough for us to get out. It'll *have* to be big enough—we've got to get out of here before the fire reaches the storage batteries!" The batteries were behind a false wall in the upstairs pantry. Matt had forgotten about the passageway, although he had looked over the plans for the farm back at the complex. He had forgotten about the batteries, too.

Once the fire ignited them, there would be a tremendous explosion that would surely blow a hole in the cellar ceiling.

Matt nodded and ran for the far wall, picking up an ax on the way. He began hacking at the wall. The lights flickered a few times and then went out. The darkness was total for a few seconds before the emergency lighting kicked on. Matt continued hacking at the wall, and the fiberglass shattered until he had made an opening big enough for them to crawl through. He peered through the opening and saw a passageway leading into the darkness. There appeared to be sufficient space for them to get through, in single file. He threw the ax to one side and shuffled back to the bed. Amanda had come out of the small shower room and was sitting there, a look of resignation on her face. She was sure they were all going to die within minutes, and had only postponed the inevitable by running to the cellar.

"Mandy, listen to me. We might have a way out. Help me get Ben and the mattress onto the floor." The two of them manhandled the mattress, with Ben on it, off of the bed frame and onto the floor. They tried not to move Ben too much but even the slight jostling sent waves of pain through him. As soon as Ben was on the floor, Matt ran to the far side of the cellar and rummaged through the supplies. He came back with a coil of rope.

"We're going to have to drag the mattress behind us, though the passage. It's the only way to get Ben, and us, out of here." Amanda nodded and watched as Matt tied each end of the rope to the top corners of the mattress. Matt grabbed the rope and pulled steadily. Inch by inch, the mattress was dragged across the floor toward the opening.

*　　　*　　　*　　　*

Outside, the townspeople watched helplessly as the flames roared skyward. The intensity of the heat had driven them all back, and although a few of the braver men still manned the hose dangerously close to the flames, it was obvious that the fire had the upper hand. A group of men were gathered around Mr. Caruthers, who was sitting on the ground with his head in his hands. Nearby, a similar group of women were tending to Mrs. Caruthers, who was sobbing uncontrollably. The fire was visible for miles, and lit up everything in the area.

The sheriff and some of the other men from town had found Green and his men hiding in the woods near the barn, watching the fire. Mrs. Higby had explained everything to the sheriff when she had gone for help, and although Green had fought like a madman when he was discovered, the men from town had overpowered him by sheer numbers. His cronies, seeing prison or the end of a rope for this night's work, had blamed everything on Green, saying that he had forced them into helping him. Green, sullen and scowling, was trussed securely and brought forward. His men had given up without a fight, but they too were bound securely and put under guard nearby.

Mr. Caruthers looked up and saw the sheriff with Green. He got to his feet and walked over, standing in front of Green.

"How could you do this?" Mr. Caruthers said, and felt himself clenching his fists as he saw the sneer on Green's face. The sheriff hurriedly stepped between them. "Jack, take it easy. We've got him. He'll not be long for this world, not after this."

But it was little consolation. Mr. Caruthers turned away and slowly walked toward his wife, looking over his shoulder at the flames engulfing the house.

CHAPTER 30

▼

In the cellar, as they reached the opening, Ben hissed through clenched teeth. "Matt, don't forget the laptop." Matt ran back to the table and retrieved the computer, disconnecting the cables and closing the lid. He also picked up the two knapsacks that held his own equipment and slung them over one shoulder. Returning to the opening, he placed the laptop and knapsacks on Ben's chest. "You'll have to hold these," he told Ben, and Ben nodded.

Playing out the rope, he looked up at Amanda. "Mandy, take this flashlight and the rope. You need to go in first. I'll be right behind you." The passage was barely big enough for them to make it through single file, and less than four feet wide. Matt had no idea of the length of the passage, but estimated that it had to be a good three hundred feet to the other end. They'd have to crouch and, at the same time, pull Ben through behind them. The power cables lined one side of the passage wall and made for a tight squeeze.

Foot by foot, they slowly made their way along the passageway. Amanda had been amazed at the large handheld floodlight when Matt had switched it on and handed it to her, but did her best to keep the beam focused ahead of them as she pulled on the rope with her other hand. Matt had draped the rope around his upper arms and pulled with all his might. Between the smoke from the fire, and the blow he had taken from Green, he was about done in. But he somehow dredged up enough strength from his tired muscles to keep going.

As they inched through the passage, Amanda in the lead, Matt had to stop every ten feet or so to rest. He figured they were at least halfway through when he stopped again to catch his breath. As he did so, a muffled explosion shook the ground around him. He looked back toward the cellar and saw with horror that a large fireball was headed straight for them along the passageway. The fire must have finally reached the storage batteries and ignited them.

"Mandy, get down!" he shouted, and dropped to the floor. Amanda looked back and screamed as she saw the fireball bearing down on them. There was nowhere to go, nothing to do but wait for the inevitable.

Above, in the yard of the house, a large crowd of the townspeople had gathered to watch the conflagration. As they watched, a huge explosion sent many of them running back. The force of the explosion knocked down quite a few of the closer observers, but the main blast had blown toward the sky.

"What the..." one of the firemen said. None of them had ever seen anything quite like this before. A few minutes later, debris from the blast began to rain down. The townspeople scattered and ran until they were out of range of the falling debris.

In the passageway below, Ben looked down between his feet and instinctively raised his hands to his face as he saw the fireball heading straight for him. He closed his eyes and felt the blast of tremendous heat pass across his body, expecting to be consumed by the flames. Ahead, Amanda had thrown herself face down and covered her head with her hands. Matt untwisted the ropes and threw himself on top of her just as the flames passed over them.

But, as suddenly as it had come, the fire was gone. The blast had blown the ball of fire along the top of the passage, but as the flames reached the vertical shaft that went up to the barn ahead of them the fireball went up the shaft, reached the top and simply dissipated.

Matt opened his eyes and cautiously looked around. Tired as he was, and in severe pain, he couldn't help but laugh. "My God," he said with feeling, "that was close."

"We're not dead?" Amanda said in a bewildered voice as Matt rose to a crouch.

"Ben? You OK?" Matt said, and he could see Ben nodding in the faint light.

"I'm a little singed. Damn, I thought we'd had it that time!"

"Let's get out of here before something else happens," Matt said, and grabbed the rope. The ground shook slightly and Matt reached for the flashlight and shone the beam back down the passageway. The passage had collapsed at the far end, sealing off the cellar. Matt was sure that the intensity of the fire would completely obliterate any trace of the remaining equipment in the cellar. Slowly and painfully, he pulled Ben through the remainder of the passageway and to the bottom of the vertical shaft. The shaft was about ten feet across, with a ladder going up at one side near the thick black power cables. He painfully climbed the ladder and tried the trap door, but it was solidly closed and nothing he did would open it. He climbed back down and sat down wearily next to Amanda.

"Looks like we'll have to sit this one out until morning," Matt said. He reached into the knapsack and pulled out three light sticks. He snapped them each in turn, shaking them, and tossed them around the perimeter of the shaft. A soft greenish-yellow glow lit up the area. Amanda had a look of incomprehension on her face. "It's like a candle, but without the flame," Matt explained briefly. Amanda said nothing. He picked up the knapsack and, moving over to Ben, saw that the flames had singed Ben's hair and clothing, but saw no burns on his flesh. He spent several minutes checking Ben over and, looking across at Amanda, saw that she had dozed.

In a low voice, Matt said, "Listen, Ben, I'm going to give you another shot for the pain. But first, do you have any idea what we're supposed to do now? The portal is gone."

"Philadelphia," Ben said, now only half-conscious from the ordeal. "Our only chance is to get to the portal in Philadelphia. I don't even know if it's still working, or if we can get it to work, but it's our only chance."

The Philadelphia portal! Matt had completely forgotten about it, and he remembered Professor Parkwood saying that the portal was dormant. Dormant, but not collapsed. At least, Matt hoped it wasn't collapsed. It would be the only opportunity he and Ben would have to get back to their own time.

He turned back to Ben and, in a low voice, said, "Listen, Ben I don't know what to do here. Remember how we were talking about that story I saw in one of those old newspapers? How Amanda was supposed to have died in a fire?"

"And you think it was the fire we just escaped?" Ben asked. Matt nodded. "Then we could be in serious trouble," Ben continued. "By saving her from the fire, we may have already changed the past, and with it our future. There may not be anything that we can go back *to*."

Matt busied himself with preparing the shot. "Not much left," he said to Ben as he filled the syringe. "Maybe two days' worth. After that…" His voice trailed off. He swabbed Ben's arm and plunged the needle home. Within a few seconds Ben's eyes closed and he was unconscious.

Matt leaned back and sighed. There had been no time, no opportunity for him to get Amanda out of the situation they had been placed in with Green. And he couldn't have known that this was the fire she had died in. Even if he had, there was no way that he could have left her to that fate.

Bottom line, though, he knew that he was to blame. If he hadn't been so selfish, if he hadn't gotten involved with Amanda, then things would have worked out the way they were supposed to have worked out over a hundred years before his own time. Now, he realized that he might have been the sole cause of altering history, and in the process dooming his contemporaries to an unknown fate.

Matt replaced the kit into the knapsack and moved over to Amanda. He lay down with his back to the wall and, placing an arm around her, pulled her to his side. She murmured in her sleep and nestled her head on his chest. Matt leaned his head back and closed his eyes, and was asleep within seconds.

*   *   *   *

At the research facility, the atmosphere was calm. Professor Parkwood and the others sat around the consoles, patiently waiting for the next communication. Suddenly, they were all startled by a blinding flash of white light from the portal. There was a moment of stunned silence, then an explosion of activity as everyone raced for their respective stations.

"What the hell was *that*?" one of the technicians said to no one in particular.

Professor Parkwood picked up the microphone for the intercom. His voice was calm as it boomed through the complex. "Everyone, give me a status check as soon as you have it."

Minutes passed, then, "I've lost all telemetry from the portal." This from Goodman, the lead communications technician. "I'm not getting any signals at all."

Calmly, Professor Parkwood nodded, then listened as each console reported its status. Throughout the room, the reports were negative.

After a while, Stinnett, the team leader, came up the stairs to where Professor Parkwood was sitting. His report was short and abrupt. "It appears we've had a total, catastrophic failure of the system."

"The portal finally collapsed?" Professor Parkwood asked, but Stinnett shook his head. "No, this is different. Everything indicates that a total system failure has occurred at the other end of the portal. We've tried everything we can think of. It's as if there's nothing there."

"Is this like what happened before?" Professor Parkwood asked.

Stinnett shook his head. "No, that was simply a system shutdown. This...this looks to be a total failure of the entire system at that end. The link is totally broken."

Professor Parkwood bowed his head and rubbed his temples. He looked up again. "Any chance of getting it operational again?"

"Not from this end—and not from that end either, I believe. It appears that this portal is dead. Permanently." He shook his head again. "I'm sorry."

Professor Parkwood sighed. "So am I, so am I." He rose slowly, dejectedly. "I'll go and tell Sandra."

"Professor, wait," Stinnett said. "There is one chance. The Philadelphia portal. If they can make their way to it, and activate it, there's a small chance we can bring them back."

"But, will they remember about it?" Professor Parkwood said. "Ben is apparently in bad shape, unconscious most of the time, and I only mentioned the Philadelphia portal to Collins in passing. Unless Ben can help him, I'm afraid we've lost them."

"Henry, we've at least got to give them the chance."

"Yes, of course you're right," Professor Parkwood said. "Assemble the team, let them know what's happened and what we propose. I'll meet with everyone in an hour and we'll decide what we're going to do."

CHAPTER 31

▼

"Matt? Matt, wake up, please!"

The voice seemed to come from far away, and Matt was aware of a rocking sensation. He finally opened his eyes and saw Amanda in the dim light, her hands shaking his shoulders.

"What...what is it?"

"Matt, I think it's morning. Those lights you lit are going out. It's getting hard to see in here."

With difficulty, Matt roused himself and tried to get up. The sudden pain cutting across his back made him wince in agony. He fell onto his side, and then painfully stood up. He shuffled over to the knapsack and, removing two more of the light sticks, snapped them. Light flooded the area, making him close his eyes at the brightness.

"Here, hold this," he said, handing one of the sticks to Amanda. She hesitated, and he said, "They won't hurt you. See, they're cool." She gingerly took the stick and watched as Matt removed his jacket and shirt. He turned around and said, "How's my back?"

He heard Amanda's sharp intake of breath as she looked at his back in the light. There was an ugly black and blue bruise across the middle of his back. "Not good," she said. "Does it feel like anything's broken?"

Matt grimaced with pain as he flexed his shoulders. "God, it hurts! But no, it doesn't feel like anything's broken." He put his shirt back on and took the light stick from her. "Let me look at you."

The side of Amanda's face was slightly swollen, but the huge welt from Green's blow seemed to have diminished. Looking at her, he said, "Beautiful as always." He took her in his arms and held her close. "I don't want to ever go through anything like that again," he said with feeling.

He released her and walked over to Ben, who was still unconscious. Matt checked his pulse, which seemed normal, but frowned when he placed a hand on Ben's forehead.

"He's feverish," Matt said, straightening. "We've got to get him some help." Matt reached into his jacket and pulled out the watch. "It's a little after 8:00 am." He replaced the watch and went over to the ladder. He activated another light stick and, with an effort, began climbing up toward the top.

With the light, he was able to see the four latches arranged around the edge of the hatch. Swinging them back, he gave the hatch a shove and it began to rise silently on the pneumatic rods. When the hatch was vertical it stopped. Matt slowly peered around the interior of the barn but saw that it was empty. He climbed out and crossed to the barn door. Through the crack between the doors, he could see the still-smoking remains of the farmhouse some distance away. The structure had been completely leveled from the blast. There were three or four men poking about the ashes with iron rods, but before long they shook their heads and turned to walk back to town, leaving the farm deserted.

Matt went back to the ladder and descended. Amanda was tending to Ben, who was sweating profusely and rocking his head back and forth.

Amanda looked at Matt. "He woke up right after you'd left. He's in terrible pain, Matt." Matt nodded and reached for the knapsack once again. He pulled out the small medical kit and opened it. Inside, Amanda saw a dozen vials and some other instruments.

"I'm not a doctor, but we'll have to chance it." Matt removed the syringe and selected a nearly empty vial. Sticking the needle into the vial, he withdrew a small amount of the liquid, removed the syringe, and replaced the vial in the box.

Matt reached for Ben's arm and, without hesitation, plunged the needle into his arm and pressed the plunger gently. Within just a few seconds, Ben relaxed and began breathing regularly. Matt replaced the syringe and closed the box.

"Matt, what was that?" Amanda said.

"A painkiller. I couldn't afford to give him too much, but that should be enough to keep him out for a while. We've got to figure out a way to get him up this shaft to the barn. He'd never make it if he was conscious." Matt rummaged in the kit and brought out a couple of small pills, which he swallowed. He looked at Amanda. "Are you feeling OK? Any pain?"

Amanda shook her head. "No, I'm fine. But, how do we get Ben out of here?"

Matt ascended the ladder again and looked around the barn. A winch and pulley swung from the ceiling, and Matt went to the handle and released the lock. The pulley slowly lowered to the ground. Matt leaned over the opening of the shaft and looked down. Below, Amanda was looking up at him.

"Mandy, I'm going to lower this rope down to you. Let me know when there's about twenty feet of rope at your end." He cranked the winch and the rope lowered into the opening. A few minutes later he heard Amanda say, "That's enough."

Matt locked the winch and again descended the ladder. Fashioning a harness from the rope, he secured the rope around Ben's chest below the arms and secured it so it wouldn't come loose. He turned to Amanda. "When I crank the rope, try to make sure he doesn't move around too much when I pull him up, especially that leg. Once he's cleared the ground, get my things and come up the ladder. I'll need your help up above." Amanda nodded and watched as Matt grabbed as much as he could carry and climbed the ladder once again.

Matt slowly cranked the winch, and felt the increased weight as Ben was pulled to a vertical position and then swung freely a few inches above the ground, his head lolling to one side. Amanda came up the ladder quickly, dropped the two knapsacks and the laptop at one side, and moved to the winch, helping Matt turn the crank. Slowly, Ben was pulled higher and higher until his body, suspended in the harness, had cleared the opening.

"Now, we've got to swing him away from the opening and onto the floor." Amanda nodded and grabbed the rope above Ben. As Matt reversed the winch, Amanda guided Ben to one side and onto the floor. Matt played out some slack in the rope and locked the handle. Going to the hatch, he closed it and turned the latches.

Ben, still unconscious, seemed none the worse for the experience, but Matt knew that they had to get help for him, and soon. Ben was getting weaker with each passing hour.

He motioned Amanda to follow him to the door. Peering outside, he saw that the farm was now deserted. He turned back to Amanda.

"I need to explain a great many things to you, but right now we only have one chance to save Ben's life. Strange as this may sound, we need to get to Philadelphia as quickly as possible. I'm going to need your help. How can we do that?"

"We have a doctor in town, Matt," Amanda said, but Matt shook his head.

"No, we can't do that. You'll have to trust me on this."

"Well, if we can get to New Milford, we can get a train."

"We can't take him on a train with a lot of other people. Too many questions, and they might be looking for him anyway. I took him out of the Scranton hospital without his doctor's permission."

Amanda said, "No, Matt, what I mean is we can hire a private car on one of the trains. That could get us to Philadelphia in no time."

Matt looked around the barn. An old wagon was parked at one end, but there was no horse to pull it. He turned to Amanda.

"I'm going out to see if I can find a horse. There should be one nearby somewhere. With any luck I'll be back soon." He pulled her close and held her for a minute, then leaned down and kissed her forehead. "Keep an eye on Ben." She nodded as he slowly opened one of the barn doors and peered out. There was no one in sight. He slipped through the opening and closed the door behind him.

It was an hour and a half later when Amanda heard the snort of a horse. She jumped up and ran to the door, peeking through the space between the boards, and was relieved to see Matt leading a large gray horse behind him. She opened the door and let him through, then closed it again.

"I had to chase him for half an hour before I could get close enough," he said to her as he led the horse to the wagon and began hitching the horse to it. "I think it would be safer if we waited till nightfall to leave."

"But why, Matt?" Amanda asked. "I told you we can get help here in town."

Matt shook his head. "There's still much I need to explain to you, but for now we need to stay out of sight. You'll understand later."

He spent the next hour putting up some blankets across one of the stall openings, and then made a few trips outside to the well, where he brought back pails of water. He placed the water into a large tin washtub.

"We'll need to get cleaned up before we leave," he said to Amanda. "I don't know what to do about the clothes, though. We're all looking pretty rough. You go ahead. The water's a little cold but it's all we've got."

Amanda nodded and entered the stall, pulling the blankets closed behind her. She cleaned up as best she could, but her dress was near ruin and her hair was disheveled. When she had finished, Matt dumped the water from the washtub and refilled it from the buckets. He also did his best to get rid of the soot and grime and came out a short while later looking almost normal.

"Luckily we have this," he said, reaching into one of the knapsacks and pulling out a stack of notes. "I'll get us all some new clothes in New Milford."

CHAPTER 32

▼

Matt guided the wagon through the outskirts of Philadelphia. He looked over his shoulder and saw Amanda holding on to Ben, trying to ease the rough jostling of the wagon. Matt estimated that it was just before noon. Ben was conscious again but he looked deathly pale. They had managed to locate a train in New Milford, along with new clothes, and had rented a private rail car and made the run to Philadelphia in good time and without incident.

"Listen, Ben, I think we're nearly there. Can you look around and tell me if we're anywhere close?"

Ben, with Amanda's help, rose to one elbow and surveyed the area. "Yes, we're almost there," he said in a weak voice. "Just beyond that small park, turn right and look for a big house with columns. Pull the wagon around to the back."

Matt nodded and followed the directions. He saw the big house, set far back on the grounds, and steered the wagon through the gate and up the drive. He pulled around to the back and set the brake on the wagon. Jumping down, he went up the small steps at the rear and looked for the false brick. It was identical to the setup at the Montrose house, and he quickly punched in the combination code. The door clicked open and Matt went inside. He reconnoitered the house but found it empty. He left his laptop and satchel on one of the tables in the sitting room and returned to the kitchen.

He reappeared in the doorway a few minutes later and said, "Looks like everything's OK. Amanda, we need to get Ben inside and down to the cellar. Do you think you can make it?"

"Yes, I think so," she said, although Matt knew she was exhausted. They each picked up an end of the litter and struggled under Ben's weight. Although Ben didn't weigh much at this point, the litter was difficult to carry, especially when they attempted to negotiate the stairs to the cellar. The ceiling lights were working but were somewhat dim.

Somehow they made it, and they gently laid the litter on the floor. Matt went to the small bedroom and returned with a mattress from one of the beds. He repeated the trip and came out with the lightweight bed frame. Setting up the bed to one side, they hoisted Ben onto the bed. Matt checked his watch and gave Ben another shot.

Amanda dropped to the floor, her back to the wall, and watched Matt as he checked the laptop that was already set up. There was no power to it. He checked the circuit breakers in the console, then went across the room to the power control panel. The master switch had been set to "Off". He threw the switch and the lights brightened perceptibly. He checked the console again and typed a command into the laptop, nodding in satisfaction as it began the initiation sequence.

Matt then rummaged around in the cabinets along the wall near the bedroom and reached in, bringing out a small black case. He set the case on the console and flipped open the latches. Inside, he saw a small supply of emergency medical equipment, along with vials of medicines and a few pillboxes. None of the items had been touched. "Thank goodness," Matt said to himself.

Matt closed the case and walked over to Amanda, reaching down to help her up. She came to her feet with a questioning look in her eyes.

"I promised I'd explain all this to you, and I will," Matt said. "But first, you can go in and take a shower, get cleaned up. I'll go in after you've finished." He took her into the small bathroom and turned on the faucets until the water temperature was adjusted. "Here's a robe for you to use when you're finished." He turned and went out, closing the door behind him.

As Amanda showered, Matt went outside and saw the horse and wagon, the horse patiently waiting. Matt had completely forgotten about the animal. He unhitched the horse from the wagon and gave it a resounding slap on the rump that sent it galloping off down the street. Someone would find it and take it in.

Returning below, Matt checked the remainder of the cellar. It was almost an exact duplicate of the cellar under the house in Montrose, only larger. The equipment was identical, with the portal sitting at the center of the room.

After twenty minutes, Amanda appeared at the door. Her hair was wet, and she had wrapped the robe around her. The robe came halfway down her calf, and Matt saw that she was barefoot. "Here," he said, rummaging through the trunk in the bedroom, "here are some slippers you can use." She slipped them on, still not saying anything. Matt knew that she was both frightened and wary of the events around her.

"Trust me," he said, and she nodded. "I'll be back before you know it. Just remember, don't touch anything." She nodded again and he disappeared into the bathroom.

Before long he returned, also wrapped in a soft robe and wearing sandals. He took her hand and led her up the stairs to the main house.

A short while later they were seated on the couches in the sitting room, a pot of hot tea and some cheese and crackers on the table between them, which they ate quietly. Amanda had still not spoken, so Matt came over and sat down beside her. Taking her hands, he looked into her eyes and said, "There's a lot, a lot that I have to explain to you. Some of what I'm about to tell you is going to sound unbelievable, some you'll understand. Some of it you won't comprehend. But, I swear on my love for you, everything I'm about to tell you is the truth. Do you understand that?"

Amanda nodded, not sure of what to think. Matt continued. "I'm a...a traveler here. I did come to Montrose from Philadelphia, and I do live in Pittsburgh—but it's not the Philadelphia or Pittsburgh that you know. I'm from a place as strange to you as if you were to travel to...well, there's nothing to compare it to."

Amanda kept looking at him but saying nothing. Matt wasn't sure how to continue. Then he thought of something. Walking across to the desk, he brought back his laptop and flipped it open. He sat next to her, the laptop on his knees, and said, "Watch this." He pressed the power switch and the computer hummed into life. Amanda shrank back and, seeing that there was no danger, leaned forward again. She watched in fascination as the computer's screen flashed in different configurations. Finally the screen was covered with small boxes.

"Touch this one," he said, and she reached out, hesitated, and then touched the icon. Classical music came softly through the speakers. She looked at him and smiled. "A music box?" she asked.

"Hardly that," Matt said, and he touched another icon. The music stopped and a video began playing on the screen. Amanda was fascinated at the moving images. The video was a simple demo for one of the programs, showing how the computer could render three-dimensional images.

"This is called a computer," Matt said. "In this small box I can store the equivalent of an entire library, thousands of books. It can perform mathematical equations. It can do many wonderful things, once you know how to use it." He closed the lid and set the laptop on the table. "Where I come from, virtually everyone has one of these. This is simply a tool. And this is insignificant compared to many of the other things we have available to use." He took her hands again. "I'm a historian," he said. "I had the opportunity to actually become a part of what I've studied for many years. So I took it. That's what brought me to Montrose. The opportunity to study something out of the past."

"Historian?" she said, not understanding. "You study history? You're studying Montrose as history? But that would mean..." She shook her head. "No, that's not possible." She looked at him, and this time there was fear in her voice. "Matt, what are you trying to tell me?"

Matt knew that there was no easy way to explain this. "I'm here from very far away...I'm here from many years in your future."

She looked at him steadily, but there was no comprehension in her eyes. Matt realized that she had no frame of reference for this pronouncement, and simply could not understand such a concept. She still said nothing, and he hoped that she wasn't coming to a conclusion that he was insane. He decided to try again.

"Look," he said, "when you were a little girl, didn't you ever pretend that you were, say, a princess in the Middle Ages, and that a handsome knight would come to your rescue? Didn't you ever wonder what it would be like to have lived then?"

"Yes," she said slowly, "but that was pretend. I knew I could never really do that."

"But what if someone found a way that you could? Would you?"

"I don't know," she said.

"Where I come from, Ben's father found a way to do just that. That's how I got here. That's how Ben got here. But it's only for a little while, a few months at the most. When they lost track of Ben, I came to find him and bring him...home."

Amanda closed her eyes and shook her head. "No, it can't be. It just can't." She opened her eyes and looked at him again. "How far have you come?"

"Over a hundred years."

She looked at him, and tears sprang into her eyes. "And you've found Ben. Wherever it is you're from, you're going back there with him, is that it?" She sprang from the couch, her voice quivering. "You used me. You used me and now you're telling me that you're leaving." Matt got up and went to put his arms around her when she began beating him on the chest with her fists. "How could you do this to me?" she said, sobbing. "After what you told me. You promised me."

Matt pulled her close. "Mandy," he said, "I did promise, and I meant it."

She was still sobbing. "If what you say is true, I'll never see you again. I'd be dead long before you were ever born. I can't go with you."

"Yes, you can," Matt said. "In fact, you have to. It's the only way to save you." Amanda looked up at him and, through her tears, said, "What do you mean?"

This was going to be dicey, Matt thought as he gently sat her back down on the couch. "Before I came here, I had to study the old newspapers from Montrose, so I'd know what to expect." He reached for the laptop again and opened it. "Those newspapers are copied in here; you can read them." He punched up the database and brought up the newspapers. She recognized the newspaper and watched as he zoomed in on some of the articles.

"This is a newspaper from last week," he said, and showed it to her. It held information that she recognized. "Now, this is a newspaper from sometime late next month. For some reason, the exact date is not on this one—some sort of problem when it copied. But, I want you to read this." He zoomed in on the obituary and turned the screen so that she could read it. He took her hand and held it, watching as she read the article.

She read it twice before leaning back. "The fire," she said in a shaky voice. "They think I'm dead." Matt could see that she was upset. Well, I guess anyone would be, he said to himself, if they had just read their own obituary.

Matt said, "I'll try to explain this. According to history, you died in that fire at the farm in Montrose. I couldn't let that happen, so you didn't die in the fire. But everyone, your parents and family, everyone in town, thinks that you did. It was reported in your hometown newspaper. It's now a part of history. You can't go back to your home. You can't stay here in 1896. If you did, then history, my history, would be changed. And that can't happen. We can't allow that to happen."

"Then why am I not dead? It's there," she said, indicating the newspaper story.

"With the intensity of a fire like that, they wouldn't expect to find any remains. I'm guessing that's why the newspaper says it was a memorial service, not a funeral." He paused. "You can't stay here. You have to go back with us— with me. If you stay here, history will be changed. If that happens, I could cease to exist. All of the future could be changed."

Amanda pressed the heels of her hands into her eyes and shook her head. "I don't understand any of this," she said. "We're here; we're alive. You're here. So, nothing has changed."

"I hope you're right. But Ben and I don't belong here. Our only way of knowing for sure that nothing has changed is to get us all back to where Ben and I came from. That is, if we can and if it still exists." It was then that Matt remem-

bered something that Professor Parkwood had told him. "There's only one problem."

"What's that?" Amanda said.

"We're not even sure if we *can* get back. The equipment downstairs is failing.
Everything may stop working before we can even try."

CHAPTER 33

▼

Professor Parkwood sat at the head of the large table in the conference room and looked around at the anxious faces. Everyone had prepared their respective reports and had them at the ready.

"Miss Craig, suppose you begin, and then we'll go around the table in turn. Besides the actual statistics, I want your personal input as well. Your opinion as to how we should proceed."

Miss Craig nodded, rose, and began reciting her findings. Each of the technicians took their turn as Professor Parkwood and Stinnett made notes. As the final technician finished and sat down, Professor Parkwood waited as Stinnett reviewed his notes. Finally, Stinnett rose and faced the group.

"With the conditions we have right now, I calculate that we have an approximately sixty-five percent chance of retrieving our people, provided that we can get everything ready within the next few days. Unfortunately, as you know, we have no way of knowing if or when Ben and Mr. Collins will be able to initialize the portal in Philadelphia. If the portal at their end is activated before we're ready, they could break the temporal link altogether without even knowing that they're doing so. We are the control; this complex has to be ready to take control and maintain it until the transfer is complete. Because of that situation, I would estimate our chances at less than forty percent right now."

Several around the table shook their heads in resignation. "Of course," Stinnett continued, "this is all uncharted territory, so to speak. Our review of the newspapers from that time period, those that are available, show absolutely nothing in reference to Ben or to Mr. Collins. In my opinion, that means one of two things: that they are already dead from whatever catastrophe befell the Montrose installation, or that we were, or should I say will be, successful in retrieving them. Otherwise, I believe that they would have found some way to communicate with us."

"Perhaps another cylinder was planted with the information," one of the technicians ventured, but Stinnett shook his head. "No, Mr. Collins may not have been able to do that, and we know now that Ben was in no condition to do it." Stinnett looked around the table. "It is my recommendation that we work around the clock to get everything ready and hope for the best."

Professor Parkwood rose. "As you know, it's going to take every last one of us to accomplish that. We'll only have one chance at it. I can't force any of you to do this. I know you're all tired. Still, I need to know what all of you have decided."

One by one, the technicians around the table nodded at Professor Parkwood. Stinnett spoke up with an optimistic grin. "Professor, I think I speak for everyone when I say, we can't quit now. This experiment isn't finished. The only way to complete this is to see it through."

"Thank you all," Professor Parkwood said. "Sandra and I appreciate this more than you can know."

CHAPTER 34

▼

It was three days later in the Philadelphia of 1896 and the weather had taken a turn for the worse with the arrival of a sudden snowstorm that had blanketed the ground with a foot of snow and coated the surrounding trees with thick ice. The sun had finally peeked through the clouds about noon, but the air was icy cold. Under these conditions, the solar cells on the roof of the house would be hard pressed to generate any current.

In the cellar of the house, Matt and Amanda bustled about, checking the settings of the equipment but also moving around to keep warm. They had been forced to disconnect the electrical heating system from the power supply so that every ounce of power could be diverted to the storage batteries. Even without the added drain of the heating system, the power readings hovered at seventy percent—and nothing they could do would make the readings go any higher.

"It's no use, Matt," Ben said. "There's just not enough sunlight to bring the charge up in the batteries."

Matt slammed his fist down on the console in frustration. "There has to be *something* we can do! We can't be this close to getting home and have the whole system become useless."

"How do you think *I* feel?" Ben said with anger. "I could still lose this leg, or even my life, if I don't get some decent medical attention!"

Matt nodded dejectedly. "I'm sorry, Ben," he said. "It's just that I didn't expect us to be stopped by something like this." He leaned across the console and activated the heating system. Soon warm air was flowing throughout the cellar. Matt looked over at Ben. "I'll just run it long enough to warm it up in here a bit. No use us freezing to death."

Ben was about to protest when he realized that Matt was right. Besides, the power drain was negligible at this point. The system had been initialized and was ready, but without at least eighty per cent power they couldn't even establish voice or data contact with the complex. And it would take at least a ninety five per cent power level to even attempt a transfer.

Matt turned to Ben. "I'm going upstairs and bring down some supplies," he said, and trudged up the stairs to the kitchen, closing the cellar door behind him. In the kitchen, he found Amanda seated at the table. Matt sat down across from her and sighed.

"This doesn't look good, Mandy," Matt said. "We may really be stuck here."

"Is that so bad, Matt?" Amanda said.

Matt sighed. "It could be. Ben and I definitely cannot remain here; the risk is too great. And neither can you. You've seen too much, know too much—and it could change history if you do. Besides, I'm not leaving you here. I would have nothing to live for."

"But is all of this worth it?" Amanda asked. "Ben's not getting any better; he needs a doctor, and soon. We've got a safe place to go to in Montrose. If not that, then we can get a doctor here in Philadelphia." She paused, then looked up at Matt. "What I'm saying is, whatever you're trying to accomplish with your equipment isn't working. And we can't afford to wait much longer." She got up from the chair and moved around the table, standing behind Matt and placing her hands on his shoulders. "My family can help us. I need to let them know I'm alive. They must be grieving terribly." The tears sprang to her eyes as she thought of her family.

Matt shook his head as he listened to her. For once he just didn't know what to do. Amanda's arguments were convincing, but Matt kept hearing the warnings from Professor Parkwood as well.

As he sat there, Matt became aware of Amanda's emotional state when he heard a low sob. Rising, he turned and saw that she was silently crying. He took her in his arms and just stood there, holding her close as if he could protect her from the hurt.

He hadn't stopped to think of the emotional toll the past few days must have taken on her: one shock after another, and being placed in near-death situations more than a couple of times. Hardly what you'd call normal, and he realized that if it hadn't been for him, she would never have had to go through all of this. Now, to make matters worse, her family thought she was dead and he was telling her that she could never return to them—all while trying to explain to her that he was a traveler from the future. He finally realized that it was only her love for him that had tipped the balance, the only reason she had remained with him. Because, otherwise, she must be thinking that he was insane.

"Mandy," he whispered, "you do believe me, don't you?"

It was a few moments before she answered. "I believe you love me, Matt," she said. "I believe that you think you're trying to do what's right for Ben. But..." she said, and her voice trailed off.

Matt nodded. "I know," he sighed, "if I were in your position, I'd probably think I was crazy, too." He held her away from him, looking into her eyes. "It's true, Mandy, all of it. It may be hard for you to understand, but I must get Ben back to his family. I must go with him. Under the circumstances, I've been told that if you remain here it could severely affect history. I don't know that for sure, but Ben and his father are the experts, and that's what they've told me.

"But I'm not going to force any of this on you. You're going to have to make your own decision on this. Who knows, we may not be able to get back. But if we can, Ben and I must go. There's no question on that. Your decision is going to be whether to remain here with your family, or go with me and never see them again. I know it's difficult, but that's the choice you're going to have to make." He held her close again, then sat her down in the chair. "I'm going to take some food down to Ben, leave you here to consider everything."

Amanda nodded silently and watched Matt descend to the cellar. With a sigh, she began to think things through.

*   *   *   *

A short while later, Matt was finishing his discussion with Ben. "So I need to know, Ben, with a hundred per cent certainty that if Amanda remains here, it could create catastrophic problems."

Ben shook his head. "I can't tell you that, Matt," he replied. "you, and I, and Barrett, are the first any only people to have done what we've done. Theoretically, we should have never done this, made this journey, because the potential consequences are so great." He shifted to a more comfortable position on the cot and continued. "Let's say we were to travel to Austria, right now, and killed, or attempted to kill, Adolf Hitler. One school of thought says that we can't, no matter what we try. We would be changing history in a big way, and as a result of that my father's experiment, the whole complex, might never have been built in the first place. So, we could never have come back to make the attempt anyway.

"My father's point of view is that, if you visit a time period, blend in and do nothing radically overt to change things, then no harm done. But, that's a very risky proposition, since every action has some sort of reaction, and so on and so on. Barrett should never have come; I should never have come. The one saving grace of all of this is that I'm pretty sure that nothing has changed, otherwise all of this equipment would simply cease to exist, along with us. We're still here— that to me means we've done nothing, so far, to alter future events."

"But what do you make of what we do know?" Matt asked. "Amanda's obituary is in that newspaper, which hasn't even been published yet. That tells me that she didn't return to her family, that she's still considered dead to this era."

Ben thought for a moment. "That would tell me that Amanda made the choice to return to the 21st century with us. But it's got to be her decision, Matt. We can't just kidnap someone from another era and take them against their will.'

Matt nodded. "I know. The problem is that I don't think she believes me; I mean, about the complex, and being from the future. She may think I'm insane, for all I know. The only way to really convince her is to show her—but that's a one-way trip for her."

At the top of the stairs, Amanda listened silently to the conversation. She had been on her way to check on Ben when she heard the two men talking, and had been listening for several minutes. It seemed pretty clear to her: either Matt and Ben were both deranged, or they were telling the truth. And there were the other things she had seen, the computer, the light sticks, the equipment in the cellars. There would be no reason for such an elaborate ruse.

And then she thought of Matt. Throughout their relationship, he had been nothing but chivalrous, kind, and sincere. Although she didn't understand how such a thing could be, how someone could come from many years away, her intuition told her to believe Matt. And, she knew he loved her with all his heart and soul. She couldn't turn her back on that.

Think, Mandy, she said to herself! You've found what you thought you'd never have, a man who loves you. And you love him too! Don't make the wrong decision!

With that, she descended the stairs and approached the two men.

"Ben, how are you feeling?"

"I've been better," Ben said ruefully, "but I'm doing okay for now."

Amanda nodded and turned to Matt. "I need to talk to you upstairs, please."

Matt followed her up the stairs and closed the door. He faced her, not knowing what she had to say.

"Matt, when you came into my life I didn't know what to think. I had resigned myself to becoming an old maid. I refused to let men into my life because I thought they would use me, and I vowed to never let that happen.

"You showed me that there was more to life than bitterness. You've been so good to me, and I feel that I haven't treated you in kind. But, I need to know exactly how you feel about me. If what you're telling me is true, I'll be leaving behind everything I've ever known."

"Mandy, like I told you that day at the farmhouse: I love you, and I always will. I think I knew it from the first time I met you; that's why I continued to try to get you to respond. I don't want to live without you. If I was from this time period, there wouldn't be any question as to what I'd do. But I'm not. Ben and I must return to where we came from. I want you to come with us—with me." Matt knew what he had to do. In the fashion of the time, he got down on one knee and looked up at her. "Trust me, Mandy," he said. "Believe me when I say I love you, and always will."

She smiled at him and motioned for him to stand up. Moving close, she put her arms around Matt and held him tight. Her decision had been made.

"So, we'll just have to figure out a way to get your machinery to work." She looked up at him. "I'm looking forward to finding out just what things are like in your world."

Matt held her close. "You won't regret it, any of it, I promise." He then remembered their predicament. "I just hope I have the opportunity to show you," he said.

Amanda nodded. "We'll make it," she said, and Matt marveled at her optimism. Especially since she had been so dejected just a few weeks before.

They returned to the cellar and were setting the supplies on one of the tables when Ben suddenly said, "Matt! I may have found our solution!"

"Well, let's hear it," Matt said, pulling up a chair and sitting down.

"I've been looking at one of the almanacs that Barrett brought back with him, the one from 1897. According to the information in it about *this* year, we've got at least a week of clear skies ahead. That should give us enough power coming from the solar panels to charge the cells."

Matt heaved a sigh of relief. "Some good news for a change," he said, smiling. Now, their only problem would be to see if they could get enough power into the system to initiate contact. They'd make it work. They *had* to make it work.

With Ben instructing him, Matt took readings at each of the readouts and brought the results to Ben, who began calculating what they'd need. After a while, Ben looked up with a smile on his face.

"If we can cut out all unnecessary power use, we should see the power levels rise enough to establish contact within two days. I mean everything: heat, lights, the appliances, whatever we don't absolutely need. That is, provided we still have enough sunshine as well, and we should."

But Matt was already going around the perimeter of the cellar, disconnecting everything that wasn't absolutely essential. The power readings jumped perceptibly but still were not high enough. They'd just have to trust that they could make this work.

Two days later in the afternoon found the power levels sufficient for contact. A short text message was sent to the complex indicating the status of the equipment at this end and the expected power levels.

Another three days found the power levels high enough to attempt the transfer. Everything was going smoothly with the exception of one component at the console. One of the accelerator circuits would not stay calibrated and had to be adjusted by hand almost constantly, as if tuning in an erratic signal on an old radio. It was decided that Matt would maintain the setting by hand until Ben and Amanda had gone through the portal, then follow them immediately. They had transferred Ben to the wheeled cart, since he wouldn't be able to walk through the portal.

As they prepared to activate the portal, Matt leaned down to Ben. "Listen, they don't know it's three of us coming through. They don't even know about Amanda. I wasn't able to send another message for fear of upsetting the parameters, and I haven't given them any specifics—only equipment data. You'll need to let them know as soon as you get through that I'll be right behind you. I figure we've got this thing working and it's now or never."

Ben nodded. "You're right. If we can keep the equipment stable for another ten minutes we'll be home free."

Matt turned to Amanda. "Mandy, listen to me very carefully. You're going to have to push or pull Ben through the portal on this cart. When you get to the other side, don't be afraid. Ben's family and my friends are there. Don't worry, you'll be safe with them. You'll see some things that will look strange to you, too. Everything will be fine. I'll be along right behind you." He looked down at Ben on the wheeled cart. "Remember, I'll hold the accelerator circuit until you two are through, then I'll be coming through. Let them know on the other end, okay?"

Ben nodded weakly. Matt knew that Ben was using the last of his strength just to remain conscious, and would be getting help none too soon. Matt doubted if Ben would have lasted another day here.

He helped Amanda line up the cart with the entrance to the portal, then paused for a second to take her in his arms and kiss her tenderly. "For luck," he said, and turned to walk back to the console.

Matt raised the power levels and was relieved to see the indicators smoothly rise to almost one hundred per cent. He grabbed the accelerator circuit control and held it to the prescribed setting, watching the static charge dance around the outer edge of the portal.

"Okay, Mandy, you can go now," he said, but saw that she hesitated. The nimbus of electricity scared her, and her instinct held her back. She froze, not moving at all.

CHAPTER 35

▼

"There's no time, Mandy! Go now!" Matt shouted as the portal came fully alive. Amanda, terrified of the dancing electricity around the framework of the portal, at first shook her head involuntarily at the diaphanous fog that swirled in its center. Then, taking a breath and squaring her shoulders, she pushed the cart toward the opening. As she neared the silvery obelisk she could feel the hair on her head standing up from the static charge, and the goose bumps danced along her bare forearms. As scared as she was, though, she remembered that Matt had told her not to worry—that this was completely safe. Steeling herself, she continued forward, her eyes tightly shut as she shuffled forward steadily.

$$* \qquad * \qquad * \qquad *$$

At the complex, Professor Parkwood watched anxiously as the portal activated. He looked over at Stinnett. "What are your readings?"

Stinnett scanned the controls and shouted back, "The mass looks right. Appears to be two people and some equipment."

Professor Parkwood spoke to the people around him. "Good, good, that has to be them. Pray that everything holds for another thirty seconds. That's all we need."

The technicians nodded in agreement. Suddenly, through the swirling vortex, an odd apparition appeared: Ben's head and shoulders, slowly emerging from the fog in a horizontal position. Soon they could see the cart below him. Anxiously, inch by inch, they saw Ben's body emerging. Then, two hands appeared at the back of the cart, still pushing it. Professor Parkwood raced from the dais and down to the floor below, to stand next to Ben. The medical personnel were already prepared to take him to the infirmary.

Professor Parkwood looked at the portal and gasped. There, coming through behind the cart, was a young woman. Her face was set in a grimace, her eyes tightly shut, and she was breathing quickly through her open mouth in wordless fear. As she cleared the portal, she felt the cart being pulled away from her. She tried to control her breathing as she slowly opened her eyes.

The first thing she saw was Professor Parkwood, a look of astonishment on his face. "Are you Ben's father?" she asked.

Professor Parkwood replied with some urgency, "Where is Matt Collins?"

"He's coming through—right behind me," she said, and fell to her knees. The experience had proven too much for her, and she swooned.

"Sandra!" Professor Parkwood called, and Sandra came running to Amanda's side to help her up. As Sandra helped Amanda toward the infirmary, Professor Parkwood looked at Stinnett with a questioning look. "Is there any way we can maintain the power settings for another few minutes?"

Stinnett shook his head in frustration. "The equipment was calibrated for what we thought was going to be the indicated mass, which was two people and their belongings. We didn't even factor in the weight and mass of the cart that Ben was on, although they made it through all right despite that," he said. "But that's not the problem. We set everything to automatically power down right after the transfer. The computer is going through its shutdown sequence. There's not enough power left for another transfer anyway, not now."

Professor Parkwood grimaced as he watched the portal lose power, the fog in its center dissipating and the static charge diminishing until the portal was dormant.

*   *   *   *

Once Amanda had disappeared through the portal, Matt turned from the console and walked toward it himself when he noticed the lights dim. The portal's activity faded perceptibly, and Matt broke into a run toward the portal. "No, no, no!" he cried in frustration as he leaped for the opening. There was the barest flicker of static electricity around the framework as Matt leaped though the opening—and found himself rolling on the cellar floor on the opposite side of it. He came to his knees and looked back at the portal, now dead.

"Dammit!" he shouted. He got to his feet and raced back to the console. The power cells were reading nearly empty, and the readouts were all at or near zero. He slumped into the chair dejectedly. He was trapped here, in 1896, all alone.

∗   ∗   ∗   ∗

Back at the complex, Professor Parkwood was livid. He strode into the infirmary where Sandra was doing her best to check Amanda.

"Who are you, young lady? Where is Matt Collins?"

"Professor, please!" Sandra said. "Can't you see she's been scared out of her wits?"

"Do you have any idea what this might mean?" Professor Parkwood said to no one in particular. "My God, we've got someone here who belongs in 1896, and one of our contemporaries trapped there—possibly forever!"

Amanda, hearing this, snapped out of her daze. "What do you mean?" she said in a near hysterical voice. "Matt said he was coming right behind me! Ben said everything would be all right!"

"Then Ben was wrong! Everything is *not* all right!" Professor Parkwood paced back and forth, frustrated at this turn of events. "It should have been Ben and Matt Collins who came back here," he said. "*Only* Ben and Collins! Collins knew that! Why did he do this?"

From behind a nearby curtain, Professor Parkwood heard a weak voice. "Dad?" It was Ben's voice. Professor Parkwood ran over and pulled back the curtain.

Two of the medical staff were busily working on Ben, who was semi-conscious. He was a mere shadow of himself, the injuries having taken their toll. Professor Parkwood's anger softened as he saw his son lying there.

"Dad, Matt didn't have any choice. The only way for me to get through was to have Amanda bring me. Matt was going to come through right behind us. He had to stay at the console until the last possible second. The accelerator circuit was faulty and he had to calibrate it by hand."

Professor Parkwood shook his head sorrowfully as he took his son's hand. "Ben, I'm so glad to see you, son. But, what happened? Who is this woman? Why is she here?"

"She had to come, Dad," Ben said. He struggled to remain conscious. "I'll explain when I'm better—or maybe she can help. Her name is Amanda Caruthers."

One of the doctors took Professor Parkwood by the arm and led him outside the curtain. "Professor, if we're going to do anything for your son, you'll have to let us do our job. He's in a bad way, very bad."

Professor Parkwood sighed and nodded. He turned and went back to Sandra, who was standing outside the curtain surrounding Amanda's bed. Stinnett was there, too, waiting as Sandra checked the entries on the patient's chart. "She needs to be in complete isolation," Sandra said. "We'll need to put the entire complex on quarantine until I can check everything out. She may be carrying God knows what kind of diseases, and she'll be extremely susceptible to everything here until we can get her inoculated."

"They're doing everything they can for Ben," Professor Parkwood said. "I'll be in my office. Let me know the minute you have any information." Sandra nodded and watched as he disappeared through the doorway.

CHAPTER 36

▼

It was two hours later and Matt still sat at the console. He noticed with relief that the power levels were a fraction higher that they had been; the solar cells were replenishing the storage batteries, but at this rate it could take days to restore enough power to even initiate communications. By then, the temporal doorway might already be collapsed permanently.

He roused himself and went upstairs to the kitchen. He checked the pantry and found sufficient food, so no problem there. He went outside and made a quick circuit around the house, noting that everything was secure.

Matt returned to the house and made sure that all of the doors and windows were locked. Until he knew without a doubt that there was no way back to his own time, he knew that it would be risky to leave the house. He vowed to spend every waking minute looking for a solution.

Four days later—an eternity, it seemed, to Matt—the power levels had risen enough so that the computer could at least be reinitialized. He activated the sequence and saw that, from its current state of complete shutdown and taking into account the rate of recharge, it would take at least another ninety-six hours to bring everything back on line at a sufficient level provided the solar panels were able to recharge the cells. At that point, he could attempt to at least contact the complex—provided that they were still operational as well. For all he knew, they had already written him off.

*   *   *   *

Professor Parkwood had found the announcement in the Montrose newspaper concerning the memorial service for Amanda Caruthers. He had never considered this possibility, and had to ponder what it might mean. He picked up the telephone and pressed the intercom.

"Stinnett? Please come up here when you get a chance." He replaced the handset and sat back with a sigh. Since Barrett's death, Stinnett had become his primary confidant on matters relating to the project.

A short while later Stinnett arrived, and Professor Parkwood motioned him to sit down.

"Two things, Mr. Stinnett," Professor Parkwood said. "First, one of our greatest concerns was if a contemporary traveler to another, earlier time was to somehow change history, or alter the course of events." He held up the newspaper. "What we seem to have here is a different type of occurrence, something we never considered. We have a human being from the nineteenth century here in the twenty first. And, according to this newspaper, someone who was supposed to have died in the nineteenth century. We need to see what potential problems this might have created. In addition, our second problem: what are the chances that we'll be able to get this portal operational again, long enough to try for a transfer of Collins?"

Stinnett shook his head and grimaced. "The chances for a transfer are not good, Professor," he replied. "As you know, these last two portals were on the verge of collapse anyway. At the 1896 end, it's getting into December in Philadelphia—diminished sunlight, clouds every day…besides that, there might not be enough power generated by the solar cells by themselves to even get the portal operational again, much less try for another transfer. And by the time the sunshine returns next spring, I'm certain that the anomaly will have long since collapsed."

Professor Parkwood nodded. "Then we need to get some input from the rest of the team. Something, anything, that might work as a power source to supplement the cells at that end. We have to try something, and soon. I'm not giving up on this until the last possible second."

Stinnett nodded in agreement. "I'll tell the others; we'll get working on it right away." He was about to get up and leave when he paused and turned. "Oh, yes. As for the girl, she was supposed to have died in 1896. Although she's here now, she would have ceased to exist back then anyway." He thought for a moment.

"What I'm trying to say is, she's been given a new life—one that she would not have had before. And there's no danger from her. It's Collins we have to worry about. He cannot remain there—it's far too dangerous."

"And if we can't get him back?" Professor Parkwood said.

"We *have* to get him back," Stinnett replied. We absolutely *must* find the solution to this problem."

"But how?" Professor Parkwood asked.

Stinnett was tired but remained optimistic. "Well, we built the damn thing," he said with a grin, "so it's obvious that the solution is here, somewhere. We'll just have to figure out what it is."

CHAPTER 37

▼

It was two days later and the technical staff was once again seated around the large conference table. Stinnett spoke to the group. "Mr. Goodman here has come up with a novel idea, which he will now explain." Goodman rose and cleared his throat.

"In our previous experiments, the equipment has always been programmed to shut down immediately after a transfer. This was, I understand, to protect the equipment. My question is, why can't we activate the portal and keep it on for an extended period?"

A voice from the rear spoke up. "Because," Jim Railsford, the lead reactor technician said, rising from his seat, "the equipment won't take it. We would have a systems failure in a very short time."

"How short?" Stinnett said, and Railsford frowned in thought.

"Twenty minutes, maybe less," he said. "After that everything would burn out, literally, and you won't have *any* equipment."

"And it takes a few hours at the very least to align the signals between the portals, provided the other portal at that end is operational?" Goodman asked.

"Yes," Railsford said.

"What I propose," Goodman said, "is that we activate the portal, take our best shot at aligning this end with the other portal—Stinnett did that when Mr. Collins initially went through, so it's at least possible—and send through a power cable of sufficient strength so that it can be directly connected to the other portal and powered up from here immediately. We keep the portal energized constantly so that the temporal doorway remains active, at least until the equipment fails."

Half the staff shook their heads silently. One by one they spoke up. "We can't know where the cable would materialize at that end. It might appear on the roof, down the street—who knows? The equipment isn't that precise."

Goodman nodded dejectedly and sat down. They all talked among themselves for a while in low tones, and finally Helen Arran, the scientist who months ago had been the first to suggest that this experiment had evolved into a temporal doorway, spoke up. "Well, if we can't get everything operational from this end, then we'll need to *take* the help to him."

Most of those present began murmuring in negative tones, and Professor Parkwood shook his head. "No, we've already discussed that. Having one individual from the twenty-first century possibly trapped in the nineteenth is bad enough. Having two there is just asking for problems. If we were sure that we could get both of them back, then I might consider it. But under the circumstances..." His voice trailed off.

Stinnett spoke up. "There is another possibility," he said. "The girl, Amanda. We could send her back. That way we'd be minimizing our risk if this fails."

Sandra nodded and spoke. "That's an excellent idea. She's had a rough couple of days. I've tried to console her but she thinks that Matt may be lost for good. Whatever happened between them back there in Montrose, she is totally committed to him. In fact, if we can't get Matt back, I doubt she'll be able to handle it. She really has no one else. Everything, everyone she knew is back there."

Professor Parkwood nodded. "Talk to her, Sandra. Let her know what we propose, see what her reaction is." He looked around at everyone. "This will definitely be our last opportunity at this. Please, give everything your undivided attention. We can't afford any errors."

They all nodded and moved off to their respective stations. Stinnett remained behind and, after the others had left, leaned over and put his hand on Professor Parkwood's arm. "Henry, don't worry. If it works, it works. If it doesn't, it won't be because we didn't try."

CHAPTER 38

▼

Another week had passed. Matt sat at the console, a blanket around his shoulders to help in keeping him warm in the cold damp of the cellar. He leaned over the console, his head in his hands, and it was obvious from his unshaven face and rumpled clothing that he had lost all hope. Patiently he had waited for some sign, some indication that Professor Parkwood and the others had figured out some way to at least contact him. But the equipment had remained silent. The power levels had reached sixty-five per cent but had refused to go any higher, and he had no way to make them.

He knew that before long he would be forced to leave the house, to go into town and try to figure out some way to survive in this era. He had no doubt that he could accomplish this, but the realization of how truly alone he was had hit him full force. He had even lost any solace he might have gotten from Amanda. To be trapped here with her would have at least been bearable. Now, he had loved and lost—twice. The only consolation he had was that she was safe, and alive.

The area around the console was taking on an unkempt look, as Matt had not left the room for some days and had let the clutter accumulate. Finally, with a sigh he leaned back in the chair and dozed.

He felt that he was dreaming. In the dream, he could hear Amanda's voice, faint but recognizable. "Matt," it called to him, "Matt, wake up!" He even felt as if someone was shaking him, and as he slowly opened his eyes he drew in a sharp breath. There, standing over him, was Amanda—but not the Amanda he had last seen. She was dressed in 21st century clothing, and her hair was pulled back and hung down around her shoulders. He smiled at her, certain that this was a dream, and murmured, "I thought I'd never see you again."

Amanda, seeing that Matt was still half-asleep, shook him again vigorously and spoke more sternly. "Matt Collins, you wake up right now!"

Matt blinked a few times and shook his head, expecting the beautiful apparition to disappear—but she remained. He reached out a hand and grasped her arm. It felt real enough, but…

He sat bolt upright in the chair. "Mandy? But how…"

Amanda was looking at him with a frown. "Matt Collins," she said in mock admonishment, "I certainly hope this isn't an example of how you live all the time."

He jumped from the chair and threw his arms around her, holding her tight. Amanda did the same, holding on as if she would never let go. After a time he held her away from him, and was surprised at the tears that sprang from his eyes. Amanda was crying, too, but the smile on her face told him exactly how she felt.

She reached up a hand and rubbed it across his face. "I can't take you back looking like this," she said. "Go, get cleaned up and into some proper clothes. I've brought your things from the laboratory. Then you can help me with the supplies upstairs."

Matt needed no further urging. He went to the breaker panel on one wall and threw the switches for the appliances. Then, picking up the knapsack that Amanda had handed to him, he made his way to the bathroom to shower and shave.

Half an hour later he emerged, dressed in his usual fieldwork clothing. He went straight to Amanda and held her close, kissing her deeply. Then, he just stood there holding her. Finally he said, "How did you get here?"

"Professor Parkwood asked me to come. They couldn't risk sending anyone else from the laboratory. And, if this doesn't work, I didn't want to live there without you." She looked up at him. "That's quite a place you came from. I didn't leave the building but Sandra took me upstairs and showed me part of Philadelphia from the windows. From what I could see, the city is very large."

Matt nodded. "There's lots more places, even bigger, and I can't wait to show them to you. But, what plan do they have to get us back?"

Amanda explained that she had brought supplies, and most importantly a generator with fuel. "The Professor said that you should be able to get all of this working by tomorrow. He said to tell you that it was most important that we do this as quickly as possible."

"Yes, I can understand that," Matt replied. "The conditions that make this possible, travel between these two places, will disappear, and very soon. Let's get to it."

As they went upstairs, Amanda explained that she had come through the portal but had found herself some six miles away from the house. She had found a local farmer and had hired him to bring her and the supplies to the house, for which she had paid him handsomely. The farmer and his family didn't know what to make of her, with the strange clothing she was wearing and the odd-looking boxes of supplies, but she had said as little as possible to them. Back at the complex, she had been shown how to deactivate the lock on the keypad at the house. When she arrived, she had come to the cellar immediately, not knowing if she'd find Matt or not.

Matt pulled the small generator into the kitchen and snaked the exhaust hose out through the kitchen window, then strung the extension cables down to the cellar. He had followed the simple instructions and had connected the generator wiring to the console at the indicated locations. He replaced the faulty accelerator circuit with a new one that Amanda had brought, then fueled the generator and started it up. After a couple of false starts it began operating smoothly. He took Amanda's hand and led her back to the cellar where he checked the readings. Already the power levels were rising.

Later that night, communications were established with the complex. Professor Parkwood explained the situation and had Matt check and recheck all of the settings. There would only be one chance.

The following day found the power levels sufficient for a transfer. Matt and Amanda approached the portal, which was already showing the static charge around the perimeter. The familiar swirling mist began to form inside the opening, and Matt watched the countdown timer on the console. He took one of Amanda's hands and held it tight. "Until this is over, I'm not letting go of you."

As the timer neared zero, Matt and Amanda walked slowly toward the opening. Pausing for only a second, they stepped into the mist together and disappeared.

CHAPTER 39

▼

At the complex, Professor Parkwood waited anxiously near the portal entrance. He glanced at Stinnett every few moments, and Stinnett nodded encouragingly. Professor Parkwood stuck his hand into one of the pockets of his lab coat and waited.

Suddenly, through the mist, two forms began taking shape. Slowly the shapes solidified, and Matt and Amanda appeared in the portal, their eyes closed but their steps firm. As they stepped into the complex and away from the portal, Professor Parkwood moved around them and stood just outside the portal's opening. Withdrawing his hand from his pocket, he punched a button on the small package he held and tossed it with some force into the opening.

"Now, Mr. Stinnett!" Professor Parkwood shouted, and Stinnett gave the signal to the other technicians. The portal's activity immediately diminished and ceased altogether after another few seconds.

There was a burst of cheers from the assembled technicians and scientists. Stinnett came down from the raised dais and held out his hand to the Professor. He leaned in, trying to be heard over the din, and said, "Well, we did it."

Professor Parkwood nodded, a smile creasing his face. "Yes, we did. An amazing experiment." He paused. "Once everyone has settled down, let's start getting this equipment dismantled."

"Amen," Stinnett said with feeling.

CHAPTER 40

▼

The following afternoon, Matt got up off of the infirmary bed and went to the adjoining room. There, Amanda was patiently waiting for him.

"Well, we've both been given a clean bill of health. We didn't bring back any diseases, and your inoculations are satisfactory." He leaned against the doorway. "I figure we'll be out of here in a couple of hours."

Amanda nodded. She looked up at Matt. "How different is it, out there?" she said.

"Oh, it's different," he said with meaning. "There's a lot, an awful lot, that you'll need to learn. And you've got over a hundred years of history to catch up on."

"As long as you're with me, I won't be afraid." Amanda got up and walked around to him.

They were interrupted by the arrival of Professor Parkwood and Sandra. Sandra went to Matt and, without a word, hugged him quickly. Professor Parkwood spoke up. "We can't thank you enough, Mr. Collins," he said. "Ben will be in rehab for a few months but the doctors think he'll be just fine."

"Professor, what was that object you threw into the portal right after we arrived?"

"An incendiary device. I had to make sure that the equipment at that end was totally destroyed. Look at this." He pulled a copy of an old newspaper out of his pocket and handed it to Matt. The story was about a huge blaze that had leveled the Philadelphia house; the date was the same date as when Matt and Amanda had left 1896. "Completely incinerated, just like the house in Montrose, except on purpose this time. I don't think we have to worry about anything at this point.

I was right, you know, about any changes to history. You and Amanda were simply a part of what occurred in 1896."

"And your experiment?" Matt asked.

"It's over," Professor Parkwood replied. "A success, and one that no one can ever know about. Who'd believe them, anyway?" He reached into another pocket and pulled out a large envelope. "This is for Miss Caruthers. Identification papers: birth certificate, everything she'll need—all dated to the proper contemporary dates." He turned to Amanda. "You, of all of us, have been given a unique opportunity. I hope you take proper advantage of it."

Amanda nodded, took the envelope, and said, "Thank you, Professor."

Professor Parkwood turned to Matt. "Your vehicle is ready. All of your belongings have been placed in it. You can leave whenever you like. And, if I can ever be of assistance to you, just contact me."

Matt reached out a hand to the Professor and shook it. "Thanks again," he said. "You were right—the opportunity of a lifetime." He paused, then said, "I just hope I never have another one like that! There were a couple of times when I thought we were going to be trapped back there for sure."

They laughed and Professor Parkwood patted Matt's arm. "Take care, you two," he said, and shuffled off behind Sandra.

Matt turned to Amanda. "Well, it's out there—my world. Care to see it with me?"

Amanda took the proffered arm and smiled. "With you? I'm ready for anything."

They walked out into the main complex. The technicians were well on their way to dismantling the equipment. Matt saw that the portal itself had already been disassembled and was lying in pieces in the center of the room. Guiding Amanda around it, he took her to the elevator and punched in the top floor. Amanda held his arm tightly as the elevator rose.

At the top, the doors opened silently and they walked out and over to the roof access stairway. Climbing the short flight, Matt opened the door at the top and they stepped out onto the roof.

Amanda drew in her breath sharply as she saw the panorama of the city around them. Far to the north, a jet was sailing across the sky, leaving a trail behind it. She watched it in wonder for a few moments. As they surveyed the city, she noticed the headlights snaking around the numerous roadways and the skyscrapers reaching for the sky.

"It's...beautiful, Matt," she said in an awed voice. As the sun dipped below the horizon, the lights of the city twinkled on.

She turned to Matt and put her arms around him, holding him tight. "Thank you...for everything." She looked up at him and said, "No regrets?"

Matt placed his hands on her shoulders. "I certainly don't have any," he said, "but how do you feel about leaving your family behind?"

"I miss them," she said simply, "but we've got each other. I would have left them anyway, if we'd gotten married..." She paused. "Sorry, I'm making an assumption."

"No, you're not," he said with feeling, leaning down to her. "As soon as we can, I promise." He kissed her, softly at first, and then with all the passion that he felt.

EPILOGUE

▼

Ten months had passed since Matt and Amanda's return through the portal. They had spent those first few days after their return in Philadelphia, Amanda shopping for new clothes and Matt showing her the sights. Everything seemed fascinating to her, like a child's fascination with every new thing learned. They had also visited a jeweler and chosen their wedding rings, and had been married within a week of their return after going through the formalities required. Since then, it had been the happiest ten months of their lives for both of them. They had also kept in touch with Professor Parkwood, and were pleased to learn that Ben had made an almost complete recovery from his injuries.

Of all the new experiences, Amanda had first and foremost been frightened by the speed and proximity of automobile traffic. It had taken her some time to get used to even walking on the sidewalk near it. But, the real challenge for Matt was in getting her comfortable with riding in a vehicle at highway speed. She had instinctively huddled below the dashboard as Matt guided the SUV toward Pittsburgh on their return. But, little by little, she had grown accustomed to automobile travel and now barely gave it a second thought.

She was awed at the size of Matt's house ("well, it's yours now too," he had told her) and could not believe that all of the nearby houses were similar in size. In her own era, it was common to find a palatial house adjacent to a run-down clapboard frame house, and no one finding it in the least odd.

In the ensuing months Matt, along with the help of a couple of cable television channels, had brought Amanda more or less up to date on the last hundred years or so of history. She had been awed at the accomplishments, appalled at the brutality of war and terrorism, and most of all amazed that mankind had survived the twentieth century. She was also amazed at the conveniences, most notably with heating and air conditioning. To be able to control the climate was almost beyond belief, and this, along with all of the laborsaving appliances and conveniences, made her feel pampered indeed.

But she wasn't so sure about the television. True, she had learned a great deal from this wonderful invention, but she also failed to understand why certain programs such as sitcoms were presented. Matt tried to explain to her that it was for entertainment but she shook her head. "Such a waste of time," she had said, preferring to look elsewhere for entertainment.

"Such destructive power," she said one evening as they sat in front of the television. A retrospective on the Hiroshima bomb was being shown, along with footage of other atomic testing from the 1940's.

"Because of that," Matt explained, "we've managed to avoid another world war, so far. But," he said, hitting the 'off' button on the TV remote, "to change the subject, I've been asked to attend a symposium up in Binghamton next month. If I drive, it'll take me right through Montrose."

Amanda froze, not looking at Matt. He had asked on a couple of previous occasions if she'd be interested in visiting Montrose, but she had shied away. Matt knew that she didn't want to confront what she might possibly find, and open old wounds. But, after a brief pause, she looked at him and nodded.

"Maybe I am ready this time," she said, and Matt nodded his approval.

"Great," he said. "Tell you what. The symposium is only a day and a half. We can go to that, and visit Montrose on the return trip. That way we won't have any deadlines and can take our time, look over the town. Okay?"

Amanda nodded, but Matt could still sense reluctance in her. He knew what it was but said nothing.

*   *   *   *

Early June arrived and Matt spent part of a Saturday morning loading the small but serviceable storage area in the Lotus with their luggage. Before long, they were on the highway and headed for New York—up I-79, then across I-86 toward Binghamton. The time flew by as the Lotus ate up the miles effortlessly.

The symposium was a predictably low-key but necessary part of Matt's continued membership in the state Historical Society. The time passed quickly and Tuesday just after noon found he and Amanda driving south on I-81. It was a perfect day.

As they pulled off the interstate and neared the outskirts of Montrose, Matt saw little that he recognized. The surrounding area was beautiful but held nothing familiar. He frowned as he checked the GPS.

"According to this, Parkwood's old farm should be right here." He pulled to the side of the road and they both got out. Before them, only rolling grassland and a few scattered trees dotted the landscape. There was no sign of the old barn, nothing to indicate that structures had ever been here.

"Let's head on into town," Matt said, and they got into the car and drove slowly toward the downtown area. Here and there, a familiar building could be seen; but, for the most part, all of the other buildings that they were familiar with from 1896 had been replaced long ago with their more modern counterparts. Matt pulled the car into a parking spot near the County Courthouse, which hadn't changed much on the outside, and they got out.

They walked along the concrete sidewalk and up the steps into the Courthouse. The interior had changed considerably, and was now brightly lit. Matt walked to one wall that held photographs. One such photo was captioned, "Hiram Higby, Mayor, 1893–1904." Higby, now a long gone memory, stared back at him from the photo. He also saw a photo of the Town Council, circa 1899, and there among the somberly posed faces was Amanda's father. Matt looked at Amanda and saw the tears that sprang into her eyes as she looked at the photo.

They walked up the stairs to the second floor and found that the old Assessor's Office was now remodeled as well. The large room was well lit and, instead of the plat books from Amanda's era, computer terminals were spaced along the counter.

Descending the stairs, Matt took Amanda's hand and led her outside and around the corner to the Library. Once inside, they were directed to the Historical Society section. Matt briefly scanned the materials and then began selecting certain folios from the shelves.

"Here's what I was looking for," he said, and placed the large volume on the table. Inside, photographs of the town's history from the late nineteenth century had been carefully arranged in more or less chronological order.

They gazed at page after page of the photos when suddenly Amanda said, "Matt, look at this one!"

It was a photo of couples dancing. There, in the background, barely noticeable, were Matt and Amanda. Near the front, slightly blurred due to their motion, were Stevie and Rebecca, large smiles on their faces.

Matt took the folio over to the counter and, after a brief conversation, came back for Amanda.

"They're going to make a copy of that photo and mail it to us. Now, let's go find a restaurant."

Outside, on a whim Matt walked toward the old hotel. Incredibly, it still stood in the same spot. They walked into the entrance but found that the restaurant had been converted into a travel agent's office. Going back outside, they walked along the street, taking in the changes. Most of the original buildings remained, although many had new facades, but when they got to the former location of the Caruthers' General Store they found an empty lot.

Throughout all of this, Amanda had been silent. Matt knew that she was trying to control her emotions as the realization finally hit her. With few exceptions, everything she had known was gone.

"Are you okay?" Matt asked, and Amanda nodded. "I know it's difficult," he continued, "but things change."

They ate a leisurely lunch at one of the franchise restaurants that dotted the main thoroughfare, then retraced their steps back to the car. "Another stop," Matt said, and slowly drove the few blocks to where the Caruthers house had been.

As they pulled up, Matt was amazed. Other than new windows, the house was in virtually the same condition as when the Caruthers family had lived there. The yard was well maintained and the house looked to have a recent coat of fresh paint.

Amanda drew in her breath as she saw it. "My house," she said as if to herself.

"Remember, other people are living here now," Matt reminded her as they got out of the car.

On the porch, an elderly lady sat in a rocking chair. Matt took Amanda's hand and led her through the gate and up to the house.

"Hi," Matt said. "I'm Matt Collins, and this is my wife Amanda."

"Hello," the old woman said. "I'm Margaret Bishop. Everyone calls me Peggy. What can I do for you?"

"We've been doing some genealogical research and learned that my wife is related to a family that we think may have lived here many years ago."

"Which family is that?"

"Their name was Caruthers," Amanda said.

Peggy smiled. "Why, yes, this is the family homestead. I own it now. It was passed down to me from my great grandmother. We called her Grandma Becca."

"Grandma Becca?" Amanda repeated, and the old lady smiled.

"Her name was Rebecca Hastings, but when she was a little girl her name was Rebecca Caruthers."

Amanda drew in her breath sharply. "Rebecca Caruthers?"

"Yes. The family has been here in town for generations. Came here in the 1800's. You say you're related?"

Matt spoke up. "We've learned that Amanda is related to Jack Caruthers, Jr." Still the truth without having to explain too much, Matt thought to himself.

"Jack Caruthers, Jr." the old lady said, thinking. "If I remember right, that was one of Grandma Becca's brothers."

Matt looked at Amanda to see how she was taking all of this, and saw that she was retaining her composure. "Can you tell me what happened to your grandmother's family, her parents, her brothers and sisters?"

"Well, I know some of the family history, but only up to a point." She got up from the chair. "Why don't you two young people come on inside? I'll make us something to drink and see what I can find."

They followed Peggy into the house. Amanda looked around in awe. The rooms were the same, although the furnishings and decorations were vastly different. The old lady showed them into the living room and said, "Make yourselves comfortable. I'll be back in a minute." She walked off toward the kitchen.

"This was my Father's study," Amanda said, walking around and looking at the pictures on the walls. She didn't recognize any of the people in the photographs.

"You realize, of course, that Margaret Bishop is your great niece," Matt said.

Amanda looked at him. "No, I didn't, but you're right." She smiled. "So my family *is* still in Montrose."

Peggy came through the doorway with a tray of drinks. "Have a seat," she said, and handed them each a glass. She settled herself in a recliner.

"Let's see what I can remember of the family history," Peggy said. "I don't know too much about some of them, but I remember when I was a little girl, Grandma Becca would tell us some stories about her family. She had the two brothers that worked for the railroad, but they were much older. I don't think she knew them too well. Her sister Sallie married a rich lawyer and moved to Philadelphia. Grandma Becca stayed here in Montrose her whole life."

"And her parents?" Amanda asked.

"Oh, they lived here, too. My great-great Grandpa Jack was a very influential man here in town. He passed away in the 1920's, but his wife lived to be almost a hundred. Lived in this very house until she passed away, too. Grandma Becca inherited everything, which was quite a bit. Her mother was able to hang onto everything through the Great Depression, and being the only child still here, Grandma Becca got it all."

Matt spoke up, asking the question he knew Amanda wanted to ask but couldn't. "Did Grandma Becca have any other siblings?"

Peggy thought for a moment. "You know, there was another sister. I don't remember what her name was." Peggy lowered her voice. "Grandma never spoke much about her; I think it was too painful. I understand she was murdered when Grandma was a little girl. They ended up hanging the man that did it. They found out that he had killed two other people some time before that, but they were never able to prove anything on those." She paused. "Grandma's parents always felt that if he had been caught on those other killings, Grandma's sister wouldn't have been murdered."

Peggy got up and went over to a bookcase. She pulled out a photo album and brought it back to the table. Flipping the pages, she stopped at one photograph. "Here's Grandma Becca and the family on her 75th birthday."

Amanda looked at the photograph. The old woman in the photograph smiled back at the camera, her family around her. It was the eyes in the photograph that Amanda recognized. "Rebecca," she said to herself in a low voice.

"Grandma had six children," Peggy said as she sat back down. "What with all the grandchildren, there's family all across this part of Pennsylvania."

"Do you have any other photographs of Grandma Becca's family?" Matt asked.

Peggy shook her head. "No, Grandma donated all of her photos and such to the State Historical Society. It's down in Harrisburg."

"I know the place," Matt said. He turned to Amanda. "We can do some looking there some other time."

Matt turned back to Peggy. "Is there a family cemetery or anything like that?"

"Why, yes, our family has a section out off of Cemetery Road." She gave Matt directions to the site.

"Thank you so much for your hospitality," Matt said as they rose to leave.

Peggy turned to Amanda. "It's good to find another relative. If you have any other questions, just call me. I can always call some of the other family members if I don't know the answer."

"Thank you," Amanda said, and she and Matt made their way to the car.

Matt started the car and they both waved at Peggy as they pulled away. They drove in silence for a few blocks.

"Are you sure you want to do this?" Matt asked.

Amanda nodded. "Yes. I've got to know, and the least I can do is pay my respects."

Matt guided the car through the streets, following the directions. Before long they saw a huge cemetery on the right. Pulling into the open gates, he slowly guided the car along the roadways until they came to a large section surrounded by an old iron fence.

As they got out of the car, Matt saw a marble monument at the entrance that simply said, "Caruthers." They walked inside and Amanda immediately began looking at the inscriptions on the headstones.

"I don't know any of these people, Matt," she said in an uncertain voice.

"Look at the dates. These are probably more recent graves. I've found that in plots like this, the oldest graves are in the back."

They moved among the headstones, briefly looking at each and noticing that the dates were earlier as they made their way toward the back.

"Oh, Matt," Amanda sobbed as she stopped at a large headstone. On it, one side of the inscription read 'Rebecca Caruthers Hastings, 1884—1968.'

Amanda knelt at the foot of the plot, crying softly. Matt came up to her and put his hands on her shoulders.

"The others are here, too," he said, pointing at the markers for Amanda's parents and brothers.

"Looks like most of your family lived well into their eighties and beyond," Matt said shortly. "See, you had nothing to worry about. They all lived full, long lives."

"I miss them," Amanda said simply, through her tears.

"Of course you do. But, like I told you once before, there's too much to life to let it pass you by. They didn't," he said, "and with the opportunity that we've been given, we shouldn't either."

She stood up and, smiling through her tears, wrapped her arms around Matt. He could tell that she had finally come to terms with whatever guilt she had been carrying. "You're right, and we won't," she said. "Let's go…and *live*. Come on."

As he followed her out of the enclosure, Matt neglected to point out the solitary weathered headstone far to the right. The stone was dark but Matt had been able to read the inscription. It simply said, 'Amanda Caruthers, 1872—1896.'

978-0-595-36682-8
0-595-36682-1

Printed in the United States
82156LV00005BA/175